DEADLY ATTACK

A SAMUEL GARCIA PRIVATE EYE MYSTERY

ALTON LYNN COOPER

ISBN 979-8-89428-386-9 (paperback)
ISBN 979-8-89428-387-6 (digital)

Copyright © 2025 by Alton Lynn Cooper

All rights reserved. No part of this publication may be reproduced, distributed, or transmitted in any form or by any means, including photocopying, recording, or other electronic or mechanical methods without the prior written permission of the publisher. For permission requests, solicit the publisher via the address below.

Christian Faith Publishing
832 Park Avenue
Meadville, PA 16335
www.christianfaithpublishing.com

Printed in the United States of America

CONTENTS

Introduction v
Chapter 1: Terror in the Night 1
Chapter 2: Enemies on the Loose 12
Chapter 3: Searching for Clues 29
Chapter 4: On the Wrong Trail 37
Chapter 5: A Sad Goodbye 68
Chapter 6: Multiple War Fronts 76
Chapter 7: Imminent Danger 96
Chapter 8: Return to Kalmajo Island 111
Chapter 9: The Head of the Snake 146
Chapter 10: Webs of Deceit 184
Chapter 11: Shocking Revelations 240
Chapter 12: Justice at Last 302
Chapter 13: Back Home at the Ranch 322

INTRODUCTION

Samuel Garcia was the debonair young Spanish associate of Davey Gibson in the novel *On the Wings of Love*. He was a dashing young man who was most comfortable in blue jeans and a brightly colored silk shirt, with his feet clad in genuine leather cowboy boots (with carved designs on them, of course). Samuel's great-grandfather had been a policeman and passed his love of solving difficult cases down to his flamboyant grandson. After Davey moved back to the States from serving in missionary work in the South Pacific, Samuel joined the local police department on Kalmajo Island to gain on-the-job experience, preparing him to return to Texas and take up residence as an elite private investigator. He launched his career in some most unusual ways before finally landing his first big case tracking down some pretty clever cattle rustlers (*In the Dark of Night*). In his next major case, he was called upon to stop the loss of millions of dollars in stolen artwork, resulting in a near-death experience at the hands of a madman (*The Case of the Vanishing Masterpieces*).

Samuel managed to remain footloose and fancy-free, even though he had a number of young lady admirers along with a loving mother who was expecting a host of grandchildren from her eldest son. Samuel established his office in the old bunkhouse on his family's sprawling cattle ranch in the Texas Panhandle after evicting numerous families of mice who had called the place home for many years. A hard case with large amounts of intrigue got Samuel's blood moving and his investigative juices flowing. He fancied himself among the best when it came to snooping, and we certainly hope you will agree after traveling with him through this latest caper. After solving his last case concerning a missing bank president and twelve million dollars in bearer bonds (*Gone Without a Trace*), he was awaiting his next snooping assignment while resting up on his family's West Texas cattle ranch.

Samuel had no idea that his next major case would come to him in a most unexpected way, resulting in him becoming his own client in need. The days and months ahead would be the most intense in his detective career as his very life depended upon him catching the perpetrators before they finished

DEADLY ATTACK

their task of eliminating him. Come along on this page-turning adventure and see if you can unravel this latest mystery before our master detective figures it out, bringing the culprits to justice.

CHAPTER 1

Terror in the Night

"I don't like it." Sofia cast an intense eye down the dining table toward her boys. "Your papa, rest his soul, would sit out in the pastures during the night the same way when we first started this ranch. A bolt of lightning struck through my whole being every time I heard that rifle sound off."

"Mother, if we don't rid the ranch of these coyotes, they will rid this ranch of our cattle. Guns are a necessary tool and are safe when handled in the right way."

"I'm not against guns, Diego, I just don't like them. The two of you better stay together out there in the night or you may mistake one another for a coyote and I will be down to five sons, no?"

Eduardo jumped into the conversation, giving his brother a brief reprieve from his mother's stern gaze. "It's a full moon tonight, Mother. Even though my dear brother Diego is not the most handsome among us, he still doesn't have the long snout of the coyote."

Diego gave his brother's shin bone a sharp kick under the table with the side of his work boot.

"You stop your kicking. I've told you before, no physical contact at my table." The boys had long ago learned that their mother's keen eyes rarely missed the smallest infraction created in her presence. "Larson Maxwell's ranch has lost more than a dozen calves to these night raiders in the past two months. Papa had to take them out in his time, and nothing has changed. We will be careful, but it's a job that must be done."

Diego went silent as he and his brothers finished the supper meal, preparing for the night ahead. He had often admired his father's rifle that hung above the large stone fireplace in the gathering room. Mateo Garcia had not only fought the coyotes in the early days of the ranch but also cattle thieves, treacherous storms, and disease among the herd in the struggle to build the ranch into what it was before his home going. He had graduated to heaven a number of years ago, leaving his wife and seven boys to carry on the work he started. The ranch now exceeded one hundred forty thousand acres, as each year required additional pastureland to keep up with the ever-expanding herd.

"What has gotten hold of the tongue of my eldest son?" Sophia gave Samuel an inquiring look. "Is it possible he is contemplating making a marriage proposal to a very beautiful young lady?"

Sofia's head maid, Valentina, had captured Samuel's heart over the past few years, but he had avoided making a personal commitment to her, allowing him to remain free to pursue his investigative career. When the rich, debonair Hector Maria Gonzalez Lopez appeared at the hacienda and hung around for a number of weeks, it sent a wave of panic through Samuel that had driven him to pay more attention to Valentina as of late. He was passing through a time of indecision, knowing that the life of a private detective was not one to sustain the kind of close relationship that marriage to Valentina would bring into his life. Something in his innermost being drove him on with a strong desire to catch criminals and see them brought to justice. On the other hand, he could marry and settle down on the ranch, helping his mother and brothers manage the demands of the large enterprise. He was caught between his deep feelings for Valentina and his desire for the excitement that a complicated case filled with intrigue and danger brought his way.

"Nothing has hold of my tongue, Mother. Just taking time to think and ponder on the days ahead."

Samuel had been silent during the supper conversations, contemplating his own future. Since he finished working on the bank case, he hadn't received any new calls from potential clients needing his snooping prowess. He wasn't a person who could sit around idle, and these times between cases caused him to become jittery as the days slipped by. After the experience of thinking he was losing Ms. Valentina to the young Hector Maria Gonzalez Lopez, he had invited her on a picnic and taken her out on a few driving dates in his jeep. It amazed him that she seemed to enjoy letting her long, radiant hair blow in the wind in the jeep after riding in Hector's bright red Ferrari. His old jeep had been rebuilt at Arnold Snuffman's automobile hospital in Amarillo, but it was still a jeep and liked to bounce its occupants over every crack in the road. He excused himself from the evening meal and began the walk down the long, curving, tree-lined driveway back to his bunkhouse office near the road. He was hoping that just maybe there would be a message from a poor soul in need of a private detective's services.

DEADLY ATTACK

Samuel poked at the blinking button on his answering machine, anticipating a potential client's call, only to hear Sheriff Joe Halstead's voice reminding him of his commitment to support the annual toy drive for the pediatric unit at the hospital in Amarillo. He had volunteered for the drive each year and enjoyed visiting the children's rooms, delivering toys and wishes for speedy recoveries to the many stricken young people housed there. He often spent time in prayer for the children and their parents who were struggling through difficult times. Samuel headed for the bathroom to brush his teeth and get ready for an early bedtime. Surely some corrupt individuals must be out sowing seeds of destruction that would send a case his way, requiring him to track down the culprits and see to it they got what was coming to them.

"Well, old boy, let's call it a night and hope that some person in distress will call us soon. We surely need something to get our blood moving and this highly rated detective's heart pumping." He often spoke to himself out loud, giving voice to his inner thoughts. Little did Samuel know that his request would be answered soon and in a most horrifying way.

"I thank the good Lord above for a beautiful full moon. Let's cover the north pasture first, and then we can stake ourselves out here closer to the barns before turning in for the night." Diego and Eduardo pulled two Winchester lever-action rifles from the ranch's gun case. They were model 1886 rifles with nine-round tubular magazines. They were part of their late father's collection and had been at the ranch since the early days. The rifles had been well maintained through the years and were excellent for hunting varmints around the ranch while protecting the herds.

The brothers drove slowly out into the night toward the north pasture, hoping to dispose of the predators threatening their cattle. They carried thermoses of hot coffee with them, along with a small bag of Ms. Valentina's delicious cookies for a late-night snack. Valentina oversaw all the household activities as well as directing the cooks in the kitchen preparing the family's meals. She was an outstanding cook herself, which always resulted in the family gathering in the large dining hall expecting the best from her culinary expertise.

The two brothers sat in the truck, scanning the pasture before them. It was a quiet night except for the sound of the night bugs sending out their rhythmic calls to one another. The warm, soft breezes caused first one and then the other to nod off at times.

DEADLY ATTACK

"We'd better talk to keep ourselves awake, my brother, or the coyote will snatch the calves right in front of us." Eduardo gave Diego a sheepish grin.

"That's a good idea. I've been wondering when you're going to get up the courage to tell our mother you are leaving ranching to pursue your building career?"

Eduardo considered Diego's question before responding. "Our dear brother Ricardo recently shared with Mama his desire to attend law school. She's struggling with that news of him leaving the cattle business behind. I was going to tell her of my desire to start up a construction company, but I think it would be more than she can handle for now. With Samuel's detective work, that would leave her with four sons managing the ranch. I'm sure she knows that we would still be available to jump in and help if the ranch needed us, but it bothers her for us to go in different directions."

"Yes, Eduardo, you may intend to go back and forth helping the ranch if needed, but that's not the same as having your focus fully on the cattle business. You and Ricardo would need to focus on your new careers, the same as Samuel does concerning his detective work if you are to be successful. It would not be the same as being involved with the ranch full time, and Mama knows that. But I do understand your desire to pursue your dreams, and I support both you and my youngest brother in your endeavors. Let's head back toward the barn area and watch there for a while before we turn in for the night."

Sofia lurched upright in bed as the sound of automatic gunfire ripped through the night air. Terror washed over her, knowing that it wasn't Diego and Eduardo's rifles sending the sound in her direction. She quickly pulled on her robe and headed down the stairs to the main entrance, running out onto the driveway and staring at the terrifying scene near the road. The horror of what was taking place washed over her as her world went dark, sending her to the ground. Lights started coming on throughout the hacienda as the brothers, along with a number of the servants, left their beds in panic to see what was happening outside. Valentina stood at her bedroom window, terrified as gunfire lit up the night near Samuel's office. Diego and Eduardo leapt from the truck with rifles in hand, running toward the backside of Samuel's office that was taking the full brunt of two automatic weapons pouring forth their deadly shelling. They could see the silhouettes of two men in the moonlight out on the road, emptying their weapons on Samuel's office. Diego leveled his rifle and fired toward the flashes of light as Eduardo ran behind a stand of live oak trees on the side of the bunkhouse and began emptying his rifle toward the shadows on the road. The assassins stopped firing and fled toward a vehicle sitting a short distance from the bunkhouse on the shoulder of the road. Diego ran around the bunkhouse, out onto the two-lane, leveling his rifle and sending the remaining shells toward the fleeing vehicle, shattering its rear window as one of the projectiles found its mark.

Samuel was awakened by the sound of bullets ripping through the thin wooden walls of the bunkhouse. His whole being went into defensive mode as he threw himself off the bed, pulling the box springs and mattress on top of his body. His bedroom was in the back of the bunkhouse, farthest from the road, providing as much cover as possible. He could hear the deafening blast of the automatic weapons as the bullets ripped through the walls, tearing apart the kitchen along with his office in the front part of the bunkhouse. He tried to reach out to the nightstand to get his pistol but didn't want to leave parts of his body exposed to the incoming fire. He prayed silently for God's hand of protection over him as rifle fire erupted nearby. He heard the squalling of tires spinning their way onto the blacktop mingled with more rifle fire, and then the night went silent.

Eduardo left his position behind the trees and ran around to the front of Samuel's office, kicking in the door and calling out his brother's name. He reached the bedroom just as Samuel pushed the bedding off him, scrambling to get his pistol from the nightstand.

"Are you hit?" Eduardo's voice betrayed the fear built up inside him.

"No. Not that I know of. Are we still in danger?"

"No. Diego emptied his rifle as they were speeding away. Whoever came calling is gone for now."

The night was split open again as distant sirens could be heard screaming out their shrill sounds as emergency vehicles came rushing from Amarillo in their direction. Valentina had maintained her thoughts through the attack, immediately dialing 911 and sending help their way.

Valentina's heart sank, thinking Sofia had been shot as she hurried out the front entrance, seeing her body lying on the ground. She knelt down beside her, pulling Sofia's limp body to her chest, weeping as she rocked her beloved mistress back and forth. Fernando was the first brother on the scene, kneeling down, picking up his mother, and rushing her back inside the hacienda. After a quick examination, he realized she wasn't injured but had apparently fainted from the night attack on her eldest son's life.

"Get a little ammonia on a napkin and bring it to me." Valentina ran to the kitchen and returned shortly, handing the soft cloth to Fernando. After two passes of the cloth under his mother's nose, her eyes fluttered open as she stared around in a daze.

"Oh my Lord, is everyone okay?" Sofia's voice was filled with the horror from the scene that had caused her to lose consciousness.

"Valentina, stay here with Mama." Fernando ran after his brothers as they rushed down the tree-covered driveway toward Samuel's office, praying that their eldest brother was still among the living.

CHAPTER 2

Enemies on the Loose

Joe Halstead slammed on the brakes of his patrol car, sliding to a stop, and jumped out, sprinting toward the bunkhouse, leaving the engine running. An ambulance and fire truck rushed to the scene, pulling into the driveway near Samuel's office. Two Texas highway patrol cars, followed by three Amarillo sheriff vehicles, stopped sideways, blocking the road in both directions. The night was lit up with flashing emergency lights illuminating the bullet-riddled bunkhouse.

Eduardo came out with Samuel in tow just as the sheriff reached the office. "Are you hurt?" Samuel could hear the stress in his friend's voice.

"No, Joe. Thanks to my Lord above and my two brothers' quick reaction, I'm okay. I'm afraid my office didn't survive the attack." The fire truck had placed its high-powered spotlights on the bunkhouse, revealing the splintered wood with some areas completely blown out. The machine guns had riddled the wall toward the road and taken out most of the kitchen cabinets, including Samuel's old reliable refrigerator. The sheriff's deputies hadn't wasted any time searching the roadway for shell casings from the attack.

"Here are some leftovers." Randy Sawyers handed the sheriff a plastic bag containing casings from the automatic weapons. Joe Halstead examined the bag with a concerned look on his face. The fleeing assassins had been sent Samuel's way with sufficient firepower to eliminate him, ending his investigative career for good.

"I'm going up to the house. I'm sure Mama is in a terrible state along with the others. I need to let them know that no one was hurt." Diego headed up the drive just as his brothers came into view, running in his direction. "Everything is good. Just a lot of cleanup to do." Diego continued his way toward the main house, feeling a strong sense of dread inside him. He could assure his mother and others that everything was okay, but in his heart, he knew that this was far from over. Whoever wanted Samuel dead would keep coming until they finished the job. This was a vicious attack aimed at his oldest brother, no doubt brought on by those whom he had put away solving past crimes.

"Do you have any idea who may have led this attack?" The sheriff watched Samuel's face closely as he turned the question over in his mind.

"I have no idea. I haven't received any threats lately, if that's what you mean. It must be someone with a powerful grudge against me. Probably from one of my previous cases. I've dealt with some pretty bad characters in the past."

"I'm going to call in the ATF to help us trace the guns used in the attack. I don't want to alarm you any more than you already are, but these shell casings appear to be from a Soviet-style assault rifle. I remember reading that these same type weapons were used in a gang war in Los Angeles a few years back involving the Russian mob."

"The Russian mob? I have solved some tough cases, but none involving the Russian mob."

"At least not that you know of." The sheriff gave Samuel a concerned look as the possibility of Russian involvement in some previous case had sent killers his way. Joe Halstead knew that if the Russians were involved, this was only the beginning, and they wouldn't stop until Samuel was eliminated. "I'm going to post my deputies nearby tonight and continue a level of protection for the next few days here at the ranch. I suggest you get some rest tonight if possible and come to my office early in the morning. We need to put our heads together and make a list of potential suspects and begin investigating their whereabouts. If some are out of prison and on the loose, we need to check them out."

Before the sheriff left, he placed crime tape around the bunkhouse and told Samuel not to move a lot of things around. He wanted to send other investigators from the Texas DPS Crime Laboratory in Amarillo out to give the crime scene a close inspection. He knew they would need every piece of evidence left behind to catch whoever had launched the attack. He instructed his deputies to block the lane closest to the bunkhouse and the shoulder of the road to hopefully preserve any tire tracks from the getaway vehicle.

Samuel watched as the deputies took up their positions at the end of the driveway and out on the two-lane. He made his way back into his shattered office, stepping on fragments of what was left of his desk and other office equipment. The automatic weapons had done their job well. He shuddered to think where he would be if his bedroom had been in the front of the building. The thin wood walls were no barrier against the force of the bullets tearing the building apart. A cold feeling spread throughout his being. He had brought death and destruction to his family's home. What if they had attacked the main house instead of his office? It dawned on him that he could have not only lost his own life but could have lost family members as well. Having his office here at the ranch was something that he needed to change going forward. He loved being here at his home close to his family, but in his line of work, he was bringing them into harm's way. If he caused them to be hurt in the process, he could never forgive himself.

He tried the microwave to no avail. It had taken a bullet on the rim of the door that had evidently taken out its power circuit. Thankfully, the stove still worked, allowing him to put on a pot of coffee. There was no way he could put his bed back together and lie down and go back to sleep. He wasn't going to wait for his meeting with Joe Halstead the next day to begin listing names of potential enemies. Whoever attacked him or sent their goons to do their dirty work had started a war. He brushed the debris from his desk and sat down with pen and paper to begin listing all those in his previous cases that had reason to come calling. He knew that his next big case was here, front and center, with himself becoming his own client. He needed to find who was behind this attack before they came back attempting to finish their work. They would soon find out that he was still among the living, which would result in them putting their next deadly attack in place.

Samuel completed his list of potential attackers and cleaned up as much as possible before going to the main house for breakfast. He wanted to assure his mother and the others that he was okay and was embarking on his next big case tracking down his would-be assassins. He knew what his mother's reaction would be, but this was why he was in law enforcement. If good people didn't capture and hold evil people responsible for their actions, no one would be safe. He would need to relocate his office to a place in Amarillo until those evil individuals were safely behind bars. He had been attacked on his own soil.

For Samuel, this was a challenge to his very being, and he would not rest until he tracked down and returned the favor to those who came to destroy him. The attack was violent, but Samuel, to his own amazement, found that he had an inward peace. God had spared his life and kept him from the murderous onslaught of the automatic weapons used against him. In the moments after the attack, Psalm 91:10–12 entered into his mind: "*There shall no evil befall thee, neither shall any plague come nigh thy dwelling. For he shall give his angels charge over thee, to keep thee in all thy ways. They shall bear thee up in their hands, lest thou dash thy foot against a stone.*"

The attack had indeed come against his home, but God had protected him through it. These verses were embedded in his mind from previous deadly situations that he had encountered in past investigations. He sent a silent prayer up to heaven asking God to lead him to the perpetrators in the days ahead, allowing him to remove them before they could mount another attack.

Sofia was still shaken from the terror launched against the ranch in the night. She sat at the head of the table with a haggard look on her face. She refused the food offered her, accepting only a cup of coffee as she sat staring at her boys. "Never in my days would I have expected this. I am thankful to our God, Samuel, that you are here at this table this morning. I am begging you to stay out of this and let the authorities handle the investigation in the days to come. This is the first time in my life that I don't feel safe in my own home." His mother's words twisted

DEADLY ATTACK

like a knife in Samuel's heart. The last thing he ever wanted to do was bring death and destruction to the ones that he loved. He chose his words carefully before responding.

"I hate that this evil has come here to the ranch. This is exactly why I entered into law enforcement. Evil must be fought against and overcome by good. I wouldn't do anything, Mama, to cause you additional grief, but I must be involved in stopping those that attacked last night or they will surely keep trying until I am eliminated. I will locate my office for now in Amarillo and work with law enforcement to track down and bring to justice those who started this war. I have prepared a long list of suspects and prayed, asking God's favor in the days ahead."

Samuel looked at the faces before him, including Valentina's, who had entered from the kitchen and stood next to Sofia at the head of the table. Tears ran unabated down his mother's face as she stood, laying her napkin on the table and leaving the room. Valentina escorted her toward the stairs, helping her mistress to her bedroom, praying for God to strengthen her in the days ahead. Tears filled Samuel's eyes as the pain brought into his dear mother's life was because of him and the profession that he had chosen.

"I think you should stay here at the ranch. Your brothers and I can stand watch and help ward off any future attacks with God's help."

"Thank you, Diego, but it would not be safe for any of you if I remained here. I plan on having the newspaper run a story on the attack while announcing that I will set up my office in Amarillo, assisting the authorities in tracking down those responsible. I'm sure the perpetrators will be watching the news to see if I was killed in their attack, and hopefully, this will divert their attention away from the ranch."

"So you intend to put yourself out there tracking down those who are obviously attempting to track you down?"

"Eduardo, that's the business I'm in. Law enforcement has never been easy. Unfortunately, this world is a sinful place. Evil walks among us. We must fight back if society is to remain. No people can long exist if there are no laws, and laws have no effect if there's no one enforcing them. It burdens my heart to see our mother's pain, but I must be in this fight until it's over."

Silence filled the dining hall as Samuel laid his napkin next to his untouched plate, leaving the hacienda to collect what he could from the bunkhouse and head to Amarillo. He would stay in touch by phone and avoid the ranch as much as possible until this business was finished one way or the other. He could have caused great injury to come to those whom he loved, and he was determined to do everything within his power not to bring danger their way again. He had begun parking his jeep on the island in front of the bunkhouse, keeping it under the shade of the large live oak tree. He noticed that a stray bullet had taken out the right headlight during the attack. If it had been parked between the bunkhouse and the road in its regular place, the old jeep would have become a casualty during the onslaught.

"Have you eaten this morning?"

"No, I'm really not hungry." Joe Halstead looked at Samuel with concern in his eyes.

"Perhaps you should take some time away and let myself and others track down these people. They are obviously set on your demise, and they no doubt will be very aware of your search for them."

"Joe, you know I can't do that. It's me they want, and it's me they will get. You can't fight evil by running away from it. This is now my case to solve, along with your help and those that you bring into the investigation. Don't ask me to sit on the sidelines when it's me that has been attacked. I intend to carry the battle to them. When this is finished, it will be to their destruction and not mine, God willing."

ALTON LYNN COOPER

"I knew you would take that position, but I had to try. Let's put our heads together and come up with a plan going forward. Let me pour us a good strong cup of brew, and we'll get to work tracking those who are tracking you."

Sheriff Halstead sat staring at the paper that Samuel had slid in front of him. "You've got quite a list here. You sure have made a lot of enemies in your short detective career."

"You should know how it is, Joe, when you bring the bad actors to justice. They all proclaim their innocence and squeal that law enforcement was out to get them. They rarely ever take responsibility for their own crooked ways."

"What is your plan to start checking them off your list?"

"I need you to check their current status in your offender's database. Some are no doubt out of prison by now, while others are still enjoying their three square meals a day at the taxpayers' expense. My plan is to track down those on the loose first and see if I can tie them to the attack. If that doesn't expose the culprits, I'll check the outside contacts of those still locked up to see if any hired killers have been brought against me by their doing. If I get to that point, I'll need your help in getting their prison com-

22

munication logs to see who their pals are." The sheriff nodded in agreement.

"The forensic team headed to the ranch just before you got here to go over your blown-up office with a fine-tooth comb. I'll let you know what we find."

"How do you plan to get started?"

"I'm going to the newspaper and putting the story of my survival out. I want to let the attackers know that I'm safe and sound and hunting them. I also want to make it known that I'll not be working from the ranch. I need to divert their attention away from my family."

"Sounds good to me, Samuel. I plan on keeping a patrol car there for the next few days, along with sending one up and down the two-lane on a regular basis. Diego said that they fled in the direction of Plainview. We have the authorities there and in Lubbock searching for a car with the back glass blown out. Hopefully, the car will show up and provide us information as to who was in it."

"Joe, I plan on setting up office here in town, leaving the ranch out of harm's way. Do you know of a good dependable realtor in the rental business?"

"I do. Are you open to a suggestion?"

Samuel considered his friend's question for a moment before answering. "It depends on what that suggestion is."

"I say we get you a storefront office on Main Street. Hang out your sign for all to see. Place security cameras in the office and across the street and behind the building to capture anyone casing out the place, and then locate your real workplace here in one of our vacant back rooms on a temporary basis. I can't make your space official here, but I can allow you to operate out of this office as a means of providing protection for you following the attack. The empty Main Street office may draw the next wave of attackers, allowing us to track who is sending them your way."

Samuel considered his friend's suggestion before responding. He had put his family in a bad position, and he didn't want the sheriff to do anything that would be against departmental rules. "Are there any rules concerning the sheriff's department that would be in conflict with your proposal?"

"No. I would not suggest that we break any rules. This would be temporary, as I said, and would be strictly in line with the ongoing investigation."

"Okay, Joe. Sounds good to me. But as you said, this is only a temporary setup. I intend to make that

DEADLY ATTACK

storefront my actual office after a few modifications over the next couple of weeks. I'm not the kind of person that hides out when the going gets rough. They brought this fight to me, and I will do all in my power to take it to them. I'm going to start working this list as soon as you get me the incarceration information. I want to eliminate who I can and then get up close and personal with those who may be hunting me."

"I'll get on it right away, Samuel. Oh, by the way, during your stay here, park your jeep in the police garage. That will help to keep your presence under wraps for the most part and maybe avoid a bomb finding its way under your hood."

"This is already front-page news. It's not every day around here we get a private eye killed." Samuel looked deep into the eyes of the gum-popping young woman behind the counter at the Amarillo newspaper office. Her name tag announced her as Ms. Emily Pepperton, Assistant Editor.

"How did you become Assistant Editor so soon? You appear to be young for the position."

Emily Pepperton gave Samuel a condescending look. "I happen to have graduated at the top of my journalism class, and I'm actually overly qualified for this position. I should be in New York running the

25

Times. How is it that you're so good at being a private investigator that you get your office blown away and run out in the night in your pajamas?"

Samuel realized that he had struck a sensitive spot in the young assistant editor's life. "I'm sorry if I offended you. You obviously are very good at what you do. How much will an ad cost me announcing my new office location when I find one?"

Ms. Emily gave Samuel a big red-lipped grin as she assured him that he would get her paper's best rate. She didn't say what that best rate would be, leaving their future business dealings open. After assuring that the front-page story included his personal comments, Samuel headed for the front door with the bell hanging above it. "I didn't run out in the night in my pajamas. I'm known as a top-rated detective, and I don't run around in public half-dressed and unprepared. I should actually be in DC at FBI headquarters, heading them up."

Samuel stopped by the store and bought a whiteboard and a pad of Post-it notes. He wanted to start putting together the board in his back room office, helping to focus his attention on the investigation in the days ahead. He found that putting his discoveries up on the wall helped him to keep his mind on what he knew while hopefully revealing holes in his ongoing investigation. He stopped by the corner delicatessen and picked up a dozen boiled eggs, a large ring of bologna, and a box of saltine crackers, topping off his purchase with a two-liter of cold diet Pepsi. He headed back to his temporary office with his investigative juices flowing at full speed, eager to get on the trail of his attackers.

Samuel hung the list of names on the whiteboard. It took him back through his past investigations, bringing up a number of unpleasant memories. He stared at each name, trying to imagine which of them might be so angry at him they would attempt to kill him. Larry Rowland, cattle thief; Gerald Wiseman, disgraced insurance agent; Hugo Salinas, corrupt butler for Larson Maxwell; Tony Rollins, dishonest insurance investigator; Andres Rafael, outlaw running the small town of Loralloes; Michael Williams, corrupt art gallery curator; Carl Sanderson, art forger; Marilyn Laski, corrupt art museum director; Wilfred Sandalson, corrupt art school employee; Rudy Goldman, Anthony Reynolds's enforcer; James Dawson and his brother Shepard Dawson, antique store workers; Anthony Reynolds, corrupt art thief and killer; Paul Gleason, corrupt bank president; Brandon Mitchell, antique store owner with mafia connections.

Joe Halstead was right. Samuel had made a number of enemies in his past cases, and any one of them was capable of wanting to get even. He went to the whiteboard and pulled the list off, writing some additional names on it from his days on Kalmajo Island: Manuel Alvera, drug dealer; Ronald Maubry, corrupt police chief; Joey Dawson, corrupt police deputy; Adam Webber, corrupt mayor.

As he looked at the list of names, he couldn't imagine some of them being so bold as to orchestrate the attack on his office, while others were capable of any atrocity. He stopped himself from prematurely crossing any of their names off the list until he could definitely rule them out. With the large list of suspects, it would take time to eliminate the ones that couldn't have been involved. He knew this was not going to be an easy task and no doubt would put him in harm's way throughout the investigation. He would not rest easy until the attackers were identified and put away for good.

CHAPTER 3

Searching for Clues

"I need to meet with you here in town if you can get away from the ranch for a while." Eduardo covered the mouthpiece on the phone and spoke to someone in the background. "Sorry about that. Sending some of the cowhands out for the day. It's good to hear your voice this morning, my brother. I can meet with you this afternoon if that works for you."

"That would be much appreciated. Meet me at Carmen's cantina, and I will buy your lunch."

"Hey, getting to see my brother who is still alive and have him buy my lunch, it can't get any better than that. What time?"

Samuel hung up the phone, placed a pad of paper on the desk before him, and began listing a number of steps needed to hopefully keep him alive over the duration of his investigation. He had been frugal with his earnings from the previous cases and had built up a considerable amount in his business bank account. It was time to put some of those funds to work with Eduardo's help.

Carmen Ortega flashed a brilliant smile in Samuel's direction as he entered the cantina for lunch. She was an attractive woman in her early thirties and had a soft spot for Amarillo's master detective. Samuel had played cat and mouse games with her in the past while staying unattached, pursuing his investigative career. Carmen, along with some other young ladies in Amarillo, had tried in vain to establish a close relationship with Samuel to no avail.

"It's so good to see you walk in here today. The news spread all over town about that horrible attack last night. You aren't hurt, are you, my dear Samuel?"

"Your concern for me is touching, Ms. Carmen. No, my assailants were no match for my bunkhouse, box springs, and mattress."

Carmen's face twisted up at Samuel's last words. "Box springs and mattress?"

"Yes. Now what is your special for the day? My brother Eduardo will be joining me shortly, and I want him to experience some of your very best."

"You must try my special chalupas. Your taste buds will never be the same again, this I can assure you."

"Will my taste buds survive and not be burned from my palate for good?"

"They are a little daring, but nothing that a strong man like you can't handle."

Samuel was always nervous when the cantina proprietor suggested something other than his regular three tacos with extra mild sauce. She had set him up before, after he sent too many teases her way. He always steered clear of her "best" after that experience, realizing that habaneros were lurking somewhere in the cantina's kitchen.

"Okay. But be gentle. I need my brother to survive lunch so that he can perform a special project for me."

Samuel and Eduardo ate in silence for a while, each reliving the attack from the night before.

"You must know that our mother remains in a state of shock this morning."

"Yes, and I truly regret that I put my family in this position. That's why I need your help. I'm moving my office to a vacant storefront on Main Street, and I need you to help with some necessary modifications."

"Are you sure about this? Your absence from the ranch will be another grief placed upon our mother."

"It's best for now until I can track down my assailants. I've already put the word out that I will no longer be operating from the ranch, hopefully to steer future attacks toward me here and not at my family's home."

"Tell me what you need and I'll see what I can do."

Over the next half hour, Samuel shared with his brother his plan to make his new office attack-proof.

"This is going to cost you a pretty penny, you realize that, right? I wouldn't charge you labor, of course, but the materials you describe won't come cheap."

"I'm well aware of that. I need to keep myself alive until I bring to justice those that have brought this terror upon my family."

"I'll get started right away. Mama's not going to like this in the least bit. That's between you and her. I will need to bring in some additional help from the local building community to get this done and meet your timeframe. Is that okay with you?"

"Eduardo, do what you feel is necessary to finish the office as we have discussed. I trust your good judgment."

"When is the last time you cleaned that coffee pot? Either you keep feeding me three-day-old stuff or that pot of yours has a life of its own."

DEADLY ATTACK

"A strong law enforcement person such as yourself should be able to enjoy the richness of the Amarillo sheriff's best brew. Now settle in and let me tell you what the crime lab has found at your deceased bunkhouse. They were able to make casts of tire tracks near the road where your attackers parked their car. They also collected a small bag of glass as a result of Diego emptying his rifle on them, blowing out the car's back glass."

Joe Halstead laid two bullets on the desk in front of Samuel. "They dug these out of the mattress that covered you during the attack. The bullets passed through the bunkhouse wall and the wood slats in your box springs and stopped just before exiting the mattress and finding you behind it."

Samuel picked up the two deformed bullets in his hand. "Do you know where they were located in the mattress?"

Joe Halstead stared at his friend before speaking. "They came from the area near the headboard."

Samuel knew immediately that his head was inches away from the bullets that tried desperately to take away his life. God's Word filled his mind once again, reminding him that God had given His angels charge over him, to keep him in all his ways.

"Joe, it was God's protection that spared me last night. I will lean heavily upon Him to keep me from harm in the days ahead."

"You will need to, my friend. This investigation will be your most dangerous, I'm sure. I will help you all I can, but ultimately, we all need a higher power's protection forming a wall around us. I'm not a churchgoing man as you, but I do understand we're not in this life alone."

"Did they locate the car that was used in the attack?"

"No, still searching. The weapons used were AK-47 Soviet-style assault guns. The shells were identified as 7.62 x 39 mm cartridges. They are capable of passing through a little over fifteen inches of solid hardwood. It's no surprise they were able to blow apart those thin bunkhouse walls of yours. These people want you dead in the worst way. If I were you, I would think through your past cases and list what major organizations could have been shut down due to your investigation. You've made yourself some powerful enemies that want payback in the worst way."

Samuel sat in his temporary office with the list of names in front of him. Following the sheriff's advice, he needed to consider which arrests of

DEADLY ATTACK

individuals from past investigations could have interrupted a major crime organization as they were brought to justice. He hung the whiteboard back on the wall with seven names highlighted on it.

Andres Rafael was busted when Samuel solved the cattle rustling case. He was controlling the border town of Loralloes, Texas. Michael Williams was the corrupt art dealer costing major galleries millions of dollars in forged artworks. Anthony Reynolds was the mastermind behind the art thefts and killed his own brother to gain access to his collection. Brandon Mitchell was the partner in the antique company's business and had known mafia ties. Manuel Alvera was the drug dealer on Kalmajo Island. The actual head of the operation was believed to be in the States and was never identified. Adam Webber was the ruthless mayor involved in the drug business on Kalmajo Island that wanted Samuel eliminated.

And last, Tony Rollins was the lead investigator for the Morales Insurance Company. He was involved in the cattle-rustling scam, costing the company millions of dollars. He was never apprehended at the end of the case, and his whereabouts were still unknown. He had set Samuel up going to the border town of Loralloes to be murdered by Rafael's gang of cutthroats.

Samuel stared at the names, realizing that any one of these would be more than delighted to send death and destruction his way. The chilling thought that crept into his mind was it may be none of those noted on the board, and someone else completely unknown to him was the true culprit.

CHAPTER 4

On the Wrong Trail

Eduardo was hard at work converting the empty storefront into a well-secured safe place for his older brother. He had brought in a number of skilled builders to make short work of the project. Following Samuel's direction, he removed the front picture windows, made the openings smaller, and then installed double panes of bulletproof glass in the openings. This still allowed a clear view of what was happening on the street and made it possible to close off the openings from inside with heavy steel shutters when needed. The front and rear doors were reinforced steel with solid wood cores and were hung using hidden hinges.

The more difficult task involved opening a portion of the back wall and creating an inside parking space for Samuel's jeep in the back of the building.

The garage door was heavily reinforced in the same manner as the pedestrian doors and could only be opened from the inside using a keypad or accessed from the outside by a separate transmitter. The inside of the structure was studded out, allowing the walls to be reinforced to repel the type of shells that were able to destroy his bunkhouse.

After completing the structural work, Eduardo brought in an electronics expert to install a high-level security system capable of monitoring the outside entrances, front and back, as well as the interior spaces. The system's cameras were set to record outside activity should any unwanted guests come calling. Security screens were installed in Samuel's office space, allowing him to monitor the outside areas when he was preparing to exit the building. His private quarters were outfitted with a bed, a small kitchen area, and a bath and shower space. The office was located in the same block as the sheriff's office with the back alley servicing both buildings. Samuel determined to make this his working and living space until this case was over, allowing him to hopefully avoid putting his family in any ongoing danger.

"Well, is this what you had in mind?" Eduardo watched Samuel's expression closely after he finished walking through his remodeled office space.

DEADLY ATTACK

"I think it will work for the time being. When will the sign be installed out front?"

"It should be up in two days. You must really want to draw your enemies to you. Are you sure this is what you want?"

Samuel had ordered a neon sign that proclaimed to anyone interested that this was indeed Amarillo's master detective's place of business.

"I want to make myself available. You can't run and hide from those trying to do you harm. Better to face them head-on if possible. You did a good job, Eduardo. I appreciate your work on my behalf and would be pleased to pay you for your labor."

"No labor charges, my brother. Just don't be taking any crazy actions that very well could bereave our mother of her eldest son. Also, it would be a blessing to see you in our family's pew at church on Sunday. Mother needs to see that you're still up and moving around."

"I'll be there. I've stayed away from the ranch on purpose to avoid drawing anyone else there seeking my demise."

"Have a seat, and we'll go over who may be out and about, seeking to exterminate you." Joe Halstead went to the coffee pot and brought back two cups of steaming brew. Samuel sniffed his before taking a sip, smacking his lips together.

ALTON LYNN COOPER

"Hey, fresh pot. Doesn't have that three-day-old burnt taste. Sorry if I insulted you before."

"Samuel, I actually took your advice and washed the pot after our last visit. I was amazed at what came out of there. I had to throw the rag away. Couldn't get the tar out of it. Take a look at this and see what you're up against."

Joe Halstead laid the paper on the desk in front of Samuel and waited for his reaction.

Tony Rollins was still on the loose and had never been apprehended nor held accountable for his involvement in defrauding the Morales Insurance Company in the cattle-rustling scheme. Andres Rafael had recently been released from incarceration and had disappeared from public view. Manuel Alvera was out and about. His last known place of residence was back on Kalmajo Island. Anthony Reynolds was serving a life sentence for the murder of his brother, but his accomplice Michael Williams was released from prison five months ago with his whereabouts unknown. Along with Reynolds, Brandon Mitchell and Adam Webber were still in prison for their involvement in the art thefts and drug business.

"This is quite a list. Four on the loose that I am sure wouldn't send flowers if I should depart this life unexpectedly."

"Here's one that you may want to check out first. It seems he was recently seen in Chicago meeting with some known hired guns that the FBI has been monitoring for some time."

Samuel looked at the name on the note and gave out a low whistle.

"His name hadn't even come to mind. He appeared to me as one that didn't have enough brains of his own to carry out any coordinated attack. I thought of him as Reynolds's pit bull, not thinking for himself but doing Anthony's bidding."

"He tried to kill you more than once when you were on the stolen art case. I wouldn't underestimate him."

Samuel stared at Rudy Goldman's name on the slip of paper. He was Anthony Reynolds's goon enforcer who tried to kill him by blowing up his rental car and then a second time by smashing his other rental car with a stolen truck. He was also the one that was preparing to drown him in the ocean in France and who almost paralyzed him by kicking him in the spine.

"What day was he seen in Chicago?"

"Wednesday last week. Four days before the attack on your bunkhouse."

"Any information on where he's staying in Chicago?"

"No. I'm not even sure he's still in the city. The FBI didn't move in on their meeting. They are waiting to make a connection between the hired guns and who the masterminds are that may be behind them. They are pretty sure they are connected to one of the organized crime families working between Chicago and other groups on the West Coast."

Samuel could sense his mother's discomfort as he sat next to her in the family pew. It tore at his heart to know he was the one responsible for her state of mind. He knew that he could take away her worry by fulfilling her wish to let law enforcement do the heavy lifting tracking down those who had tried to kill him. He also knew that he could not ignore the burning desire inside him to bring those to justice that brought terror to him and his family. His thoughts turned to the pastor's message as he announced the subject that God had laid on his heart for that day.

*****

"This world is filled with those that seek their own way. God's Word tells us that man's ways are

DEADLY ATTACK

right in their own eyes. I encourage you to ask yourself what God wants you to focus on and seek His path for your life." The pastor's voice drilled its way into Samuel's heart that morning as he opened God's Word and read the passage of scripture before him. *"But seek ye first the kingdom of God, and his righteousness; and all these things shall be added unto you. Take therefore no thought for the morrow: for the morrow shall take thought for the things of itself. Sufficient unto the day is the evil thereof."*

The pastor went on to explain that the last phrase taught us that we have enough in our lives to deal with today. We don't need to bring tomorrow's challenges our way before tomorrow comes. "God will be in your tomorrow and has enough grace to carry you through whatever may come your way. Our God has promised to supply all our needs if we will seek Him first in our lives."

Samuel bowed his head and asked God to be with him, not only tomorrow but in all the days ahead. He also asked his heavenly Father to bring peace and comfort to his dear mother's heart. His mother's soft voice sounded next to him, drawing him from his prayer.

"I don't care who is after you. I still expect to see your face at our family's dinner table this afternoon.

Don't you dare tell me no, my son. I've never shot one of your dear papa's guns, *rest his soul*, but I can learn if necessary."

*****

Samuel made airline reservations to fly to Chicago on Tuesday morning. He hated flying but didn't want to drive two thousand miles round trip there and back from Amarillo. He reserved a rental car at O'Hare International and made hotel reservations at the Hilton near the airport. He didn't like to stay in such an expensive place but wanted to get into Chicago, locate Goldman, determine if he was the one that sent killers his way, and then get out of Chicago as soon as possible. If it was Rudy Goldman, he would send the Chicago authorities to apprehend him and then have him sent to Texas for trial. He shared his travel plans with Joe Halstead, keeping him informed just in case he met with certain individuals in Chicago that would require him to call in the cavalry. He realized that the Amarillo sheriff couldn't do anything for him personally in Chicago, but he could send help from the Windy City's authorities if he sent an SOS the sheriff's way.

Samuel left his jeep in the parking lot and flew out of Rick Husband Airport in Amarillo early

DEADLY ATTACK

Tuesday morning. He made a mental note to have Arnold Snuffman at the Amarillo Car Hospital repair the blown-out headlight when he returned from Chicago. He swallowed two Dramamine tablets while waiting for his flight to board, hoping to help the butterflies in his stomach take a break.

This was the worst part of being an elite private investigator for him. He would rather be in a shootout with a desperate criminal or be stranded on some remote island waiting to be rescued than ride in the air at thirty thousand feet, being hurled through space at over six hundred miles an hour in a tin can. He took his window seat, pulled the shade down, closed his eyes, and willed the flight to be over while the plane waited its turn on the tarmac for takeoff.

"Are you asleep?"

Samuel slit one eye open and looked at the person with the squeaky voice in the aisle seat next to him.

"Yes, I am asleep."

After a few moments, the squeaky voice returned. "That's so clever of you. How can you answer me if you are asleep?"

The giggles that followed sounded like some of the girls back in Samuel's fourth-grade class at Amarillo's elementary school.

ALTON LYNN COOPER

"If I stop answering you in my sleep, do you promise to stop talking to me?"

A burst of squealing laughter broke out in Samuel's ear.

"You are so cute. Are you married?"

Samuel turned his head to the window shade and began snoring in a snorting whooshing sort of way that drowned out his admirer's giggles in the seat next to him. He eventually did go to sleep and woke when the plane bounced its way onto the O'Hare International runway in Chicago. His young admirer stuffed a crumpled-up piece of paper into his silk shirt pocket, looked at him from behind large speckled-rim glasses, and popped her gum one last time before singing out, "Toodle-oo!" as she departed the plane.

*****

Samuel checked into his hotel and asked the bald-headed desk clerk if he knew where the best Mexican restaurant was in town. The portly man turned his back to the counter, digging in a pile of brochures, and then handed one to Samuel with the picture of a chili pepper blowing out flames.

DEADLY ATTACK

"Is that place safe? It looks like you might need to carry a personal fire extinguisher with you."

"It's harmless. I've been eating there for years." The clerk gave Samuel a wide, lopsided grin while slapping his protruding stomach. "A little caution may be due, however. Before I became their regular customer, I had a full head of hair just like you. It would be a shame if you lost that glorious mop on the top of your head." The man rubbed his bald head as if he were remembering the time when he had a rich head of hair in days gone by.

Samuel turned toward the elevator to go to his room and freshen up before heading to the Flaming Pepper.

"Hold on, cowboy. You've got a message waiting here." The clerk pulled a note from the box with Samuel's room number on it, handing it to him.

"Why did you call me cowboy?" Samuel wondered if the man knew that his family owned one of West Texas's sprawling cattle ranches.

"Saw your boots, heard your Southern drawl, and you are sun-tanned. Didn't get that here in our fair city."

"You're pretty observant. If I need to hire another person as my assistant in my line of work, I may give

ALTON LYNN COOPER

you a call. Of course, that all depends on whether or not I survive my visit to the Flaming Pepper joint."

"What kind of work are you in?"

"I stay on the move, hunting people who are hunting me."

Samuel left the desk clerk with a look of wonder on his face as he watched the tall, sun-tanned Texan head for the elevator.

"Hey, Gregory, how is fighting crime in your neck of the woods?" Gregory Lawrence was the FBI agent who had helped Samuel during his previous case tracking down the missing Amarillo banker.

"Keeping busy. Never enough time in the day to hunt down all the crooks. Seems when you put one away, two more pop up to take their place."

"How did you know where to find me?"

"Our good friend Sheriff Halstead contacted me to let me know what happened at your office and your travel plans. He thought I may be able to hook you up with the two agents here who have been monitoring individuals they believe are involved in an organized crime family here in Chicago. Seems the crooks they are keeping an eye on had a visit from one of your old acquaintances."

"You said here. Does that mean you are in Chicago?"

DEADLY ATTACK

"For tonight. I'm heading back to DC tomorrow."

"Do you have time to meet for dinner and catch up on old times?"

"Sure. What greasy spoon do you have in mind?"

Samuel gave the agent the address for the Flaming Pepper joint and headed for the shower. He hung his silk shirt on a hanger, placing it on the small rack near the bathroom to air out. He had only packed two of his shirts and would have to alternate between them to avoid offending Chicago's citizenry. He hadn't had time to go shopping for more clothes after the attack on his bunkhouse and, much to his dismay, a number of bullets had air-conditioned four of his silk shirts and four pairs of his favorite blue jeans. He determined to collect damages from his would-be assassins and replace his lost wardrobe before sending them off to enjoy a few years of jailhouse hospitality in new wardrobes of their own.

*****

The Flaming Pepper joint was hopping when Samuel arrived.

"Have a seat, sir, and we'll call your name when a table opens up."

"How long do you think that may be?"

"Hard to say. Depends on how many tacos, tamales, and nacho chips get consumed tonight. Some people order, eat, get their second wind, and order again."

Samuel took his seat, smelling the rich aroma of the Flaming Pepper's fine cuisine drifting his way. Gregory Lawrence entered a few minutes later and slid in alongside Samuel, letting out a whooshing sound. Samuel looked at his friend's tired face that seemed to have aged a bit since their last meeting.

"Rough day?"

"Long day! I've been in town, following up on a robbery attempt at one of the banks. An alert security guard thwarted the robber, causing him to flee the scene. I was sent to review the security video to see if this was the same person that we've been chasing on three other holdups."

"Was he your man?"

"No. Just another person choosing not to work while trying to get other people's money."

"Your table is ready, sir. Follow me." Samuel and Gregory followed the tall, thin waiter to a table in the middle of the restaurant and took their seats.

"What's good here?" Gregory asked.

Samuel looked at Gregory's face before responding. "Depends. Do you want to buy pants with an elastic waist and lose your hair or try to stay as you are?"

"What does that mean?"

"Advice from the clerk back at my hotel."

Samuel ordered a platter with samplers of the restaurant's best and was surprised at how tasty the food was. It had a slight burn to it but nothing like the picture on the front of the brochure. Gregory Lawrence played it safe and ordered an all-American cheeseburger with fries. The curly-haired waitress stared at the agent, shaking her head back and forth as she took his order.

"You need to live a little, amigo. Get some of that good south-of-the-border cuisine in that body of yours."

"I'm not familiar with the two agents working the case here in town where your man was spotted. I'll find out how you can set up a meeting with them. Most of these guys play it close to the chest and are reluctant to share their information with outsiders. I have to head back to DC early in the morning, so I can't stay and smooth the way for you. I will let them know that you can be trusted to not blow the case they are working on. Hopefully, they will share what they know about your pigeon."

"I have a list of those who may have orchestrated the attack on me. He's one that tried to kill me three times before. I don't think he has the brains to pull off anything on his own, but maybe those gang-related individuals he met with may have been involved in the attack against me."

"Here's where you need to be very careful. The agents here in town have been watching the men they believe are tied to a vast money laundering outfit operating here in the States, shipping large amounts of cash out of the country. They won't share anything with you that would lead you to the men they've been tracking. Sorry to say, but your bunkhouse getting blown up is the least of their concerns. Don't take that the wrong way."

*****

Samuel spent a restless night's sleep, waking several times, hearing the automatic weapons sending their deadly bullets through the bunkhouse. He awoke the next morning, feeling as if he'd not gone to bed at all.

"This is going to be a long day, old boy. Better get a lot of strong brew in you."

DEADLY ATTACK

He sat in the hotel dining room with the morning newspaper, having a large pancake breakfast with his own pot of rich, dark coffee on the table. He had requested three boiled eggs at the breakfast counter, only to be told his choices were scrambled, fried, or made into an omelet.

"We don't boil here. It takes too long."

The morning paper had the story of the attempted bank robbery on page three, indicating that the FBI agent assigned to the case was leaving town with no suspect in tow.

Samuel finished his breakfast and dialed the FBI agent's number that Gregory had given him. The voice on the other end of the line was less than cordial, informing Samuel that he and his associate had no relevant information concerning his near-death experience.

"I need to meet with you. The man you observed meeting with those you are watching has tried to kill me in the past. He is a prime suspect in the attack against me, and I will track him down with or without your help. I'm pretty good at finding people myself, and I'm sure I'll be able to find your pigeons that he met with and ask them questions about my case. I don't want to interfere with your investigation, but pardon me for being selfish. My staying alive is

ALTON LYNN COOPER

more important to me than your money laundering problems."

The silence on the other end of the phone let Samuel know that he had not made a friend of the agent he was talking to.

"Where and when?"

Michael Robertson was a burly, hard-looking man with a dark birthmark on his right cheek. The man with him was equally imposing, with dark brooding eyes that were half-covered by drooping eyelids. Samuel wasn't sure whether these were the mafia individuals the agents were monitoring or if they were the agents themselves. The men before him could easily fit into either world—crooks or keepers of the peace.

"You Garcia?"

"Yes, and you are?"

"Lawrence told us about you. As I said on the phone, we know nothing about the attack on you. I'm warning you: don't stick your nose in where it's not wanted. We've been on these guys for over two years. Our case is almost ready to bust wide open. We don't need a small-town investigator to come in here and mess up our work."

"I don't intend to mess up anything. I intend to find the man that you saw meeting with your goons.

DEADLY ATTACK

As I said, I will find him with or without your help. If I have to find your two birds and get them to sing out his whereabouts, then so be it."

Both of the agents standing in front of Samuel gave him a look that could kill if they were indeed mafia men.

"One thing, Garcia: your goon that met with our goons wasn't exactly their close relation. He got smacked around real good in an alley five blocks from here and was left bleeding on the ground. I think our two tried to kill your man. The last we saw of him, he staggered out of the alley and flagged down a cab. Now that's all we've got for you. Stay out of our investigation and don't force us to arrest you."

Michael Robertson and his fellow agent turned and left the hotel, letting Samuel know their interaction with the small-town detective from Texas was finished.

Samuel left the hotel and walked five blocks to the south, not finding any alleys in the last block. He turned and went back to the north, walking amongst different groups of individuals talking on cell phones while dodging in and out of passersby on the sidewalk. Before he reached the fifth street from the hotel, he had been approached by four different individuals asking for money. One of the men was staggering along and smelled of sour whiskey when he came up close to Samuel's face.

"Pleeseee miser, me daughter iss siccckk and needs er medecineee."

Samuel knew that the only medicine the beggar was after was another bottle of the same poison that had put him in his present condition. He had walked beyond five streets, and still, there was no alley in the last block. He continued north and finally came upon an alley in the seventh block from the hotel. He turned into the alley with waves of foul dirty odors filling his nostrils. This alley reminded him of those on Kalmajo Island near the Lost Sailor Saloon. He had entered that place for the same reason he was here in Chicago—searching for those that had tried to destroy him and Davey Gibson.

He walked slowly up the alley as large rats scurried along in front of him. The stench of the trash and filth was overpowering as he continued deeper into the alley. Broken liquor bottles spread here and there, mixed with human urine, filled the place. The dumpsters were full and overflowing, providing the rats plenty of rotting food. He stepped on shards of broken wine bottles and other small pieces of debris, making his way deeper into the forlorn place.

DEADLY ATTACK

Samuel stopped short, staring at the splattered red spots on the ground and against the brick wall near a dumpster. It looked like blood that had been shed there recently. He had no idea if it was from Rudy Goldman or some other unfortunate individual. A rough voice called out behind Samuel, asking what he was doing in their alley. He turned to face three squat Chinese individuals in dirty, stained clothes.

"Is this truly your alley?"

"Are you deaf? I already told you this is our alley." The man pointed to his two comrades and gave Samuel a grimacing smile, showing two rows of yellow, broken teeth.

"Do you see this blood here?" Samuel pointed to the floor of the alley and the wall. "Do you know how it got here?"

"Your blood will be added to it if you don't give us your money for trespassing on our property." The squat man in front of Samuel spread his legs and flung his arms wide in an arc, apparently trying to show off a kung fu move.

"Are you sure you want to do this?"

The little man let out a howl that was supposed to scare his opponent into submission as he stomped his feet in place, circling his arms and preparing for attack.

Samuel spread his legs and stomped his cowboy boots, making arm moves himself, went into a crouched position, and then threw his face to the sky, letting out a bloodcurdling scream that echoed off the walls of the alley, sending the rats fleeing in different directions. Samuel bugged his eyes wide open in their sockets, pulled his lips back in a snarl, and started clacking his two perfect rows of pearly white teeth together. The three squat men's eyes bulged from their heads as they turned, fleeing in the direction of the street. Samuel let out another bloodcurdling scream, sending them pumping their short legs toward the end of the alley and out onto the street.

"Your alley indeed." He looked deeper into the dank recess, seeing blankets along the walls with shaggy-haired heads lifted out from under them, staring in his direction out of bloodshot eyes. "Nothing wrong here. False alarm. Go back to sleep." He pulled his pocketknife out and scraped some flakes of the blood into his handkerchief, placing it back in his pocket, and then made his way back toward his hotel.

*****

DEADLY ATTACK

"That's right, Charles Street, near Madison Place." Samuel watched as the man flipped through sheet after sheet on his clipboard.

"When was this again?"

"Within the last week."

"You can't be any more specific than that? We gotta lot of cabs in and out of this place."

"This would have been a big man bleeding. I'm sure your cabbie must have complained about the mess left in his back seat."

"Jerry, git over here!" The flustered cab manager yelled at an old bent-over man across the garage as he was wiping down the inside of a cab near the wall. "Did one of the boys bring a bloody rig in here sometime last week?"

"Bloody? Looked like a hog died in the thing. It was Wally's rig. Couldn't get all of it out. Smeared it around and told him to think of replacing the back cushion."

"What is the cab number and where can I find Wally?" Samuel's investigative juices kicked into full speed ahead. The cab manager scribbled down the requested information and handed it to Samuel.

"Might not find him. Been off the last few days. Plays the horses, you know."

"Where is his cab now?"

ALTON LYNN COOPER

"Jerry, show this man Wally's rig and git him off my back."

Samuel used a cloth from the old man's cleaning cart, pressing it into the cab's back cushion, drawing out some of the blood that no doubt used to be in Rudy Goldman's body. He hoped he could get enough of the blood remaining in the seat foam onto the cloth to enable the lab to test it against the blood in his handkerchief.

*****

Wally Morrison's small house hadn't seen a coat of paint in many years. The lawn was long deceased and had given itself over to numerous weeds that now called the place home. Samuel knocked on the door and waited, not hearing any movement inside. He knocked more vigorously again and heard a faint stirring inside. The door swung slowly open, and a tall, skinny young man with bloodshot eyes peered into Samuel's face. Wally Morrison looked as if he hadn't eaten for the last month. He was a weak-chinned individual with long skinny arms protruding out of a yellowed wrinkled T-shirt hanging loosely at his side.

"What you want?"

"Are you Wally Morrison?"

DEADLY ATTACK

"Yeah, I guess. You come to my house, right?"

"Right. I need to ask you some questions."

"Who are you?"

Samuel flashed his detective license in front of Wally's bloodshot eyes.

"You tha law?"

"I'm the law, Wally. Where did you drop off the bleeding man that messed up your cab last week?"

Wally's face screwed itself up in a wrinkled shape that matched the T-shirt hanging off his bony shoulders.

"Dropped him at a boarding house."

"He didn't want to go to the hospital?"

"Nope. Said stay away from the cops and drop him at the boarding house. What happened to em? Did he die?"

"Not that I know of, but I need to find him. What is the address of the boarding house?"

"Ain't got it. It's in the log in my cab back at the station."

"Thanks, Wally. Go back to bed. You look like you need to get plenty of rest."

Samuel called the cab manager and got the address of the boarding house and headed in that direction. The traffic was terrible, causing him to dread, possibly getting a scratch or ding on the rental car, costing him when he turned it in at the airport. He moved slowly, obeying the twenty-five-mile-an-hour speed limit as other cars raced around him, laying on their horns.

"Get off the road, Granny, and take you a nap."

"Get out of the way, you out-of-towner."

"Where'd you learn to drive, meathead?"

The Chicago drivers continued darting around the slow-moving rental car, throwing their remarks back in Samuel's direction. He finally reached Litchfield Road, turning onto it and heading for the boarding house. The old clapboard building looked like it may have been related to Wally's rundown house. The painted surface was long worn off, and the front yard was rutted from being used as a parking lot. The ancient wooden front door was heavily cracked, with a rusty knocker hanging on for dear life with one rusty screw holding it to the old door. Samuel raised the knocker into a level position, giving it a loud thumping, hoping it didn't come off in his hand or, worse, the old door gave way, crashing into the boarding house lobby.

A short older man opened the door, looking up into Samuel's face.

"Full up, bud. You need to make an advanced reservation if you want to stay here. I can check my book, but you're looking at three to four weeks out, I'm sure."

"I don't need a reservation, but thank you anyway. I'm looking for one of your guests who may have come in a little under the weather."

"You mean the big ox that almost got himself killed?"

"Yes. Is he still here?"

"Came in a hurry-like, packed his stuff, and fled the scene. Said if anyone came looking for him, tell them he died and I buried him in the backyard."

"Is he buried in the backyard?"

"Ain't got one. Parking lot, you know."

"So you don't know where he was going?"

"No. I ain't no social club, you know. I don't give a hoot where they come from or where they go after they leave here, just as long as they pay their bill. Gotta go. Cabbage boiling on the stove. Making a nice lunch for the guests. Today's special: cabbage and chopped-up boiled wieners. Could sell you a bowl if you want one, even though I don't normally do that for unregistered guests."

"Thank you, but I already ate yesterday."

*****

ALTON LYNN COOPER

"Rudy Goldman. G-o-l-d-m-a-n." Samuel waited for the nurse to check her records.

"Sorry, Mr. Raceria, no one was admitted under that name."

"Garcia, not Raceria. Did you have anyone fitting the description I gave you check into the hospital in the last week?"

"Big, bloody, beat up pretty bad—nope. That normally describes all our patients here in Chicago, but this one doesn't ring any of my bells."

Samuel hung up the phone, trying to think of his next move. He had called all the hospitals and health clinics, but none of them had treated a man in Rudy's condition. He picked up the phone and dialed the Chicago Police Department. After being placed on hold and forced to listen to advertisements about Billy Bob's fine used automobiles, followed by a few serenades of elevator music, a voice finally came on the other end of the line.

"If this is an emergency, please hang up and dial 911."

"Lady, if this was an emergency, I wouldn't need 911. I'd need the number for the undertaker."

"If you continue in that tone of voice, young man, I'll hang up and send the undertaker to the

DEADLY ATTACK

number you're calling from. Now how may I assist you?"

Samuel asked his question and was surprised to learn that the good city of Chicago had twenty-three bodies in the morgue from the last two weeks.

"Sorry if that number disappoints you. It's been kinda slow around here lately."

"How many are still in the morgue unclaimed?" Samuel pulled the phone from his ear as the receiver on the other end was dropped on the counter at police headquarters, allowing the clerk to rustle through a stack of papers near the phone.

"Four are still currently the guests of our fair city. Do you want to come down and take one or more home with you today?"

Samuel stood watching the attendant as he pulled open one drawer after another, removing the sheet covering the face of the body on the shelf. He let out a low whistle as the third drawer was opened and the sheet pulled back, revealing Rudy Goldman's swollen face that had definitely taken a horrific beating.

"Looks like whoever beat him up sent him your way."

"He didn't die from the beating." Samuel looked at the attendant expectantly.

65

ALTON LYNN COOPER

"What did he die of?"

"The two nasty gunshot holes in the back of his head."

"Have the police caught anyone that you know of?"

"Mister, our police are still trying to find a whole list of killers that have been sending bodies our way for a number of years now. You are in the beautiful city of Chicago, you know."

"Has anyone claimed his body?"

"It's still here, isn't it? No one has contacted us as of yet. Check back next week if you're interested. If no calls by then, you can have him if you want."

"Would it be possible to get a sample of his DNA?"

"You a cop?"

Samuel showed the attendant his private eye license while explaining the reason for his request.

"I guess since no one has claimed him, I could make that available for your investigation."

Samuel slipped his folded handkerchief and the rag from the cab into the plastic container along with the sample that was offered to him. He would have the samples tested back in Texas to determine if the blood from the alley and the cab was indeed Goldman's. It would also come in handy as a comparison if any other evidence showed up in the future that would reveal his attacker's DNA. Another thought entered his mind at that moment. He pulled the pad from his pocket and made a note to give Gregory Lawrence a call.

*****

Samuel packed and headed to the airport. In his detective heart, he wanted to track down the two goons that were seen with Rudy Goldman, hoping to find out why they gave him a brutal beatdown. He also would like to know if they were the ones that later caught up with him and finished the job. Evidently, Goldman was after something from them that they weren't willing to give. Samuel wondered if they might be connected to Anthony Reynolds. He was still in prison, and Goldman had been his goon enforcer in the art theft ring. It had been rumored that Goldman ratted out his old boss, who was still in prison, while Goldman received a lighter sentence and was on the loose again. If Reynolds did, in fact, reach out from prison and have Goldman killed, could he also have reached out, sending the gunmen Samuel's way? The one thing he knew for sure was that he could scratch one name off the list of his would-be assassins.

CHAPTER 5

A Sad Goodbye

Samuel retrieved his Jeep from the airport parking lot and headed to the sheriff's office. He wanted to keep Joe Halstead apprised of his ongoing efforts as much as possible. He reasoned within himself that if something happened to him along the way, his good friend could send the authorities to the last known contacts in his investigation.

"Draw up a seat. Made a fresh pot this morning."

Samuel took his place in front of the sheriff's desk, pulling his notes from his pocket along with the plastic container holding the blood samples he had collected in Chicago.

"I need you to send these to the crime lab if you would. They seem to respond to the sheriff's office more quickly than they do to the request of a lowly private investigator."

DEADLY ATTACK

Samuel spent the next hour filling the sheriff in on his findings in Chicago.

"Sounds like the FBI agents didn't appreciate you sticking your nose into their business. If, as you say, it was Anthony Reynolds reaching out from prison to do Rudy Goldman in, his thirst for revenge definitely could have sent the gunmen your way."

"Goldman's off my list, but Reynolds is still a prime suspect. I'm planning on giving Gregory Lawrence a call to see if he can help me with the two goons that went after Goldman. If I can find out who they associate with, it may lead me to the person who ordered the attack on the bunkhouse."

"I'll get these samples in today, Samuel. Hopefully, their results will give you something to go on and send you off in the right direction."

Samuel went down the street to check on the progress Eduardo and his crew had made on his new office space. His previous walk-through with his brother had identified a few small items requiring finishing touches along with getting the sign hung on the front of the building. To his satisfaction, the sign was not only hung but was lit up in deep red letters that would surely let people know this was the home base for "Samuel Garcia, Private Investigator." He thought, as he stood staring at the sign, it was like hanging out a bug zapper drawing in the unsuspecting guests to their doom. If any enemies came his way, he prayed to the Lord above it would be their end and not his own.

"Hey, my brother, I'm back in town standing in front of my new office. How do I get in?"

Eduardo's voice filled Samuel's ear. "I'm at the building supply. I'll be there shortly."

Samuel returned the phone to his pocket and stood with his back to the office building, scanning the street before him. He realized that if his killers were still out and about, he would always be a moving target for them. His mind returned frequently to the promises in God's Word, reassuring him that he had a greater level of protection surrounding him than was visible to the naked eye.

Eduardo pulled into the parking space in front of Samuel and climbed out of the farm truck.

"Great detective you are. Can't get into your own office."

"Be careful, my brother. Our mother is not here to protect you if you get my emotions worked up."

Eduardo handed Samuel a small remote and began instructing him on its use. It had separate buttons that would open the front entrance, the rear garage door, and close the steel shutters over the office windows from the inside.

DEADLY ATTACK

"There is a lockout button at the bottom that sends secondary bolt locks into place that would require a powerful, well-made bomb to blow them open. You could rent out some of your space for the bank to store gold if you wanted."

"I just need to keep out the bad guys long enough to catch them. I don't know if they will come calling again, but if they do, I want to be well prepared."

"Mama is expecting you for supper tonight along with a lonely señorita that has been pining away in your absence."

"I'll be there. I need to get some items out of the bunkhouse and bring them back here. I plan to begin working out of this location now that you've got it *killer proof*. I know that it's going to trouble Mama, but I won't be at the ranch after this evening until I can wrap up this mess and know that I'm not a threat to her or my family. What were you doing at the building center? Have you started on your new career without Mama knowing it?"

"No. Just got a special project in mind."

"Now what's happened to that salvage yard refugee?" Arnold Snuffman stared hard into Samuel's eyes, waiting for his answer.

ALTON LYNN COOPER

"It got caught up in a gun battle and lost one eyeball in the process. Can you check it out and tell me how long the surgery will be?"

"Be cheaper to junk her. For the life of me, I don't know what you see in that thing that causes you to want to save it from the crusher over at the yard. Junk metal is selling at a good price, you know."

"Arnold, don't talk like that in front of my ride. I happen to think that even though it is a machine, it may possess feelings that you or I can't understand."

"Listen, Garcia, the only thing these old worn-out machines understand is the need for money. Lots of it, if I may say so."

*****

Two hours later, Samuel left the automobile hospital with the Jeep once again able to shine forth its light out of both eyes. The old mechanic had to replace the electric socket along with installing a new headlamp. The bullet had damaged the connector on the wiring harness, requiring Arnold Snuffman to splice on a new plug. Samuel let out a low whistle when the automobile doctor handed him the bill.

"Told you it'd be cheaper to junk it. I figured that you would have learned by now it costs a lot to

DEADLY ATTACK

keep an old patient, near death, alive and rumbling up and down the streets of Amarillo."

Samuel stopped the Jeep next to the bunkhouse that still had crime tape surrounding it. Seeing it again brought back the terror that erupted in the night during the attack. It sat as a sad bullet-riddled place that was the result of his chosen profession. Tears welled up in his eyes, thinking of his father, who had built it many years before to house the cowhands as he started establishing the ranch. His father's hands had felled the trees and sawn up the wood as he labored in making a place for his family. Amidst the tears, a surge of anger started building up inside him. He would not rest until he tracked down and brought to justice those who had destroyed what his father built. This was personal and would drive him on in the days ahead to get his hands on all those involved.

*****

The supper meal that night was a solemn affair. Sofia was still deeply affected by the attack and Samuel's determination to track down those responsible. Valentina lingered near Samuel's seat with her hand resting gently on his shoulder. She seemed to have moved past her position as his mother's head maid and on to showing her deep affection for him in the family's presence.

"It's so good to have you here, Señor Samuel. The meal times aren't the same in your absence."

Valentina removed her hand and returned to the kitchen, leaving the family to talk among themselves.

"Eduardo tells me you are set on staying in town."

"I'm set on not bringing any more unwanted danger to my family."

"If you were a rancher, no one would want to kill you for raising cows, no?"

Samuel realized that nothing he could say would bring peace to his mother's heart. It tore at him inside to see her in her present state because of him, but this war was cast upon him, and he would do all in his power to see it through. At the end of the meal, his mother laid her napkin next to her plate and rose, leaving the room without speaking, making her way up the winding staircase to her room. Valentina wiped the tears from her cheeks as she watched from the kitchen doorway. Samuel rose, making his way out of the dining room into the entrance hall, leaving his family's home behind.

DEADLY ATTACK

Samuel picked through his desk in the bunk-house and then went into his bedroom, collecting his clothes that had escaped the gunmen's shelling. His underclothes were untouched in the dresser drawer, but four of his prized silk shirts along with four pairs of his blue jeans were riddled with holes from the attack. He always pressed his jeans and hung them on hangers on the clothes rod in his bedroom along with the shirts. The food in the refrigerator was spoiled and beginning to give off a foul odor, with its juices joining with the melted ice forming a hazy puddle on the littered floor. He was once again deeply touched as he stood in the doorway staring at what once had been his home. He sensed a sadness spreading itself through the silent old bunkhouse as he turned to leave. The mice would no doubt move back in as they had done in the past. He dreaded the day when this place would be torn down, leaving the entrance to the ranch without the little outpost that had weathered many storms in years gone by. The door hung half off its hinges as a result of Eduardo kicking it in on the night of the attack to see if he was dead or alive. He pulled it partly closed and walked slowly to the old Jeep, leaving the ranch behind.

CHAPTER 6

Multiple War Fronts

"I've got to come up with a plan on how to go about finding out which of my enemies tried to kill me. I can't just track them down and ask them straight out if they were the ones that sent the gunmen my way."

Joe Halstead looked across his desk at Samuel before responding, "I agree. Instead of approaching them, you need to contact the individuals involved with them to hopefully glean information on their recent activities."

"So you're recommending that I talk to their hoodlum buddies to rat them out?"

"No. Most of the ones who have been released from prison will be assigned parole officers. I would start with them and then follow any leads they can give you concerning the parolee's recent contacts."

DEADLY ATTACK

Samuel headed to the coffee pot to refill his cup. "I like that idea, Joe. I was also thinking about the assault weapons used. You said they were Russian-made, isn't that right?"

"Yes. I don't know if they were the same ones involved in the attack against you, but four years ago, there was a gang war in Los Angeles where a number of people were killed. It was the same type of weapons used in that attack."

"Did the LA police arrest anyone in that melee?"

Joe Halstead went to one of the file cabinets on the back wall and thumbed through a number of folders before returning to his desk. "If they did, it wasn't reported to the press. The same type of guns were used in an armored car robbery six weeks after the gang war. The FBI was involved in that case. Maybe your buddy Gregory Lawrence could assist you in chasing down any evidence collected on the weapons used."

"Thanks, Joe. You've given me some good ideas to pursue. Any word on the getaway car?"

"Nothing yet. I'll let you know as soon as it turns up. I have my counterparts in Plainview and Lubbock watching for it. I'm sure your attackers would want to ditch it as soon as possible after your brother took out the back glass."

ALTON LYNN COOPER

Samuel stopped at the delicatessen and stocked up on snack foods for the small kitchen in his new office. It always seemed to help his thought processes if he had potato chips, ring bologna, saltine crackers, Diet Pepsi, and boiled eggs. He was already missing Valentina's delicious meals back at the ranch. He had to admit to himself he was also missing Ms. Valentina herself. That would no doubt give him an extra sense of urgency to solve this case as soon as possible, along with his strong desire to stay alive and thwart any future attacks coming his way.

"You know you're starting to give me more assignments than my boss back at headquarters. What do you need this time?"

"Sorry, Gregory, but you are a valuable resource for me. I appreciate all of your help and don't want to be a burden."

"I was pulling your leg. What do you need?"

"I need to know if the FBI has DNA and fingerprint information on the two mafia men they're watching in Chicago and if they have evidence collected from the gang war and armored car heist in Los Angeles four years ago."

"What kind of evidence are you interested in from Los Angeles?"

DEADLY ATTACK

"Anything involving the automatic weapons used in both crimes."

"I'm tied up for the next few days, but I'll see what I can do."

*****

Samuel pressed the lockout button on the remote and heard the deadbolts slide into place. He tried the steel shutters on the windows, watching them silently move into place. He gave the monitoring screens a glance, watching the back alley as well as the street scene out front. Eduardo had done a very thorough job providing him with a secure office space. Of course, it all came at a significant price, dropping his bank account somewhat. But if it kept him alive, the cost was well worth it. He turned in for the night, wanting to get an early start the next day, hoping to receive some of the requested information that would send him in the direction of his attackers.

"Well, folks, it should never come to this, but when emotions run high, these types of things unfortunately happen to the best of us."

*****

ALTON LYNN COOPER

Samuel woke at the sound of the clock radio going off and sat on the edge of his bed, scratching his scalp.

"The free-for-all broke out when the council voted to repave Main Street over Edgar Melon's objection. Seems Edgar was the lone holdout wanting to add more picnic tables to the city park along with building a new pavilion. Sheriff Halstead was called in and sent the council home for the day, hoping to let tempers subside, allowing for cooler heads to prevail at the next meeting. This is WWTYZ News with your good buddy Colonel Jimmy George coming at you from smack dab in the middle of Amarillo signing off for now. Remember, folks, have a good one and keep your cows off the road."

Samuel pushed the off button on the radio and headed for the bathroom to get in shape for what he hoped would be a productive day in the detective business. He had just settled down at his desk with a steaming cup of black coffee and three boiled eggs when his cell phone started buzzing.

"Come over to my office, I've got some info for you."

Samuel seated himself in front of Joe Halstead's desk with a second cup of coffee, waiting for the sheriff to finish a phone call.

DEADLY ATTACK

"Ms. Myers, you know I can't do that. There's public parking on your street from 8:00 a.m. to 10:00 p.m. on weekdays."

Samuel couldn't hear the words, but he could hear the frustrated voice on the other end of the phone giving the sheriff a stout scolding before hanging up on him. The sheriff replaced the receiver in its cradle and bowed his head, running his hand through his hair.

"Maybe I should come and work for you as an assistant private eye. These people in Amarillo are starting to wear me thin. Ms. Myers's dog spends all day on the back of her sofa, staring out the picture window, barking at cars parked on the street, thinking their owners are coming up to her house. She wants me to ticket the cars and have them towed away at the owners' expense."

Samuel gave his friend a warm smile. "I heard on the news this morning you had to break up a free-for-all at the city council meeting."

"Edgar Melon wanted me to arrest the chairman of the council for threatening to have his brother-in-law run against Edgar in the next election. Said it was election interference in a public election, even though it doesn't take place until next year. Enough of my woes, let's get down to yours.

ALTON LYNN COOPER

"They found the car involved in the attack on your bunkhouse in Lubbock last night. It had been ditched in back of an abandoned feed store on the outskirts of town. Diego did indeed blow out the back glass along with putting two bullet holes in the trunk lid. I don't know if he hit one of the men inside the car or if the man got hit while your brothers were shooting at them on the road, but there was blood on the front passenger seat back up near shoulder level. Sheriff Wilson is having the crime team go over the car for fingerprints and is sending a sample of the blood to the crime lab."

"Do they know who owns the car?"

"Yes. It was stolen from the Lubbock Preston Smith International Airport the day of the attack. The owner returned from a business trip and reported it missing. The airport police are reviewing security video of the parking areas to see if they caught the culprits on tape. I'm going to drive over and take a look at the car myself and take the tire cast with me. Thought you might want to ride along."

*****

Samuel stared at the car, wishing that Diego's bullets had found their mark in both of the attackers.

DEADLY ATTACK

It was a hard thought, but if he had their bodies, he could more easily find out where they came from and who they were associated with. The back seat was covered with blown-out glass, and there was an angry red stain where the person in the front passenger seat had lost a considerable amount of blood. The stain was at the person's left shoulder level in the top corner of the seat back. Joe Halstead called Samuel over and introduced him to his friend Bill Wilson. Sheriff Wilson was a stout-built man in his late fifties with graying hair at his temples. He walked with a limp, coming Samuel's way as he gave him a slight smile and grasped his hand with a tight grip.

"Heard a lot about you from Joe. Nasty business what happened at your place."

"It's nice to meet you, Sheriff. Did anyone come in contact with a wounded man here in town?"

"One of my deputies checked with the doctors in town along with the local hospitals and clinics but came up empty. However, the pharmacy reported a man entering the store when he first opened the morning after your attack, buying a large amount of gauze and some over-the-counter pain medication. Said he bought two bottles of antiseptic also. The bad news is there were no surveillance cameras in the store in working order. The pharmacist was able to give us a pretty good description of the man. We have an artist in town that's helping us come up with a sketch. We're still working the car for prints and anything else that may lead us to your assailants. Excuse me." Sheriff Wilson answered his cell phone as he turned his back, separating himself from Samuel and Joe Halstead. He returned after a brief conversation, shaking his head.

"Well, we may have found out how they got out of Lubbock. Eddie Rolston phoned our office, reporting his pickup truck missing. I've warned him a million times not to leave his keys in it but to no avail. Last year, some high school boys took it for a joy ride and left it down by the lake after blowing a tire off the rim. My deputy has put out an all-points bulletin on it."

*****

Samuel was quiet on the ride back to Amarillo. It seemed that he had a lot of pieces of information that were leading him nowhere. He wanted to take off after his attackers but didn't know who they were or what direction they took leaving town. Prayerfully, the truck would show up and provide some fingerprints leading him in the right direction.

DEADLY ATTACK

His cell phone buzzed just as he entered his office, flashing Gregory Lawrence's name on the screen. He answered, hearing his friend giving directions to someone in his office.

"Sorry about that. Your two favorite FBI agents in Chicago don't think too much of me either. They very reluctantly shared some news with me after I threatened to file a complaint against them for impeding our ongoing investigation."

"You said our investigation. Does that mean you're teaming up with me in the hunt for the goons who shot up my place?"

"I am now. I'll know more tomorrow when the LA agents FedEx me the information concerning fingerprints and DNA along with the hoodlums' mug shots. It seems that they may have been involved with the armored car stickup in LA a few years back. Nothing could be proven against them at the time, but our buddies in Chicago are persuaded that they have some high-up connections with shady individuals in Los Angeles. They don't know who the connections are at this time and still have agents trying to track down those leads. That is one of the reasons my associates in Chicago don't want any outside interference that may jeopardize their investigation. They've been on this for a long time and believe there are

85

some major players involved in money laundering and other illegal activities. They're hoping the two birds in the Windy City will eventually lead them to the head of the organization."

"You said one of the reasons. What are their other concerns?"

"They don't like private investigators. Calls them 'wannabe cops.' I'll give you a call tomorrow after I receive the stuff they're sending me."

Samuel sat at his desk, staring at the whiteboard on the wall. He felt that the individual pieces of information must be connected in some way. His problem was finding those connections. He pulled the notepad from his pocket and made himself a to-do list, hoping that he wasn't heading off in the wrong direction. This case, so far, was not like any others he had worked on. He felt frustrated as if he were spinning his investigative wheels, not knowing which direction to go in. Samuel pulled out his cell phone and called the sheriff in Lubbock.

"I can't remember if you told Joe and me where Eddie Rolston's truck was stolen from."

"I don't remember mentioning that. It was two blocks from the empty feed store where the stolen car was found. Eddie goes to a local restaurant there every morning for breakfast. He was parked on the

DEADLY ATTACK

side of the place away from view of the front windows. Why do you ask?"

"Have your men checked the airport parking lot for the truck?"

"Yes. That was one of the first places they searched. It wasn't there."

"Can you share the description of the truck with me?"

Samuel jotted down the information on his notepad and thanked the sheriff for his help. He had that strange tingling inside that let him know one connection in this case might just be coming together, sending him off on the right trail.

*****

Samuel pushed the Jeep faster than he should have, heading south on I-27 toward Lubbock. The flashing red lights in his rearview mirror let him know he had gained the attention of Plainview's finest.

"Where ya going, cowboy? Is tha seat of your britches on fire? License and insurance, please. Keep your hands where I kin see 'em, ya hear?"

"I'm a private investigator from Amarillo. I'm hurrying to Lubbock on a lead following a deadly attack on my office."

"Did your office git killed?"

"It's in bad shape."

"Well, cowboy, if ya keep driving tha way ya are, that office of yours may be in better shape than you. Our little town here is small. No budget ta speak of. Iffen ya end up in our lockup, bologna and stale bread is all y'all get. Most of our clients waste away on it after tha first week."

The deputy ambled his way back to his patrol car just as a school bus rolled past Samuel's Jeep.

"Loser!"

Samuel watched the floppy-haired boy's head hanging out the side window of the bus as he shouted and then pulled his lips wide with his index fingers, wagging his tongue back and forth. He silently hoped that the deputy would have mercy on a brother who was also in law enforcement.

"Here ya are, cowboy. Ya got fourteen days ta pay or protest. I recommend ya pay. My cousin is tha local magistrate, and he never lets me down on appeal. Ya understand? Have a nice day and slow that horse down until ya clear tha city limit sign. After that, you're highway patrol's problem."

Samuel looked at the ticket and flung it on the passenger seat of the Jeep.

"Twenty-five over? No way!"

DEADLY ATTACK

In his mind, he added twenty-five and thirty-five, the city speed limit, and came up with sixty.

"Well, maybe."

After all, the old Jeep was running strong after Arnold Snuffman overhauled the engine back at the automobile hospital in Amarillo.

*****

Samuel did his own inspection of the airport parking lots and then started fanning out to the stores nearby. If the car used in the attack was stolen from the airport, he felt sure that his attackers must have flown in and would head back out the same way. They no doubt stole the truck to return to the airport, planning to ditch it nearby. He was about ready to give up after traveling quite a distance when he spotted the truck in a mall parking lot fifteen miles from the airport. There was a large puddle of antifreeze on the ground underneath the engine where the rig had evidently overheated, causing the two culprits to abandon it. He searched the inside of the cab, not finding anything of importance, and pulled out his cell phone to contact Sheriff Wilson.

"You calling a wrecker?" Samuel turned around, seeing a swarthy young man staring at him from an old Chevy Impala that had definitely seen better days.

"Why do you ask?"

"I dropped the owners off at the airport this morning. I drive for Uber. Tipped well too. Owed me twenty-eight and tossed me a fifty. One of 'em wasn't doing so good. Looked real pale and had his left arm in a sling."

"Was there blood on his shoulder?"

"Couldn't say. Had on a jacket. In this weather. Go figure. Saw the sling on his hand hanging out from under the coat."

Sheriff Wilson came rushing into the parking lot with lights flashing on the police cruiser, pulling in front of the Uber driver's car.

"Whoa, what's going on here? The guy didn't ask for his change back. I didn't cheat him for sure."

"What's he talking about?" The sheriff gave the Uber man a curious look.

"He drove the men from the truck to the airport this morning. Said one of them looked bad and was wearing an arm sling with a coat over it."

"You stay here with him. I'm heading to the airport. With any luck, their plane hasn't departed yet."

DEADLY ATTACK

"Sheriff, I'd rather follow you. I want these guys bad."

"Wait until my deputy shows up." The sheriff squealed off in the direction of the airport, leaving Samuel with the shaken-up Uber man.

"The truck was stolen. The men you gave a lift to were involved in a very serious crime in Amarillo. You will need to give the deputy a description of them and turn that fifty-dollar bill over to him to be fingerprinted. Don't handle it anymore until it has been checked out."

The Uber man held a McDonald's bag up for Samuel to see. "He'll have to get it from the eating place at the airport. I really tanked up. Not much of the fifty left."

*****

Samuel joined Sheriff Wilson at the ticket counter as the ticket agent finished tapping in some information on the computer.

"Those two flew out shortly after they got here on a flight to Colorado Springs."

"What airline are they on?"

"United flight 4031. It will make a stopover in Denver at Denver International before proceeding on to Colorado Springs."

"How long to the Denver layover?"

"That's a little less than two hours. The layover is about one hour before going on to Colorado Springs."

"I need you to print me out two copies of the information on the men." Sheriff Wilson handed Samuel a copy of the information and headed back to his cruiser.

"I'm going to contact the authorities in Denver and Colorado Springs to nab these two at one of the locations. With them leaving early this morning, it's possible that they're already through the Colorado airport barring any flight delays. We may have already missed them."

Samuel stared at the names on the paper, not recognizing either one of them. Harold Langford and Eric Hendricks could very well be aliases for all he knew. The ticket agent had indicated it was Eric Hendricks that wasn't doing so good with his arm in the sling. He sent a silent prayer up to heaven that the men would be apprehended at one of the airports, giving him a much-needed lead in the case.

DEADLY ATTACK

"Why are you asking for a fifty-dollar bill from us? We are the ones the customers normally give their money to." Samuel gave a quick explanation to the young man behind the counter at the airport McDonald's.

"Sorry. The boss took our proceeds to the bank this morning. Your fifty is probably mixed in with a lot of its family members over at Lubbock National." Samuel left the airport and headed for the bank in downtown Lubbock. After explaining to the assistant bank manager why he needed the bill, he was told to wait in the lobby.

"Mr. Garcia?"

"That's me."

"Please follow me."

Samuel dutifully followed the older lady as she led him to one of the enclosed customer rooms on the east side of the main lobby. "Mr. Morris will be in shortly."

Randal Morris was a short, bald-headed man with a nervous twitch on his face. He eyed Samuel from behind thick prescription glasses that made his eyes appear much larger than they actually were. He was an older man in his mid-sixties and seemed to not only have a facial twitch but also operate in an ongoing state of anxiety.

"Tell me again why this particular bill is important to you. My assistant tells me it may have been involved in a crime. Please assure me it isn't counterfeit."

"It's not that I know of. It came from one of two men who launched a deadly attack against me a few days ago in Amarillo. It was given to an Uber driver to pay their fare when he took them to the airport. He used it at the airport McDonald's. I need it for evidence."

"That explains it. One of my associates called my attention to the bill when it was passing through our counting machine." A strong tingle shot its way down Samuel's spine.

"Why did it catch your person's attention?"

"Wait here." The bank manager returned after a few minutes and laid the bill on the desk in front of Samuel. It had a nasty red blotch on it that very much appeared to be blood. Randal Morris spoke in an anxious voice.

"I've called the authorities. Does that look like blood to you?"

"Considering where it came from, absolutely." Samuel pulled out his cell phone and called Bill Wilson. This was one of the critical leads that would hopefully get him on the right trail of the men that

DEADLY ATTACK

shot up the bunkhouse. Whether the blood came from the injured man himself or off the hands of his accomplice from trying to close up the wounded man's shoulder, it definitely was a major piece of evidence.

Sheriff Wilson arrived a short time later and took possession of the fifty-dollar bill. "I'll get this to the lab and put a rush order on it. Bad news. Our two pigeons never arrived at the airport in Colorado Springs. They apparently landed at Denver International and then disappeared from there. I have the authorities checking all sources of ground transportation from the airport, but so far, nothing has turned up. They're checking video also. Hopefully, we'll see them on film."

CHAPTER 7

Imminent Danger

Samuel added the information to the whiteboard and hung it back on the wall. He wanted to start tying some of the loose ends together. He had a feeling in his gut that the pieces so far were pointing in the direction of the West Coast. The automatic weapons used against him, the background of the two goons who apparently eliminated Rudy Goldman in Chicago, and the FBI agents working on a connection to a money laundering ring with high-up individuals in the Los Angeles area. A thought was trying to work itself into his mind, but the details from some of his previous cases eluded him for the moment. He was pulled from his thoughts when his cell phone rang.

"If you're not tied up at the moment, I may have some recent information of interest for you."

DEADLY ATTACK

"Is your coffee pot perking as we speak?"

"My pot's always on. Only thing that keeps me sane in this job."

Joe Halstead gave Samuel a faint smile when he entered the sheriff's office.

"Have a seat and I'll pour us a cup." The sheriff took his seat across from Samuel and laid some papers on the desk in front of him.

"Whose names are these?"

"Those names belong to the two mafia-related guys that our friendly FBI agents in Chicago are keeping a close watch on."

Samuel stared at the names on the paper, drawing a complete blank.

"William Darby and Cecil James? I never heard of them."

Halstead laid pictures of the two men on the desk in front of Samuel. He stared intently at them, realizing he had never seen either of them before. The sheriff spread other sheets of paper out in front of Samuel.

"Here's the info I requested on them. Their DNA and fingerprints don't match anything that we have recovered so far in the case. We have the blood test results that you collected in Chicago, and they are all Rudy Goldman's. Gregory Lawrence contacted

ALTON LYNN COOPER

me, letting me know that they pulled the slugs out of Rudy's head that sent him into the next world. They were from a .22 caliber revolver. That's one most preferred by hit men. They don't eject out shell casings the way an automatic does."

"The interesting thing about Darby and James is that Lawrence recognized them from a previous case involving a major drug investigation on the West Coast. They were caught up in that investigation, but there wasn't enough evidence to tie them to the syndicate involved. In fact, they never found the head of the organization to make any major arrests. A number of the lower-level suspects ended up in the same kind of place as your buddy Rudy with the same kind of holes in the back of their head. We are having the slugs pulled from Rudy analyzed to see if they match those from the other shootings. I'm expecting the Uber man's sketches tomorrow along with any info from the videos from the Denver airport."

Samuel studied the mug shots again, hoping they would spark a memory, but nothing came up.

"I'm beginning to think that this may be related to the drug problems that Davey Gibson and I got tangled up in on Kalmajo Island. There were two DEA agents from Sacramento involved in that investigation. To my knowledge, they never identified

DEADLY ATTACK

the top individuals running the drug ring here in the States. The mayor on the island was on the take, along with the police chief and others who got taken down, but the big dogs were never caught."

Samuel was awakened the next morning with an urgent call from his friend Joe Halstead.

"I'm coming your way by the back entrance. Watch for me."

The tone of the sheriff's voice sent a chill through Samuel. The sheriff was not a man that got nervous easily nor rattled during intense moments. Samuel watched the rear cameras on the screen from his office and quickly released the rear door locks, letting the sheriff in. He knew something serious was in the wind by the look on his friend's face.

"Just got a call from Gregory Lawrence. You must have had your cell off. He tried you first. The agents contacted him from Chicago late last night. They were taping conversations on their two mafia men when one of them stated that he heard the rat in Texas was still, in his words, 'a job to be done.' The person they were conversing with was on an untraceable burner phone and quickly told the man to keep his mouth shut. His comments indicated that the rat would be taken care of soon by professionals that knew how to finish the job. Are you ready for this? The body of your buddy who bled in the stolen car was found off a rural road near the Denver International Airport with two holes in the back of his head. There was no identification on him, and get this, his hands and teeth were all nicely removed from the body."

Samuel stared at the sheriff in silence for a moment, trying to absorb the horror of the information he had been given. These people were vicious and would go to great lengths to keep their identities unknown.

"How do you know he was the man involved in the attack against me if his body was in that condition?"

The sheriff handed Samuel the sketches from the Uber man and then the snapshots taken from the Denver International Airport. Samuel knew instantly that he was staring at one of the men who had blown apart the bunkhouse. The snapshots showed him being shoved along by a muscular built man and then roughly pushed into the back of a black town car, waiting near the passenger pick-up area outside the airport.

"I should have copies of the video itself soon and you can take a look at it. The Denver authorities have his body. A local man was out bicycling and

DEADLY ATTACK

came across it in a ditch along the road. They are taking DNA samples from it to see if he is in the system. Gregory will have his blood sample compared to the one taken from the stolen car to make sure. If you will take my advice, we need to relocate you to an undisclosed location, putting you into protective custody until we can track down the professionals they are sending your way."

"Joe, I can't do that. I can't run and hide. They won't stop until they get a shot at me. I will arm myself as best I can and pray that I get first crack at them."

"You won't know who they are, Samuel. These people make a living out of killing. You are in *imminent danger*. Staying visible will make you a duck in a shooting gallery."

"There is something you can do for me if possible, Joe. Outfit me with one of your department's bulletproof vests and set me up with a tracking device both on my body and on my jeep. I have to stay in this hunt until the end."

The sheriff gave Samuel a sorrowful look.

"I don't like this at all, but I understand how you feel. I'll do what I can."

*****

101

Samuel sat at his desk, staring again at the whiteboard on the wall. A thought began forming in his mind that he felt would send him on the right trail. He needed to make plans to go into the lion's den and remain undetected as much as possible. This would require him to gather up some supplies that would hopefully keep him alive until he could find and expose the head of the snake. He picked up the phone on his desk and called one of his high school acquaintances from many years ago that would hopefully be able to set him up for the days ahead. Even though he had gone to a cell phone, he still maintained a landline and an answering machine at his office to receive calls in his absence.

"Hey, Raymond, how's life treating you?"

"Let me think. Do I know this voice from the past? Great, Samuel, it's good to hear from you again. What do you want?"

"Ouch. What makes you think I want something?"

"Listen, bud, you always came to me in our high school years when you wanted something. Are you telling me you've changed in your later years?"

"Well, mellowed a bit but not much. Are you still in the business of putting together stage productions for the local theater?"

DEADLY ATTACK

"Indeed, I am. Got a lot of nice awards for best plays of the year, if I might say."

"Congratulations, Raymond. I'm proud of you. Can we meet somewhere and have a chat? I'll buy lunch and make it worth your while."

Raymond Stevens was a tall, handsome man with blonde hair and a long attractive face. He reminded Samuel of some English lord watching over his lands. He carried himself with an air of sophistication that had always eluded Samuel and his brothers in high school. They were known as the "ruffian gang" while Raymond received all the accolades from the school staff. He had pursued the theater and had become known in various circles as an excellent producer of stage and film productions, earning high awards. His wavy, thick blonde hair, dashing attire, and gold-rimmed glasses set him apart in a crowd. Samuel waved to him from his seat in Carmen's Cantina, motioning him over to his table.

"Is this place safe? I've never eaten here before. I prefer the steakhouse over on Grand Street."

"You'll like it. Same idea as the steakhouse. Ms. Carmen grinds up the steak and adds her secret touches to it that will make your mouth water."

"You order for me, Samuel, and I will let you know whether you will get my help or not. If my

ALTON LYNN COOPER

mouth doesn't water but my stomach turns, no help from me."

Samuel gave his friend a big smile.

"Fair enough."

The two caught up on old times, and then Samuel made his request for Raymond's help. He had watched his friend during the meal and noticed that he did indeed enjoy Ms. Carmen's ground and seasoned beef wrapped in a nice corn tortilla. In fact, he liked it so well he placed a second order, realizing Samuel was buying.

"Is that all you needed?"

"I'll need the full-blown appearance package and the documents to go along with the new me. With this makeover, what kind of profession do you think would fit my new appearance?"

"You could pass as a college professor or maybe a newspaper man. As a last resort, you could go as a doctor, but if someone needed medical attention in your presence, you may get sued or shot."

"I'll go for the college egghead or the pesky newspaper man. Do you think you can set me up?"

"Samuel, I can set you up so that your own dear mother wouldn't know who was coming to dinner. Stop by my studio tomorrow afternoon, and we'll see what we can do. By the way, the next time you feel

DEADLY ATTACK

a strong urge to buy, meet me at the steakhouse. I'll introduce you to the best beef in Amarillo that hasn't met Ms. Carmen's grinding machine."

Samuel used caution as he left the restaurant, looking up and down the street before heading for his jeep. He had parked it in front of the cantina where he could keep an eye on it during his meeting with Raymond. He determined to proceed with caution when he was out and about. He recognized many of the people in Amarillo and hoped that if a complete stranger popped up, he would see them before they noticed him. He headed to the sheriff's office to share his future plans with Joe Halstead and hopefully catch up on other news he may have.

"Are you sure that's a good idea? You'll pretty much be on your own over there. None of our tracking devices will do you any good halfway around the globe." The sheriff looked at Samuel with concern on his face.

"Well, it'll get me out of Amarillo for a while. I think the information that we have so far is leading to the drug activity that infested the island. Exposing that may have really angered someone here in the States when they lost a lot of their market. Some of their close associates were locked up for a few years as well."

"How's the sheriff there? Is he a person you can trust?"

"Yes. Bobby Lambers became chief after Ronald Maubry was sent to prison for being involved in the drug operation. Maubry was the chief and was connected to the mayor who also got caught up in the drug racket. Lambers was one of the honest deputies left in the department trying to keep the peace on the island. I served with him for a while after Davey Gibson returned to the States. He's a good man."

The sheriff opened a folder lying on his desk.

"Our man found in the ditch was indeed one of those that shot up your place. The blood in the stolen vehicle, along with the blood on the airport fifty-dollar bill, matched his. I've just received a copy of the video from the Denver airport that I think you will find interesting."

Joe Halstead fired up the monitor on his desk and swung the screen Samuel's way. Samuel watched intently as the two men exited the terminal, making their way to the town car. Their backs were to the camera, concealing their faces until they turned sideways to get into the car. The large man shoved the injured man into the back seat and then slammed the door. Samuel looked at their faces from the side but couldn't recognize them from any past interactions. The car

DEADLY ATTACK

sped away, resulting in the video camera catching only a blurry image of the tag plate. The plate had California colors on it, but those colors also matched other states, including the state of Louisiana. Even if they could determine it was from California, the numbers were still blurred to the point it probably wouldn't lead them to the car's owner. For Samuel, knowing that it was a California car would at least let him know those seeking to kill him were potentially from the West Coast.

"Rerun that again and stop it when you get to the place where the sides of their faces are visible."

Samuel stared intently at the faces on the screen. There was something about the big man that seemed familiar, but he couldn't put his finger on what it was.

Joe Halstead poured two hot cups of coffee, preparing to share more information with Samuel.

"They removed the bullets from the ditch man's head and sent them to the crime lab in Chicago to compare them with those taken out of Rudy Goldman. It's a long shot that the two men connected to the mafia there could have killed the man in Colorado. They probably are the ones that did Rudy in and are still in the city under FBI surveillance. That doesn't mean that the two situations aren't connected in some way. Did you notice something curious about the airport video?"

107

"I noticed that the big man got into the front passenger side after shoving our wounded guy into the back seat. That means the car was sent to pick them up, and someone else was chauffeuring them."

"Good observation, Samuel. That means that their plans all along were to book a flight to Colorado Springs and then disappear at the Denver layover. They are doing everything necessary to cover their tracks, including eliminating some of their own."

The sheriff looked at Samuel with deep concern on his face. "When do you plan on leaving for the island?"

"I'm pulling some things together and hope to leave in a couple of days. By the way, you and Gregory Lawrence are the only two people stateside that know where I'm heading. I'll keep both of you posted on what I uncover on the island. I plan to call you each day at 9:00 a.m. and again at 6:00 p.m. If you don't hear from me, send in the cavalry. Chief Lambers knows the island and those on it. I'm sure if certain individuals are up to no good, he will have an eye on them. I'll check in with him when I get there and then give you his contact information. Lambers will be the only one on the island that knows my true identity."

DEADLY ATTACK

Joe Halstead gave Samuel a curious look but didn't question his last comment.

*****

Samuel spent the next two days preparing to leave for Kalmajo Island. His friend Raymond Stevens went over and beyond what Samuel expected. When he stood in front of the mirror at Raymond's studio, even he didn't recognize himself. The documents that Raymond had prepared were all in order and should serve his undercover investigation well. He stopped at the sporting goods store and bought an ankle holster and another one that would fit in the small of his back. He also bought some brightly colored travel shirts made to be worn on the outside of his slacks. He went further and splurged on some very classy khaki slacks that looked as if they belonged to an elite college professor. The shirt and pants would serve to maintain his look provided him by his high school buddy.

As he was finishing his packing, he decided to throw in one pair of his blue jeans and one of his silk shirts that survived the bunkhouse attack. He thought that there might come a time in his investigation to ditch the disguise and reveal himself to his pursuers

ALTON LYNN COOPER

to draw them out. He knew that he couldn't carry his guns on the plane but would use them along with the holsters when he returned to Amarillo. The disguise would also come in handy if strangers showed up in Amarillo. He could follow them in his getup without them knowing he was the guy they were sent to kill.

CHAPTER 8

Return to Kalmajo Island

Samuel left his jeep safely inside his office complex and hitched a ride to the Amarillo airport with Joe Halstead. He left his two sidearms and holsters in his office safe. He planned to have Sheriff Lambers outfit him with the weapons he needed when he reached Kalmajo Island. The two were quiet on the drive to the airport, each lost in their thoughts concerning the days ahead.

Just before dropping Samuel off at the terminal, the sheriff spoke up with some parting words of advice for his good friend.

"If I don't receive your two calls each day, know that the good police chief on the island will pull out all the stops looking for you. Keep him informed of your activities while you're there. If you don't call, he needs to know your last location so he can get to you as soon as possible."

"Got it, Joe. Thank you for your concern. I plan to exercise a great deal of caution. I don't know if there is an island connection concerning the attack on the bunkhouse, but my gut is telling me to start there. The island, along with its past drug problems and their association with California, seems to be sending tingles up and down my spine. Must be something to it. When I get these feelings, it usually means a nest of *rats* is nearby."

Joe Halstead gave Samuel a serious look. "Just make sure the *rats* don't get those same feelings when some private investigator gets close to their nest."

Samuel was always nervous waiting in an airport, thinking of the upcoming flight. He wasn't afraid of flying; he just didn't like it. That reminded him of his mother's words to his brothers concerning their use of guns at the ranch. A twinge of guilt flooded his heart, thinking about distancing himself from his family over the last few weeks. He knew, however, it was to protect them from the danger he was in until those seeking his life were apprehended. He wasn't sure if those pursuing him were connected to the island and hadn't ruled out Rollins, Rafael, or Michael Williams as potential suspects.

Of those three, Andres Rafael would be the most likely villain after his and Samuel's confronta-

DEADLY ATTACK

tion in the town of Loralloes, Texas. He was an angry, ruthless man controlling those around him and had a deep hatred for Samuel for interfering with his gambling operations south of the border. If the island information turned up empty, he would fly back to the States and seek out Rafael's current location as a next step in the investigation.

*****

Samuel swallowed two Dramamine tablets and chased them down with a chili dog from the airport snack stand. He hoped they would get along and calm down the butterflies having a good time buzzing around in his stomach. He was pleasantly surprised not to be accosted by any young tow-haired boys or starstruck young ladies being seated next to him. Instead, he was blessed with a silver-haired older lady in her mid-seventies with cheeks bursting forth with a heavy layer of rouge and lips red enough to put to shame a juicy, ripe tomato. He wasn't sure if the smell coming from her was some exotic perfume or an extra coating of Bengay. He decided that it would be better not to ask, just in case he guessed wrong. He noticed that she had given his khaki outfit a good going over, looking from his slacks to the untucked, brightly colored floral shirt.

ALTON LYNN COOPER

"Do you fly often, young man?"

Samuel looked into the hazel eyes seated next to him before responding. "Only when I take a plane."

That set his elderly passenger off into a fit of giggles. "Oh, that's so clever of you. My Oliver was like that when he was your age. Said the silliest things, you know, rest his soul."

"I'm sorry to hear that he's gone. How long were you married?"

"We've been together for almost sixty years."

"What did he pass away from?"

The silver-haired lady stared deeply into Samuel's face. "Oh, he's not dead. At least not yet. Left him at home with three of our great-grandkids. I'm getting a well-deserved break from that old coot and those loud, rambunctious boys. He may survive it. They like to wrestle a lot, you know. Last time I went away, they got to tussling and busted up my coffee table in the living room. Hope Oliver can hold his own. He got wounded in the war, you know."

"I'm sorry to hear that. What happened? Was he wounded in combat?"

"You might say that. He was the cook for his platoon and cut himself peeling potatoes. Got a nasty infection in his peeling finger."

DEADLY ATTACK

Samuel's seatmate gave him a big toothy grin and patted his arm.

"I'm headed to a wonderful South Pacific island. Gonna enjoy myself, get some peace and quiet, and see the sights. Well, it's been nice talking with you, but I need some shut-eye now. I nap every day at this time, don't you know?"

Samuel pulled a magazine from the seat back in front of him and began thumbing through it. A few minutes later, a burst of ragged snores mingled with periodic snorts began emanating from the dear elderly lady next to him. He thought that dear old Oliver would no doubt also get some peace and quiet while his sweetheart was out and about enjoying her South Pacific paradise.

The flight experienced brief periods of turbulence, but other than that, it was uneventful. During some of the jostling around, Samuel's silver-haired seatmate fell over against him, resting her head against his shoulder. She took his arm in her hands, squeezing it as she continued to snort and snore her way through her daily nap. He surely hoped she didn't think he was her Oliver on the way to bask in the sun with her on the island.

*****

ALTON LYNN COOPER

The landing was smooth with Samuel waiting in his seat for the plane to taxi its way up to the terminal. As soon as it stopped, he grabbed his carry-on bag and headed to the bathroom in the back of the plane, making his way through the bodies filling up the aisle. He received more than a few nasty stares as he made his way through the crowd. One curly red-haired, gum-chewing man blurted out, "Exit's in the other direction, bubba. Watch where you're going."

He went into the bathroom and quickly prepared himself to exit the plane as an auburn-haired tourist wearing gold-rimmed glasses with an unlit cigar sticking out of his mouth. He looked one last time at his beautiful handlebar mustache before pulling the razor out and removing it from its home of many years. If he survived his hunt for his would-be killers, he could always grow another magnificent one in its place. The stick-on auburn mustache and beard caused an itching to flare up on his face immediately, but he knew that scratching at it was out of the question. He had applied a good coating of Spirit Gum to his face that Raymond Stevens had assured him would leave his skin intact when he was ready to rid himself of the fake beard and mustache. One last glance in the small mirror let him know he was ready to deplane on Kalmajo Island and not be recognized as the young, dashing

DEADLY ATTACK

Spaniard that had left a few years ago. He picked up a rental car from the airport, checked into his room at the inn, and then headed for police headquarters.

"I recognize that voice of yours, but the sight of you sure has changed."

Samuel gave Chief Bobby Lambers a warm smile. "I'm running undercover. I intend to visit some of the old haunts and prefer not to get shot in the process."

"We've been working diligently to clean up some of those old places. There's still plenty of work to be done, but I think you'll experience a different environment here on the island from a few years ago. I believe if we can upgrade our streets and buildings in the rougher areas, the crime associated with those neighborhoods will decrease. We're not out of the woods yet, but we are making steady progress. Your friend Sheriff Halstead filled me in on your visit and the attempt on your life. What makes you think it may have originated from the island?"

"There seems to be some connection between the gangs in Los Angeles, drugs, and Soviet-era weapons."

Samuel took the next half hour and filled the chief in on what he had uncovered in his investigation to date.

"I know Davey and I had interactions with the drug guys on the island and that the trail appeared to lead back to California. The head of the organization was never identified and could be the one or ones behind the attack on me."

Bobby Lambers gave Samuel a concerned look. "I'm sure you are aware that Manuel Alvera is out of prison and has set up shop here on the island again."

"Does that mean he's back in the drug business?"

"Not that we know of. He has a place near the Lost Sailor Saloon that appears to be in business to rescue those going down the wrong road in life. We've been keeping a close eye on him. The rescue business very well could be a front for his ongoing drug operations. People are coming and going through his place on a regular basis."

"That's where I plan to start my investigation. I will keep you posted on my movements here on the island. If I fail to call Joe Halstead twice a day as we agreed, you can come to the rescue. I need to ask you to outfit me with a couple of sidearms while I'm here. Mine are back in the States."

"That won't be a problem if you permit me to swear you in as a deputy on a temporary basis. I can't place firearms into a private individual's hands."

"That's no problem, Chief, just as long as my identity is kept secret while I'm here. You will be the only one that knows who I am."

"Where are you staying?"

"I'm registered at the Sundowner Inn on Maubry Street under the name of Francis Bennett."

"Okay, my friend. Stay in touch and stay safe. I'm always here if you need me."

Samuel left the chief's office and drove around the island, seeing a number of changes since he and Davey had returned to the States. He drove past their old office and warehouse, wishing that he could stop in and say hello to the team who had taken over the work supplying the missionaries on the islands. He didn't want to go to obvious places from his past that might expose him to someone watching his movements. He had learned a long time ago that the unscrupulous people on the island kept tabs on who came in and what they came in for. He didn't know if their intentions were the same as before, but if Manuel Alvera was indeed back in the drug business, he would no doubt be watching strangers in his presence.

He drove through the seedy part of the island where he had met and put Manuel Alvera out of the drug business a few years back. The place looked as run-down and dirty as he remembered it, obviously not sharing in the chief's modest improvements as seen in other areas on the island. The Lost Sailor Saloon looked as lost as it was when he met Alvera there for the first time.

There was something different about an older building across the street from the saloon that caught Samuel's eye. It seemed to stand out from the other run-down structures and had a more recent coat of paint brushed onto its cracked siding. The small sign on the front of the building indicated that it was a place of refuge for those seeking a better path. There was a bench in front of the building holding two rough-looking characters giving Samuel an intense stare as he rolled by.

"I sure hope those two aren't the caregivers in that place." Samuel often talked to himself out loud, releasing his thoughts to himself, hoping if anyone should overhear him, they wouldn't think he was going senile.

*****

"It's good to hear your voice. Have you trapped any *rats* yet?" Samuel was back at the inn, making his 6:00 p.m. call to Joe Halstead, assuring him he was still alive.

DEADLY ATTACK

"Not yet. The place here looks the same for the most part. I met up with Chief Lambers and then spent some time driving around the island. The seedy part of town is just as seedy as it was before. I plan to go back there tonight and see what's crawling around the place."

"Isn't that where you first ran into those peddling drugs in the past?"

"It was. The kingpin at that time was Manuel Alvera, and he's back here on the island. I need to track him down and determine if he's still in the same business as he was before. Sheriff Lambers seems to think he may have gone straight after his years in prison but said he's still keeping an eye on him."

"The crime lab analyzed the two slugs pulled out of the ditch man's head. As we suspected, they did not come from the same gun as the one that sent Rudy Goldman on his way out of this world. But get this: Gregory Lawrence had them checked against those in evidence in LA that dispatched three low-level drug dealers a short time after you moved back to the States from the island."

Samuel waited for Halstead to continue. He heard voices in the background when the sheriff covered the mouthpiece as he was talking to one of his deputies. "Okay, I'm back. The slugs that killed our ditch man came from the same type of gun that killed those low-level drug guys in LA. Without the actual gun, we can't know if it was the same one, but we know from the ammo it was the same type of weapon. I have a feeling that when Alvera's drug activities on the island were exposed, someone in California began a systemic elimination of dealers in the pipeline that could lead the authorities to the head honcho."

"Joe, this is beginning to make a lot of sense. If I can get a lead on whether or not there's ongoing drug activity here on the island, it may lead all the way back to California to who is directing all this business."

"Samuel, one last thing before we disconnect. My deputy just informed me that two men were noticed here in Amarillo paying special attention to your office from a restaurant across the street. We will keep a close eye on them and get some pictures when they pop up again. My guy had stopped to get lunch in the restaurant when he noticed them seated at the table near the front window. He watched as one of them clicked pictures of your office on his cell phone. Unfortunately, my guy had to make a quick trip to the restroom, and when he came back out, they were gone."

DEADLY ATTACK

"Thanks, Joe. I'll keep in touch. If you are able to get their pictures, please forward them here to Chief Lambers."

*****

Samuel grabbed a quick supper in the inn's dining room, waiting for night to settle in. He knew that the Lost Sailor Saloon would be in full swing after sundown and wanted to watch the clientele coming and going and hopefully see if he could spot any evidence of drug business going down. The Spirit Gum felt as if it were trying to eat into his face underneath his stick-on hair, causing him to fight the urge to tear the phony stuff from his face. He couldn't scratch through the fake beard or mustache and was doing all in his power not to rub it vigorously in fear of sliding it off his face and onto his brightly colored island shirt. He had read where the gum was non-toxic and normally didn't bother the skin. He wondered to himself if all the itching underneath his false beard and mustache indicated that the skin on his face wasn't normal. He was quickly realizing that this undercover work was not all it was put up to be.

He returned to his room before going out for the night and looked again at the printouts of the big man shoving the wounded guy into the back seat of the limo at the Denver airport. Something dug deep in his memory as he stared at the man's rough features. He knew that he had seen him before but couldn't remember where.

The streets and alleys near the Lost Sailor Saloon were in full swing. Samuel's attire was certainly drawing a lot of attention from the winos and others in the seedy area of the island. He had the gun tucked in a holster attached to his belt, carrying it in the small of his back. He had practiced reaching and pulling it out in his room at the inn to make sure he was fast enough, hopefully to avoid being killed. He entered the saloon, making his way up to the bar and taking a stool on the end where he could keep an eye on the room.

"What'll it be, bub?"

"Sparkling water with a nice plump olive in it."

The bartender gave Samuel a disgusted look and went to fill his order.

"Stomach bothering you? Or is it just that you can't handle a man's brew?"

"I've seen enough bodies sleeping in the alleys outside to know what your 'man's brew' can do to the men who think they can handle it."

After giving Samuel one last sneer, the man moved down the counter, offering more poison to

DEADLY ATTACK

those hunched over the stools leaning on the bar. Samuel gave the room a good look over but didn't observe any apparent illicit transactions taking place. He continued to sit and sip his water before pulling the olive off the toothpick, giving it a nice chew before sending it to his waiting stomach. After watching for an hour and consuming another two glasses of sparkling water adorned with its olives, he slid off the stool and headed for the front entrance.

"Hey, sweetie, where you taking those fancy britches to?"

The man at the table guffawed with his two drunken buddies, sticking out one leg in front of Samuel, trying to trip him. Samuel lifted his foot and placed it down on the man's shinbone with enough force to send a shrieking scream from his antagonist's throat. The room went quiet as all eyes turned toward the action near the front door. The injured man's drunken buddies tried to scramble up from the table to attack their friend's assailant but fell down, tipping their chairs over on the filthy floor.

"You boys had too much of this place's 'man's brew.'"

Samuel made his way back out onto the sidewalk, heading up the dimly lit street to one of the other dives along the way. He passed across the mouth of one of the rat-filled alleys with his eyes fixed on two men across the street, lounging on an old bench in earnest conversation. The crushing blow to the back of his head sent brilliant rays of light shooting through his brain just before his world went dark.

*****

Samuel could hear mumbling voices near him but couldn't understand their words. A searing pain shot through the back of his head as he tried turning it toward the voices.

"He's coming around."

"Can you hear me, my good amigo?"

Samuel's hearing was coming back enough that he recognized the words coming toward him. A rough hand shook him as if trying to bring him out of his dazed condition.

"That's enough, Sylvester. We don't want to dislocate his shoulder, adding that to the gash in the back of his head."

Samuel knew the voice speaking near him, and it sent a coldness spreading through his being. He reached around to his back, searching for the gun, finding it missing from the empty holster.

DEADLY ATTACK

"You'll not be needing that here, my good friend. We are peaceable men, no?"

Samuel opened his eyes, willing them to focus on the men watching him. As his blurry vision cleared, he stared into the face of Manuel Alvera, smiling at him, flanked by two large burly men who had obviously enjoyed the brew at the Lost Sailor Saloon for many years. Their facial features were rough and carried the scars of many brawls from their past. Samuel could see his fluffy auburn wig and gun lying on a small table near Alvera's seat. He reached his hand up, touching the back of his head, finding crusted blood caked in his hair where the crashing blow had taken place.

"We had to remove the lovely hairpiece to stop the bleeding for you, my friend. Try not to open that up again."

Hearing Manuel Alvera's voice brought the face at the airport shoving the wounded man into the town car flooding back into Samuel's mind.

"It was him, wasn't it?"

The sound of Samuel's voice in his ears felt as if his head was exploding all over again.

"It was who, my dear colleague?"

"Your goon who tried to bury his blade in my back before escorting me into your presence."

"Oh, yes. That was years ago. You have a sharp memory. That was Rollie Jenkins. He did work for me for a while, I'm afraid."

Samuel's mind was racing, sending spasms of pain shooting through it from the wound on the back of his head. If the man at the Denver airport was Alvera's enforcer and had the wounded man with him, it must have been those two that shot up the bunkhouse. Now he was here in Alvera's presence with two of his other henchmen, no doubt getting ready to end his detective career. He tried desperately to think of a way of getting to the gun on the table before Alvera's men got to him. Samuel had made his call to Joe Halstead at 6:00 p.m. before heading out for the night, letting him know everything was fine. He knew in himself that his need of the cavalry was at this moment long before the 9:00 a.m. call the next morning.

*****

Joe Halstead sat in his office, looking at the report from the crime lab. The bullet taken out of the ditch man's shoulder was from a Winchester 1886 rifle. He knew that either Diego or Eduardo's bullet had caught up to the man. He turned and placed the

DEADLY ATTACK

paper in his file cabinet in a file marked as pending. Samuel's brothers had acted in self-defense, and no further investigation was necessary. He didn't need to find out which brother's rifle had sent the bullet into the dead man's shoulder. The bullets that killed him were those taken out of the back of his head. He was relieved to receive Samuel's evening telephone call and know that things were in order on the island thus far. He turned off his coffee pot and prepared to head to Ms. Carmen's for supper and then home to watch a good movie before turning in for the night. The men that had been observed taking pictures of Samuel's office hadn't resurfaced. Things had been relatively quiet in Amarillo. Just the way he liked it.

Sofia looked up and down the supper table, feeling a hollow burning in her stomach. It wasn't the lack of food that she was missing but the empty chair where her eldest son had always sat. The bunkhouse attack was still as raw as if it had just happened. The dread that filled her was as if she were already in mourning for Samuel as if he had passed out of the land of the living. Ever since he had moved his office into Amarillo, his absence at the ranch had taken its toll not only on his mother and brothers but also on the head maid, who moved through her days in a state of despondency. Her heart was heavily burdened, feeling the same sense of loss as that of her mistress. Samuel had avoided the ranch, not wanting to bring more danger to his family, but his absence was more painful than the thought of another attack.

*****

"I did exactly what you told me to do. I took care of the loose ends. There's no threat coming your way because of any of my actions."

The fear in the big man's voice was palpable. Sweat broke out all over his body as the car continued making its way out of the city toward the deserted countryside beyond. The plastic zip ties dug deep into his wrists pinned behind his back. He tried desperately to assure the men in the front seat that he was not a threat to them or to anyone in their organization. The car lurched to a stop near a large ravine with its steep slopes covered with scrub trees and boulders of varying sizes. The light was faint as dusk settled in over the deserted landscape. The rear door was flung open with the terrified occupant being ordered out. The big man began to shake violently as he pleaded with his captors to just let him go.

"You'll never hear from me again. I promise."

DEADLY ATTACK

"This ain't nothing personal, you understand. Just following orders."

The pistol's discharge caused a large flock of birds to wing their way skyward out of the scrub brush spreading itself down the steep banks of the ravine. The man's body rolled down into the depths below, bouncing off the rocks along the way.

"Buzzards will get some good eating off of that one."

The car pulled away, disappearing into the descending darkness on its way back into the city.

"You men go out and work the street. We'll begin our meeting at the usual time."

Samuel watched as Alvera's two henchmen left the room, heading out into the darkened streets. He wondered to himself what meeting Alvera was referring to.

"Samuel, you did me an amazing service sending the DEA agents my way. Going to prison was what I needed at that point in my life."

Samuel was confused at the words coming from the man before him. He briefly thought that the blow on his head was interfering with his ability to understand what he was hearing.

"My dear mother and grandmother were both devout Christians, but I followed my father's ways and ended up in the same business that took his life. A godly chaplain at the federal prison guided me back onto the right path. It may be hard for you to understand, but I trusted Jesus as my Lord and Saviour, and He has sent me back into this place to rescue those whom in past times I helped send down the path of destruction. I am no threat to you. I owe you a great debt of gratitude."

Alvera arose and came to Samuel, handing him back his gun.

"Be careful with that, it's still loaded. You know, when we first met, there was something special about you. I could sense your goodness compared to my evil ways. Yes, my dear friend, your life cast conviction into my heart even back then.

"The gash was not real deep. I have removed a small portion of that luxurious hair of yours and pulled it together with butterfly tape. It should be fine within a week or so. Keep it as dry as possible. Wash the front of your head if you must, but leave the back alone."

The man gave Samuel a crooked smile.

"Tilt your head back."

Samuel dutifully looked up into the small flashlight shining into his eyes.

"No concussion that I can detect, Manuel. Your man here should be fine."

Manuel Alvera thanked the man as he placed his things into the small bag on the table.

"Samuel, this is Dr. Alfred Lambright. He works alongside our group here at the mission to supply the medical needs of those coming off drug and alcohol addictions. He is also a servant of our Lord and is truly a blessing to our ministry here."

Samuel was still at a loss for words, realizing that Manuel Alvera was truly a changed man. He spent the next hour in the small meeting room where a number of street people were gathered as one of Alvera's helpers led the singing of "Amazing Grace" along with "Victory in Jesus."

Alvera then rose and shared the gospel of the Lord Jesus to the blurry-eyed men and women before him. As he finished his message, he called out, "*But as many as received Him, to them gave He power to become the sons of God, even to them that believe on His name.* My friends, open your hearts tonight and invite Jesus to come in and give you a new life. A life of hope and freedom from the destructive forces trying to destroy you. There is a better path. Take it tonight and begin your life anew, walking with Jesus our Lord."

Samuel could hear muffled sobs emanating from those in the room. His own eyes filled with tears as he looked at Manuel Alvera, a man born again by the precious blood of the Lord Jesus Christ. A life changed from destroying others to sending out the lifeboat of the gospel to bring them in from the storms of life.

After the meeting, Manuel sat with Samuel, sharing a cup of hot chocolate.

"This is now one of the biggest weaknesses in my life. If there's anything better than hot cocoa, I don't know what it is. I am only here because I was never close enough to the top to know any of their identities. I was truly a small cog in a big wheel pushing their poison here in the islands. Samuel, you need to proceed with extreme caution. I have heard that they are systematically eliminating all those underneath the head of the group to assure they are never exposed. They will stop at nothing to keep themselves above the law while continuing to make millions in their illicit businesses. When I was still in their employ, whoever the head person was, they were heavily invested in opening up the entire South Pacific through Kalmajo Island."

Samuel stared deep into Manuel Alvera's face. "You said businesses. Does that mean they are into more than drugs?"

"I can't be sure of that. However, when I was still pushing the business here in the islands, I sensed that they were also in the money-laundering business. I don't know how they are doing it, but they had to have a way of taking the drug money and making it legit. No one can generate enormous amounts of cash from the drug business and not try to conceal it from the authorities. All of these groups must find a way to wash the cash, so to speak, to avoid detection. I always felt that the main power source was coming from the West Coast back in the States."

Manuel spent the next hour sharing what he knew with Samuel to hopefully help him get onto the trail of those that sent the gunmen his way.

"All the interaction that came to me in the business came out of California. Again, I never knew their identities beyond those moving the drugs to me for distribution."

"Manuel, it was Rollie Jenkins that was seen in an airport video with one of the men who shot up my office. I believe he was the other man involved in the attack on me. What I can't figure out is why would that first meeting and our short scuffle cause him to hate me enough to come after me years later?"

Alvera considered Samuel's words before responding.

ALTON LYNN COOPER

"He was one who didn't go away quietly. After I was arrested—thank you once again—Jenkins returned to the mainland and moved further up in the drug organization, to my knowledge. If that is the case, then someone from the top sent him and his associate your way to get even for destroying their business here in the islands. They are known to carry grudges, with murder being one of their normal operating methods. They seem to wait a while and let things cool down, then send out destruction. This helps to conceal the motive behind the attack when the authorities begin their investigation. If you can find Jenkins, you will find him hooked up with others in California if he is indeed still in the business."

"One last question, Manuel. Who cracked my head open? And how did I end up here in your place?"

"Good question. One of my men was watching the street when a robber slipped in behind you. My guy yelled, and your assailant disappeared into the night. My man brought you here to keep you from further harm."

*****

Samuel placed his 9:00 a.m. call to Joe Halstead and filled him in on the happenings from the night before.

DEADLY ATTACK

"How's your head?"

"It has a nice dull ache keeping it company, but things could have been much worse. It's amazing to me how God sent a man whom I helped send to prison years ago to come to my rescue."

"Sounds like he's put you on the trail of some mighty nasty people in California. You had better proceed in conjunction with the authorities there. Don't try and go this alone."

"I plan to reconnect with Jeremy Simmons and Lemuel Rollins. They were the two DEA guys that were involved with Davey and me on the island. I don't know if they are still on the case in LA, but if so, they will be a good resource."

"Samuel, you should also keep Gregory Lawrence involved from the FBI standpoint. The armored car heist was never resolved, and that could still link him into the investigation there."

"Good idea. I'll try and get enough cavalry around me to hopefully thwart any future attacks against my person. I'm sure as I get closer to the head of the snake in California, they will send a lot of firepower my way."

*****

Samuel stopped by Bobby Lambers's office on his way to the airport. "You can stop worrying about Manuel Alvera being back in the drug business. His operation in the seedy district is for real." Samuel shared with the chief of police his experiences from the night before. "He actually saved my life from additional harm if his man hadn't run off my attacker. You may want to hook up with him in your efforts to continue cleaning up the island."

"That's a good idea. I need all the help I can get, for sure. It seems every week or so some new faces appear on the island as if they are scouting out the place. They are mostly flying in from the West Coast. My men and I are keeping a close eye on them when they are here, hopefully to identify what contacts they're making so we can watch those as well."

"Well, my friend, stay safe. I'm off to California to continue my efforts in exposing the head of the drug business there. I'm convinced they are the ones who tried to eliminate me. If I'm successful, just maybe you'll see fewer people coming your way trying to reignite their business here in the islands."

Samuel had rescued his wig and cleaned the blood from it. Fortunately, the blow to his head hadn't torn a hole in it. His plan was the same as before: go to the bathroom before deplaning in Los

DEADLY ATTACK

Angeles and put on his new look. He chuckled to himself, wondering if that was the way Superman used the phone booth in his day. He knew the danger he would be in if anyone recognized him while he spent time in the Golden State. It wasn't the same as roaming around Kalmajo Island. He knew that when he started making contacts with drug agents and the FBI in Los Angeles, some unsavory characters very well could begin to investigate him. No doubt Jenkins had given the bosses above him Samuel's description before they sent him to shoot up the bunkhouse.

The plane ride was without incident. To his surprise, the plane wasn't filled to capacity coming from the island, leaving him alone in the window seat without a seatmate. There weren't any yipping young passengers seated around him, resulting in his falling into a deep snooze, missing the in-flight snack. He was jostled awake when the wheels touched down at Los Angeles International, sending him and his carry-on bag to the restroom to become his new self.

He determined to remain undercover as much as possible during his stay in California. If the two men observed taking pictures of his office in Amarillo had waited around there for his appearing, they no doubt had told their superiors by now he was no longer in Amarillo. He had no idea whether or not eyes had been on him on the island, possibly watching for anyone arriving there from the Lone Star State. During past investigations, launching into a dangerous mission like this normally sent tingles up and down his spine, anticipating putting away a nest of *rats*. This time was different. After the near-deadly attack on him at the bunkhouse, his entire being was filled with a sense of uneasiness.

California was a big place with over thirty-nine million people running around. Finding the one or ones of those that tried to end his life would be like hunting for a needle in a haystack. He would definitely need God's help along with His protection in the days ahead.

"Enjoy your stay here in Los Angeles, Mr. Bennett. If I can assist you in any way, feel free to ask." The young desk clerk smiled as she handed Samuel his room key.

He almost slipped up and asked where the best Mexican restaurant was in town. It was hard for him to imagine, but he would have to constrain himself to regular cuisine that more identified with his auburn looks. He realized that many people enjoyed Mexican food, but he didn't want to do anything publicly to show his Spanish roots. He had checked into the Hyatt Regency near Los Angeles International

DEADLY ATTACK

after picking up a rental car from the Hertz counter at the airport. He hoped that he wouldn't get into any high-speed chases as he nursed the four-cylinder Toyota Corolla out into the stream of fast-moving commuters.

It wasn't bad for a small car, but its quickness left a lot to be desired if he needed to flee from any would-be killers. He watched the rearview mirror to see if anyone was tailing him in his trip to the seafood restaurant known as "The Shrimp Lover." The brochure in his hotel room indicated that it served Thai and Cajun seafood. He reasoned within himself that a good dose of Cajun just might quench his desire for his tacos smothered in mild sauce that he dearly loved at Ms. Carmen's Cantina back in Amarillo.

"Is your Cajun interesting while not destroying one's palate?"

The older waitress gave Samuel a curious look. "Have you eaten at seafood restaurants in the past?"

"I must admit, not many!"

"Might I recommend to you a nice plate of fried green tomatoes or a good salmon salad? If you're in the mood for a more breakfast-related meal, we have a good savory spinach and mushroom Cajun omelet."

Samuel's mind worked, trying to think of how any of the waitress's recommendations might rest in

ALTON LYNN COOPER

his stomach. Seeing his struggle, she spoke up, hoping to encourage him in his selection.

"We have many different sauces and spices that you can add to your meal to tailor it more to your taste."

"What is your most frequently ordered item?"

"Our boudin sausage, gumbo, and jambalaya are all excellent choices. You can order any one of those and add a side of dirty rice. It would make a very nice meal for one of your first adventures into our restaurant."

"What do you mean by dirty rice? Did someone drop it on the floor?"

The waitress was beginning to show her frustration with the auburn-haired man scratching at his bearded face, trying to make up his mind.

"I'm sorry. Just bring me what you think would please my palate without keeping me up tonight."

Samuel gave the stern-faced lady before him the menu back and smiled brilliantly as she left to place his order, whatever it was. Her snatching the menu from his outstretched hand didn't go unnoticed by Amarillo's top-rated detective operating undercover in Los Angeles's popular seafood restaurant.

*****

He sat in his hotel room, staring at the whiteboard before him. He had added Rollie Jenkins's name to it, identifying him as one of his attackers. He would contact the drug agents here in Los Angeles in the morning and see if he was on their radar. If he could catch up to Jenkins, he knew it would open up new directions in his investigation, hopefully leading him closer to the top of the drug ring. He was pleasantly surprised how the Cajun food had settled down peacefully in his stomach. His waitress had brought him a nice bowl of jambalaya with chicken, andouille sausage, rice, and Cajun seasonings. It had a small nip to it but not the bite that he feared after causing her a little discomfort at his inability to make a decision. He thought that just perhaps he still needed to enroll in some classes back in Amarillo to improve his interpersonal communication skills.

Wednesday morning came in, pouring rain with occasional crashes of thunder shaking the hotel. Samuel sat in the hotel restaurant, finishing his breakfast, waiting for a return call from Gregory Lawrence. He wanted to pick his brain on who could be trusted, to the best of his knowledge, here in the FBI organization. He would have to divulge his true identity to the authorities, including the DEA agents, whom he would need full cooperation from in solv-

ALTON LYNN COOPER

ing the case. He fully understood that where millions of dollars were involved, many times, those in law enforcement charged with bringing the criminals to justice had gotten caught up in accepting payoffs to allow the bad guys to continue undetected. This was an ongoing problem in a number of South American countries where government officials had been compromised by the cartels operating in their midst. He had finished his breakfast and was on his third cup of coffee when his cell phone vibrated in his pocket.

"Hey, Gregory, it's good to hear your voice. A few minutes longer, and I would have become coffee-logged."

"Sorry. Departmental meeting. What do you need?"

"I'm in LA. I believe my investigation is leading to the top of the drug organization here that was never identified during the drug arrests on the island. I'm convinced that the attack on me was payback for Davey and my involvement in exposing the drug activities there. I need some secure contacts here in LA. I need to know who I can trust to team up with, both in the FBI and DEA, if you have that insight."

"Are you suggesting that these organizations may have corrupt individuals operating within them?"

DEADLY ATTACK

"No. I have no evidence of that. I'm here concealing my identity and need to know who I'm dealing with when I expose who I actually am."

Lawrence was silent for a few moments. "I'll be in LA on Friday if you can hold off until then. We are still on the armored car case, and I've been assigned to reopen it as a cold case. Some additional facts in that case seem to be sending the department in a new direction."

"What do you mean a new direction?"

"I'll tell you more on Friday. Where are you staying?"

CHAPTER 9

The Head of the Snake

It was very difficult for Samuel to spend the rest of Wednesday and all day Thursday hanging out until his meeting with Gregory Lawrence on Friday. He had a strong desire to move as quickly as possible but knew that Lawrence would give him sound advice on his path forward. He sat in his room staring at the whiteboard. He had jotted the names of Tony Rollins, Andres Rafael, and Michael Williams on the board at the beginning of the investigation as potential suspects. He wondered to himself if he had focused on Kalmajo Island too soon, leaving the possibility that those seeking his life had nothing to do with the drug bust and Manuel Alvera.

Alvera's previous employee, Rollie Jenkins, could be working for someone other than the drug kingpin in California. It was obvious that he was

DEADLY ATTACK

associated with the man found dead in the ditch who was involved in the attack on the bunkhouse, but he didn't actually have any evidence that Jenkins was the second shooter. He made that assumption by seeing them together in the airport video. What if Jenkins was after the ditch man for some reason other than the drug operation?

Samuel wondered if it was possible that the dead man and Jenkins may have been working for one of the other three names on his whiteboard. It was a stretch for sure but was still a possibility. He sent up a silent prayer hoping that he wasn't spinning his wheels here in California while his real attacker was in a different part of the country. The plate on the limo at the airport wasn't clear enough to say for sure it was a California plate, and even the best analyst at the FBI couldn't get a set of clear numbers from it. Samuel knew also that many times, vehicles could be stolen and plates changed or altered to avoid detection. That had already happened on two different occasions with the car and truck back in Texas. His eyes stayed on Andres Rafael's name for a few moments as he remembered his trying to kill Samuel in the border town of Loralloes, Texas.

Rafael was involved in the high-stakes gambling racket there and could very well be involved in the money laundering business. It wouldn't necessarily draw attention from the authorities for a gambling operation to be moving large amounts of money. While the gambling business was indeed seedy, if it was properly licensed, the authorities would ignore it for the most part.

Samuel woke up early on Thursday morning and decided to spend his day touring Los Angeles. He thought it would be a good idea to get the lay of the land and scope out some of the nightspots in the shady part of town. He knew that high rollers normally lived high on the hog and patronized the nicer establishments while their underlings hung out at the more base locations. Outside of the DEA and FBI connections he was hoping to establish, he didn't have any other ideas of how to uncover leads in his investigation.

Going in and out of bars in a big city was different than visiting the Lost Sailor Saloon on Kalmajo Island. The island was small enough for the seedy part of town to attract most of the misfits wanting to engage in illicit activities. Los Angeles had enough nightspots to keep you hunting for years and still not making any of the right connections. He never liked going into the bars, realizing they were dens of iniquity and went totally against his Christian beliefs. His parents had never visited those places and had taught their boys growing up to avoid even the

DEADLY ATTACK

appearance of evil. He knew, however, that his profession required him many times to go and hang out in the places that the crooks frequented.

"Where do you want to meet? I'm waiting in the lobby. Or do you want me to come up to your room?"

Samuel looked at the clock radio through groggy eyes that he had forgotten to set the night before. "Sorry, Gregory, late night. Grab a breakfast in the dining room on me, and I'll get myself in order and be down soon."

Samuel hated being late for anything. It went back to his childhood with his dear mother expecting her boys to be seated at the table before the big clock sent out its last bong. That was still the case back at the hacienda, keeping Sofia's crew in check. He showered as fast as he could, forgetting to go gentle on the back of his scalp that still stung a little if he forgot and ran a brush over it. He donned his undercover attire and rushed to the elevator on his way to meet Gregory before he had too much breakfast added to his room bill.

The young girl stared at him in the elevator and then sent out squeals of laughter, shouting, "Look, Mama, that man's hair is upside down."

The exquisitely dressed lady holding the little girl's hand cast a quick look in Samuel's direction and

149

ALTON LYNN COOPER

then struggled to control her face, trying not to burst out laughing as her daughter had done. They exited the elevator, leaving Samuel to look into the small mirror above the floor selection buttons. In his haste, he had indeed stuck his mustache on upside down, causing its side wings to curl up as if they were trying to wrap themselves around his nostrils. He quickly pulled it loose and stuck it back on right side up, hoping that his spirit gum had enough staying power to avoid it falling off in public.

"Master detective indeed."

"What was that, young man?"

A bespectacled older lady was boarding the elevator, staring at Samuel with big eyes magnified by her oversized glasses.

"Nothing. Just having a conversation with myself."

"That's normal for me and my Harvey, but you, young man, you better watch out. Your kids will be trying to put you away in some shady rest old people's hangout the same as our bunch is trying to do to us. My Harvey and I are here on the lam. He says they won't catch us if we stay on the move."

"You must have really had a night. Your eyes look like you spent too much time out on the town." Gregory Lawrence gave Samuel a curious look.

150

DEADLY ATTACK

"Wasn't a night on the town that got me. It was one of those movies on TV that went on and on with me trying to hang on till the end."

"Must have been quite a show to keep a man like you interested that late at night."

"Detective movie. I wanted to know if Stephen McElroy ever solved his case trying to find out who robbed his office. At first he suspected his mother but then started focusing on other family members. I went to sleep with the crook still on the run."

Lawrence gave Samuel another sideways glance. "By the way, I know you mentioned that you were running undercover, but I never imagined you looking like some professor vacationing from one of those prep schools out east."

Samuel flinched as his spirit gum gave up the ghost, sending his mustache for a swim in the hot cup of coffee sitting before him. He quickly grabbed it up, squeezed the hot liquid from it, and stuck it in his shirt pocket. As fate would have it, the mother with her young daughter in tow walked by just at that moment with the little girl calling out, "Look, Mama, he shaved his lip."

Gregory Lawrence gave Samuel another curious look. "What was that all about?"

"Nothing! Can we get down to business?"

ALTON LYNN COOPER

"That's fine by me, but you better hope that rug don't fall off your head. The hotel staff will be using it as a dust mop cleaning up the lobby."

*****

"Carla saw it first. We had just finished our lesson and were preparing to board the school bus when she came and got me. I brought our class here today on a field trip, studying the formation of ravines as an on-site geography lesson."

"Thank you, Ms. Crawford. I need you to go ahead and take the children back to your school. My deputies and I need to seal this area off as a potential crime scene. We will be in touch with you if we need more information."

Lewis Dalton had been with the California Highway Patrol for over twenty-five years, and he knew from looking at the body near the bottom of the ravine it didn't get there from a hiker losing his footing and going over the edge.

"Lester, start inspecting the rim for tire prints. Gordon and I are going to make our way down and see what we have at the bottom."

The body wasn't in good shape after lying in the elements for a number of days, caus-

DEADLY ATTACK

ing the patrolmen to cover their faces with their handkerchiefs.

"Been here awhile. What do you make of that?"

Dalton kneeled down, looking at the small boulder next to the body. It had a red letter *M* marked on it with what appeared to be the number *1* next to it.

"Our victim attempted to leave a message behind. Those letters are written in his own blood."

"Look at the index finger on his right hand. He wasn't done writing."

The deceased man's finger had a dried clump of blood on it and was stretched out toward the rock.

"He was trying to add more to his message but succumbed to his injuries before he could complete it."

"It's obvious that he had help getting to the bottom of the ravine. His shoes aren't hiking shoes, and there were no other vehicles present when the school bus arrived."

"Got something up here."

Dalton and his deputy returned to the rim of the ravine after a difficult climb to the top. Lewis Dalton had recently turned fifty-two years old, and his days of climbing up steep rock-strewn slopes were quickly coming to an end.

153

ALTON LYNN COOPER

Lester Collins held up the shell casing in his gloved hand for Dalton's inspection.

"Humph! A .38 Special! Not the usual .22 automatic used by most of your run-of-the-mill hit men. Our shooter didn't bother to pick up their leftovers. Not only that, he wasn't a very good shot. Our man down below lived long enough to try and leave a clue to his killers even after his tumble to the bottom."

"There's more over here, boss." Collins pointed to a set of tire tracks near the rim and then two sets of footprints leading away from the tire marks to the ravine.

Dalton studied the tire and footprints for a few moments before speaking. "It appears to me that our big fellow at the bottom was sent from this world by a very small person by their foot size. Could have even been a lady. The crime lab's on the way. We want casts of these prints. Hopefully, the fellow's DNA at the bottom of the ravine will tell us who our writer was."

"So what is this new direction you and your crew are looking at concerning the armored car robbery?" Samuel watched Gregory Lawrence's face as he seemed to go back in time with his thoughts.

"When it first happened, we thought it was what it appeared to be: a hold-up to rob the armored car of the cash it was transporting. The car had run its normal route that day, picking up cash from four different companies, and then was diverted to pick up a load of pharmaceuticals. Normally, the car would pick up one or the other—cash or pharmaceuticals. Further investigation revealed that the car company was short-handed on the day of the robbery and had combined the route to cover the companies on the regular schedule, with the pharmaceutical company being a late addition. The cash disappeared, and the pharmaceuticals were sold on the black market for somewhere around two million dollars. We are now trying to determine who may have been involved that would have known what the armored vehicle was hauling. We are also trying to discover if there was some link between the gang war and the pharmaceutical robbery."

Samuel considered Gregory's information for a few moments before responding. "Do I understand you right that the crooks were after the drugs being transported more than the cash?"

"The cash in the truck was a little over six hundred thousand. Your average criminal brazen enough to rob an armored car in broad daylight normally waits for one hauling federal funds to one of the larger banks. Most of the time, they watch the routes for a period of time

ALTON LYNN COOPER

and figure out which one has the large amounts available to them, making the robbery worth their while. These guys hit a vehicle with a smaller amount of cash versus a payload of drugs. This armored car didn't have the pharmaceutical stop on its regular schedule. Our new direction is to try and figure out who may have tipped the robbers off as to what the car was hauling on that particular day and take another run at trying to tie the car robbery to the prior gang war."

Samuel's cell phone vibrated in his pocket, causing him to jump. "I hate this thing doing that when I'm not expecting it. Feels like a mouse on the loose."

"Garcia here."

"This is Sheriff Wilson. The blood on the fifty-dollar bill was from our man in the ditch. I think we all assumed that it was from him, but now we know for sure. Have you caught today's news from your location there in LA?"

"What news are you referring to?"

"They found a body at the bottom of a ravine a short distance out of town. The news is reporting that he was shot in the back before being sent down to his resting place."

"Do you think the man in the ditch near Denver and the body in the ravine here in LA might be connected?"

DEADLY ATTACK

"For now, the only comparison that I see is both of them were hauled a short distance from town and sent out of this world. Thought you might want to check it out there with the local authorities."

Samuel shared the sheriff's information with Gregory Lawrence and then asked him if he could contact the highway patrol and find out the information about the body in the ravine.

"You're the private eye. I'm here on the armored car case, remember?"

"I don't want to sound paranoid, Gregory, but I don't want to call telling them I'm a private investigator from Texas. I don't know how deep this drug ring's roots run here or who may be in on the take. I prefer to stay undercover until I know who I can trust."

"Are you telling me you don't trust the California Highway Patrol?"

"After almost getting killed in the bunkhouse attack, yes. I don't know who I can trust at this point other than you and a few other close associates."

"I'll see what I can find out."

Samuel and Lawrence parted ways, promising to stay in touch and share any information that may come their way concerning their two different cases. Samuel didn't know at that moment that their two cases had more in common than he or Gregory Lawrence realized. Samuel returned to his hotel room and applied a fresh layer of spirit gum to his upper lip. He was truly beginning to hate the stuff, noticing that little red bumps were visible on his upper lip. He determined to sue the gum company for false advertising if this stuff started taking off patches of his skin. He took one last look in the mirror, winked at himself, scratched his beard, and headed out to begin his day of investigating.

"DEA, here I come."

"What did you say your name is?" The receptionist behind the desk at the Los Angeles DEA office complex stared deeply into Samuel's face.

"My name is Francis Bennett."

"And exactly why do you want to talk to one of our agents?"

"I'm a freelance writer, and I want to do a story on the bravery and cunning of your agents. In my estimation, they are true American heroes working day and night to protect society from the deadly drugs trying to destroy lives across this country. I want to write their story and give them the honor due them."

The receptionist smiled broadly at Samuel and then commented, "That sounds too good to be true. I need to see some identification."

DEADLY ATTACK

Samuel dutifully held up his reporter's card with his picture on it. The young lady behind the desk squinted her eyes and spoke in a low voice to herself, "Francis Bennett Publishing Enterprises."

"So you write and publish?"

"Yes. I do my best to make my subjects famous. When I look at you here protecting the entranceway to this critical American operation, I see you as a strong part of the DEA organization, keeping people like myself safe every day of our lives." Samuel flashed Ms. Gloria Stumpfester a brilliant smile, showing off his pearly white teeth in the midst of the beard that was eating away at his skin coated in spirit gum.

"Please take a seat in the lounge, and I'll see who may be available to talk with you."

Samuel took his seat after getting a cup of coffee from the small table in the corner of the lounge.

"Here. I thought you might need this for your story." Ms. Stumpfester handed Samuel her receptionist business card along with sending a broad, admiring smile his way.

"Oh yes, that is very thoughtful of you. I will need the correct spelling of all the individuals' names that become a part of this amazing exposé."

Gregory Lawrence flashed his FBI badge to the man behind the thick glass window at the Lincoln

ALTON LYNN COOPER

Armor Car office and waited for him to finish his phone call.

"How can I help you?"

"I need to speak with the people responsible for scheduling your vehicle routes."

"May I ask why that would be of interest to the FBI?"

"I'm looking into the robbery that occurred four years ago when cash and pharmaceuticals were taken."

"Please have a seat, and I'll get you to the right people."

Samuel sat with the magazine in his hands, deeply involved in the story of a missing shipment of raw diamonds from South Africa that had never been found. He thought that those diamonds just might need the services of a first-rate private detective such as him to once again come into the light of day. The squeaky voice coming from above pulled his eyes from the magazine to look up into the slender, slightly pinched face before him. Samuel noticed the young man's name tag announcing him as Steven Dawson.

"Mr. Bennett, please follow me."

Samuel stood and dutifully followed the young man through four different doors, with him sliding

DEADLY ATTACK

his DEA card through the card reader on the wall, releasing the doors one by one as they passed on their way into the inner chambers of the DEA office complex.

"Please take a seat in here. I'll be with you shortly."

Samuel sat in one of the soft leather armchairs that surrounded a long, heavy oak conference table with its feet sinking into the thick carpet covering the room. After a few minutes of listening to the pendulum clock on the wall ticking its way toward 11:00 a.m., Steven Dawson returned, setting a fresh pot of coffee on the table along with a tray of ginger snap cookies and two small containers of milk and sugar cubes. Dawson slid his DEA business card toward Samuel and sat down across the table, flashing him a brilliant smile announcing that he was ready to be deposed.

"Steven, this isn't a deposition. It's an interview. Are you an active DEA agent?"

"Oh yes, Mr. Bennett. I'm an agent in training. I've been assigned to watch over headquarters here after finishing my last field agent exam."

"If you finished the field agent exam, why are you assigned to watch over the office here? Why aren't you working in the field?"

Steven Dawson's face cast a red blush as he reached to pour himself and Samuel a cup of coffee.

"My uncle is one of the senior agents here, and he felt it may be better for me to stay out of the field until I gain more experience protecting the home office."

"Steven, I don't want to hurt your feelings, but I need to interview seasoned agents who have a number of years of field experience. I need to find out what major drug operations they may be investigating at the present time. Not that I need to know specifics but just to understand what is holding their interest here in LA and across the state."

The blush left the young trainee's face as he brightened, informing Samuel that he was aware of a number of ongoing investigations.

"That's wonderful, Steven. Pour us another cup of coffee, and let's get started."

Samuel sat in his hotel room with the whiteboard lying on the floor. He pulled his notepad from his pocket and wrote the four ongoing investigations on the board that were keeping the DEA busy both here in Los Angeles and in Sacramento. He remembered that the two agents who showed up on Kalmajo Island interrogating him and Davey Gibson in their drug investigation a few years back were out of the

Sacramento office. Jeremy Simmons and Lemuel Rollins were trying to identify individuals that were involved in the drugs flowing into the islands from California. That was when he went undercover and then exposed Manuel Alvera's operation, freeing Davey from jail. He smiled to himself, knowing that Alvera was now involved in the business of saving souls instead of destroying them.

Dawson had given him insight into the four active investigations but couldn't provide him with any details or the status of each one. All four had one thing in common: the mafia was involved in moving large amounts of drugs into California and beyond, sending them throughout the States. There had been a few smaller busts of lower-level operatives, such as the one Samuel was involved in with Manuel Alvera, but the top players had never been identified. The DEA was also working closely with other law enforcement at the national and local levels investigating a number of recent murders, such as the man found in the ditch near Denver. Samuel was convinced that the individuals who tried to kill him must somehow be involved in the drug business and that the attack on him stemmed from his involvement with Alvera's arrest, interrupting their business in the islands. The head or heads of the organization must be aware of

ALTON LYNN COOPER

the DEA and FBI's ongoing investigations, resulting in them killing off the middlemen to eliminate any evidence leading back to them. Samuel knew that the attack against him was payback and not because he had any knowledge of whom the head honchos were.

"How are things back at the home front?"

"It's been pretty quiet here since no more private eye offices have been blown up lately."

"How are things going on your end?"

Samuel was placing his 6:00 p.m. check-in call to Joe Halstead back in Amarillo.

"I'm trying to find the right trail here in LA to kick start my investigation. I seem to have a lot of loose ends with bits and pieces of information that don't form any type of pattern at this point."

"Did you hear the news concerning the body found in the ravine outside LA?"

"Yes. Sheriff Wilson mentioned something to me this morning."

"Did you hear the latest?"

"What do you mean the latest?"

He was the same guy that was seen with our ditch man pushing him into the limo at the Denver airport. A deep coldness swept through Samuel as he suddenly realized that Alvera's man from Kalmajo Island was no doubt the second man that shot up

164

DEADLY ATTACK

his bunkhouse, and now he was dead at the bottom of a ravine a short distance from where Samuel was staying.

"You still there?"

"Yes. I know who that man was."

"Are you going to share or keep that information to yourself?"

"Joe, that was Rollie Jenkins who worked for Manuel Alvera on Kalmajo Island. I had a run-in with him when I was in the seedy district on the island trying to uncover the drug business going on there. This means that whoever was behind the attack on me has eliminated the two men sent to kill me. They are getting rid of anyone that could possibly lead law enforcement back to them."

Joe Halstead was quiet for a moment. "I don't want to put any more on your plate, but the two guys that were staking out your office were seen back in town shortly before noon today. Randy Sawyers was on patrol and saw them leaving the alley behind your office. They sped off toward Main Street, and by the time he turned around and started after them, they disappeared in traffic. He cruised up and down, checking out side streets, but they were nowhere to be found."

165

ALTON LYNN COOPER

"Was he sure they were the same men that he saw in the restaurant before?"

"Yes. There was no doubt in his mind."

"Thanks, Joe. I'm meeting with Gregory Lawrence in the morning to compare notes. I'll share the news of who the ravine man is with him if he doesn't already know."

"Be safe, my friend. I don't like the feel of this."

*****

Samuel had a light supper in the hotel restaurant and returned to his room. He turned on the TV, hoping to hear the local news announcing any updates concerning the dead man in the ravine. There were a number of stories concerning elections coming up and who was leading in the polls but nothing on Rollie Jenkins's untimely passing. He shook his head, listening to an advertisement proclaiming a newly released blood pressure medication stating that you could take it and eat and drink anything at any time you wanted.

"Folks, you don't need to change your lifestyle. Instead, simply change your medication. Blood pressure is no longer your burden. Take Benodol and end your days of struggling to keep your blood pressure

DEADLY ATTACK

under control. A long and healthy life is yours for the living."

Samuel listened as soft background music began playing, showing a number of older people smiling while jogging, riding jet skis, and then laughing with groups of their friends at a nighttime luau. All during the smiles and soft music, the announcer was reading off a list of the side effects of the new wonder drug that could cause death or serious stomach and lung complications. After the announcer finished reading off the dire warnings about ingesting the new wonder drug into your body, a bouncy, energetic voice spoke up in a soothing tone as the picture of the Macrone laboratories flashed on the screen.

"If you need help with your medications, Macrone Pharmaceutical Laboratories are here to assist you. We've been developing world-leading medications for the last century here in sunny California for you and your family. And remember, *you can trust Macrone as one of your own!*"

The news announcer came back on, preparing the audience for the next onslaught of information coming their way.

"Now stay tuned for your latest five-day weather report, followed by Billy Burton with your sports update."

ALTON LYNN COOPER

Samuel turned off the TV and headed for the bathroom to place a warm washrag over his face, trying to soothe his spotted skin one more time before turning in. He had already set the alarm for 6:00 a.m., allowing him a full hour to get ready before his breakfast meeting with Gregory Lawrence.

*****

"Yes, I'm doing fine, Mother. I'm working with the FBI to continue the investigation on the attack. We are making some progress but have a lot more to uncover. How's everything at the ranch?"

Sofia was quiet before responding, "Oh, everything at the ranch is fine except for a mother who is carrying a heavy load of worry for her eldest son and a young señorita who is pining away a little at a time."

"Please don't worry about me. I need to stay here in LA until I find the head of the organization that sent their goons after me. And one other thing, tell that lonely señorita that I miss her too."

Samuel hurried to the elevator on his way down to the hotel restaurant and his meeting with Gregory Lawrence. He had placed the call to the ranch feeling guilty for not staying in touch, realizing that his mother would be in a constant state of worry over him. He felt fresh pains of regret again for the horror that his family had passed through from the attack. He definitely wanted to solve this case and put away those who caused his family such grief.

"Well, it's good to see that my good detective friend remembered how to set his clock and join the living at a respectable hour."

"Good morning to you too, Gregory. Have you ordered yet?"

"Not yet. I wanted to make sure that your credit card showed up first. I feel like one of these all-American breakfasts that I see advertised on the early morning news programs."

"Order what you want. I'm putting this on my room bill and will be sure to write it off as a business expense on my taxes. Now, tell me, what were you able to find out about our man in the ravine?"

"I talked with Lewis Dalton this morning. You remember he's the California Highway Patrol chief that's working the case. They were able to fingerprint the man, and he was in the system."

Samuel interrupted his friend before he could go on. "His name is Rollie Jenkins, correct?"

"How did you know that? I thought you wanted me to get the scoop on him."

"I talked with Joe Halstead last night, and he filled me in. This means that whoever sent the men to attack me has eliminated both of them. I am wondering if they know that I am on their trail and you are back on the armored car robbery case."

"That could be. I doubt that they know who you are in that get-up. They probably have been searching for you in Amarillo with no luck."

"Two men have been observed there on two different occasions, scoping out my new office."

"You had better proceed with great caution, my friend. Whoever is at the head of this operation wants you gone in a bad way. Let's eat up and take a drive. I have something I think you need to see."

Gregory Lawrence pulled the car to a stop a short distance away from the ravine. "Got your hiking boots on?"

"Do you mean hiking or climbing? If you mean we are going down into that ravine, you may have to carry me back up."

"You look pretty fit even in that dapper outfit. I'm sure you'll find your way to the top, especially when it gets close to suppertime."

The two men reached the bottom and squatted down, looking at the blood marks on the stone. Samuel was first to speak.

DEADLY ATTACK

"What do you make of that?"

"Well, to me it could either be *M1* or *ML*, with the *L* being in the lowercase. What do you think your man was trying to spell?"

Samuel stared at the blood marks on the stone with a complete blank filling his mind. "Honestly, I have no idea. But one thing for sure, it must have been something very significant if he used his own blood and last moments of his life trying to send a message to those who would find him down here."

The climb back to the top was indeed a workout for both men. Samuel felt sorry for the men from the coroner's office who had to haul Jenkins's body back to the top. The markings on the rock would haunt his mind in the days to come. Lawrence shared with him the information that he had received from the coroner. The person who shot Jenkins had not killed him immediately, hitting him in the back with the bullet passing through under his right shoulder blade. The fall down the steep slope covered in large rocks and scrub brush delivered the fatal blows to his body and head.

"Well, let's get you back to the hotel. I've got to track down my runaway armor car worker, and I'm sure that you have some trails of your own to snoop down."

ALTON LYNN COOPER

Gregory Lawrence had shared with Samuel the information that he received during his visit to the armor car company. The individual who set up the schedule for the car that was robbed was a man named Jimmy Winters. He had worked for the company for eleven years and had an impeccable record. All their employees had to pass a criminal background check prior to being hired, and his was totally clean. He lived alone in an apartment complex in downtown Los Angeles and came up missing three months after the car was robbed. He scheduled the car to pick up the pharmaceuticals that day because the regular driver for that route called in sick. A number of workers were off sick with the flu, requiring certain routes to be combined or moved to a different day.

Winters had initially been interviewed by the FBI and was being called back in for a follow-up meeting with the agents when he disappeared. His personal belongings were still in his apartment, including a safe containing his checkbook, a few government bonds, and ten thousand dollars in cash. He and his car came up missing, with the police listing his disappearance as suspicious since the contents of the safe were left behind. Currently, he remained

DEADLY ATTACK

listed in the Los Angeles police file as a missing person of interest concerning the robbery.

*****

Samuel had a quick lunch in the hotel restaurant and went to his room to update his whiteboard before setting off in the afternoon to pay a visit to the Port of Los Angeles. The trainee at the DEA, Steven Dawson, had shared the four active investigations that were ongoing, trying to uncover the drug activity passing through Los Angeles. He wrote each one on a yellow sticky note, placing it along the bottom of the whiteboard. The DEA had undercover agents at the Port of Los Angeles monitoring shipping activities, other agents at LAX International Airport, others at the leading pharmaceutical companies in Los Angeles, and last, they had agents assigned to monitoring the armor car routes picking up and delivering pharmaceuticals to the over one hundred pharmacies in Los Angeles. According to Dawson, the agents had been working these locations for over six months, and nothing illicit had turned up to date.

There was something about the blood message on the stone that kept poking at Samuel's mind, but he couldn't figure out what it was. He knew Rollie

ALTON LYNN COOPER

Jenkins left Manuel Alvera's employment to move to Los Angeles to become more involved in the illegal drug business. Samuel knew if he could trace Jenkins's movements over the last few years, that might help him figure out the message on the stone. He pulled his notepad from his pocket and wrote down the thought that had just popped into his head.

"Long shot, old boy, but you never know, do you?" That note would add a stop to his afternoon snooping trip.

Samuel nosed the rental car toward the Port of Los Angeles, a little over twenty-eight miles away from downtown. He stopped in one of the snack shops as he entered the complex and picked up a brochure describing the port and the commerce that it supported. It was a large sprawling place covering 7,500 acres of land along 43 miles of waterfront on the coast of the Pacific Ocean. Samuel learned that the port had seven major container terminals along with six intermodal rail yards. The rail yards had direct access to what is known as the Alameda Corridor, which was a twenty-mile express railway connecting the port to the rail hubs in downtown Los Angeles. According to the trainee at the DEA office, their organization had undercover agents watching the docks for the presence of illegal drugs coming into the country.

DEADLY ATTACK

Samuel reasoned to himself that there were evidently a large number of drugs making their way into Los Angeles and then being moved on throughout the US. The DEA was focusing on the port and the Los Angeles International Airport as potential locations for the incoming drug shipments. He was puzzled as to why the agents would be monitoring the pharmaceutical and the armored car companies in the city itself. There must be some kind of link to the illegal drug business that they knew about that he didn't.

Samuel joined himself to a group that was preparing to ride a tour bus around the terminal with a tour guide, learning about the port and its importance to the US. She stated that the US imports about 145 billion dollars of goods each year. His ears perked up when the tour guide talked about drug imports. He learned that the US imports pharmaceuticals from China, Mexico, India, and Canada, with China being the largest at almost 24 percent. The tour ended back at one of the port's terminals, giving Samuel an opportunity to catch the tour guide before she prepared for the next group.

"How do you know what is actually in all these incoming containers?" The young lady considered Samuel's question for a moment before responding.

ALTON LYNN COOPER

"Why do you ask?"

"I'm a reporter considering doing a piece on the port and its operations."

"The Customs and Border Protection people inspect around 4 percent of all incoming containers at random. The exception is if you are a new company shipping into the US. More of your containers will be inspected until you have established a track record over time. Also, the shipping companies themselves must file necessary documents with Customs and Border Patrol at least twenty-four hours before the shipments leave their facility."

"Have there been containers found coming in with illegal drugs concealed in them?"

"You need to ask those questions to the port personnel that manage the docks. If you want more information, you can pick up a booklet in the snack shop that provides a good overview of the port's operations."

Samuel caught up with one of the dock managers and asked him if he was aware of any illegal activities going on at the port. The man gave Samuel a quizzical look before responding.

"Who are you? And why do you ask?"

Samuel repeated his story of being a reporter thinking of doing an article on the port's operations.

DEADLY ATTACK

"So let me get this right. You want to write a story, hopefully exposing wrongdoing here at the port?"

"Not if there isn't wrongdoing going on. I'm just curious with all the things passing through this place if there are those trying to send things into the country that may not be legit."

"Are you sure you are a reporter? Or are you with law enforcement?"

Samuel gave the man a surprised look. "Why do you ask? Are you aware of any law enforcement personnel operating here at the port?"

"We have certain individuals that are visible and others that are not. Any port or places of entry, where things come into this country, will always have people watching. If you want more details, talk to the port manager."

Samuel was left standing alone as the dock boss moved off to other duties. He would like to find out what illegal items had been caught coming in but knew that information would not be made available to the public, especially to a reporter with his beard eating a hole in the skin on his face. Samuel was beginning to realize that he couldn't stay in Los Angeles for a long period of time in his false hair, beard, and mustache. The spirit gum and his skin had now entered into an ongoing battle that he was sure the gum was going to win.

*****

"What information are you searching for?"

Samuel sat at the computer terminal in the Los Angeles library, trying to get on the Internet. He looked at the badge hanging on the cord around the neck of an elderly lady staring at him with a forced smile on her face.

"Ms. Carlisle?"

"That's what the tag says if you can read."

"How could I have guessed your name if I couldn't read?"

"Do you need help, young man? Or did you stop in to waste my time and yours?"

"I need to get on the Internet and review some tax records."

"Don't you keep copies of your tax records at home?"

"These aren't my records that I'm after. I need to take a look at a dead man's records."

Ms. Carlisle gave Samuel a stern look with one of her eyebrows cocked higher than the other. "You want me to help you intrude into a dead man's private affairs? Did he die owing you money?"

"No. I need to find out where he earned his money from, if indeed he earned any money."

"You mean you want to know where he worked if there's any record of him working?"

"Yes." Samuel could feel himself beginning to sweat in his reporter's dress shirt under the ongoing questioning by the librarian.

"Get out of the way."

Samuel dutifully got up, giving Ms. Carlisle the control seat in front of the computer.

"Name, first and last, with the correct spelling."

Samuel watched as the information filled the screen before him. Rollie Jenkins had worked in three restaurants, a convenience store, and then at the Macrone Pharmaceutical Company for a short period of time. His last place of employment leapt out at Samuel, causing those familiar tingles to work themselves up and down his spine. He needed to find out what job Jenkins did for Macrone and why he didn't last long at the company.

*****

Samuel sat in his hotel room at the small desk, writing down what he hoped were some of the pieces of information that would begin to show him a pattern in the case. The two men who attacked his office had both been murdered. They both were from Los Angeles. Rollie Jenkins came from Kalmajo Island to Los Angeles to become more involved in the illegal drug business. Jenkins worked for a short period of time at the Macrone Pharmaceutical Company. The person who sent Jenkins to the bottom of the ravine had small feet. Jenkins's last message before he died was the letters "ml" on a stone in his own blood. Jimmy Winters was a trusted employee of the armor car company and scheduled the route for the car that got robbed, with it picking up pharmaceuticals not normally on its route. Winters came up missing three months after the robbery, leaving behind ten thousand dollars in cash at his apartment. The same type of automatic weapons that destroyed Samuel's bunkhouse were used in a gang war in Los Angeles and also in the armor car robbery. He sat staring at the list on the notepad, trying to determine how the various items were related. There was a thread in front of him, but his mind couldn't connect the dots. He pulled the notepad from his pocket, jotting down his question for Gregory Lawrence. The answer to

DEADLY ATTACK

it could add one more piece of information, helping him link the notes on the paper together.

"When did it happen?"

"Last night, sometime after 9:00 p.m., Alvera had just sent his men out to start encouraging those on the street to come to the meeting. They had worked the areas near the Lost Sailor Saloon and were going further away from the mission when they heard the gunfire. They ran back in the direction of the mission, but when they got there, it was on fire. Jordon Milton, one of Manuel's helpers, rushed inside the building and found Manuel bleeding on the floor of the chapel. He carried him out of the burning building and called 911."

"So Manuel had been shot?"

"Yes."

"Did he survive?"

"Yes. He's in the hospital here on the island in critical condition."

"Do you have any idea who was involved in the attack?"

"Not at this time. I've checked the airport off and on today, but no suspicious individuals have shown up there taking a flight back to the mainland. I've stationed one of my deputies there just in case."

"Please keep me posted on what you uncover and on Manuel's condition. It's a sad day for humanity when a man who had been involved in criminal activities turns his life over to the Lord and dedicates himself to helping others and receives this in return."

"Samuel, God doesn't always work in the ways we think. He has a purpose in this, I'm sure, just as he did all those years ago when you were gunned down at the mayor's meeting."

Samuel hung the phone up after hearing Bobby Lamber's report with a sick feeling in his stomach. Manuel Alvera had devoted his life on the island to saving souls, and now someone had tried to send his out into eternity. Alvera had thought of himself as a small cog in the drug business, not knowing any of the top individuals in Los Angeles, but they apparently thought that he knew more than he did. Here was another example of those at the top attempting to erase anyone that might have the slightest knowledge of their identity. They were systematically wiping out those in their organization that might lead law enforcement their way.

Samuel knew that he desperately needed to link the information on the whiteboard together enough to send him in the right direction going forward. The trip to the Port of Los Angeles was interesting but didn't add any worthwhile information to his investigation. He knew that the DEA agents were watching the port and the airport for incoming drugs, but that was common practice for law enforcement when they were trying to find the route or routes being used to move illegal drugs around the country. He needed something to link the deaths of the two men that shot up his bunkhouse, the missing armored car employee, the message in blood on the rock in the ravine, and the attack on Manuel Alvera. Samuel was sure of one thing: someone high up in the illegal drug racket was directing death and destruction against any individual that posed a threat to their identity.

CHAPTER 10

Webs of Deceit

"I'm safe so far."

"How are things back at the ranch?"

"Mama worries about you constantly. Valentina seems to be pining away in your absence. You'd better get your business done there and get back to Amarillo soon or all these ladies are going to go into a deep depression."

"I'd like nothing better than to uncover the head of this organization and do just that. I know one thing for sure: whoever is running the drug business here in LA is a bloodthirsty murderer. They are killing off a number of individuals to cover their tracks."

Diego was quiet for a moment before speaking. "Samuel, are you in over your head on this one? If the DEA and FBI and all these top law enforcement

DEADLY ATTACK

people can't find these people, how are you going to sniff them out?"

"They tried to kill me and they blew up the bunkhouse that our father built with his own hands. This is personal for me, Diego. I don't know how this will turn out, but I'm praying that God will keep me safe and lead me to those who are responsible for all this death and destruction."

"Be safe, my brother. If you should end up as one of those taken out by these madmen, our family here will never be the same."

Samuel made an appointment to meet Gregory Lawrence at one of Los Angeles's famous seafood restaurants for their supper meal, allowing them to compare notes. In the meantime, he decided that he needed to expand his wardrobe to continue the masquerade as a newspaper man since his stay in Los Angeles was taking more time than he originally thought. The tweed suit was in need of cleaning, and the khaki pants and island shirt were in need of a serious washing and didn't exactly fit in on the streets of Los Angeles. He asked the hotel desk clerk where a reasonable men's clothing store was near the hotel and was directed to the "Gentleman's Apparel Shoppe" two blocks away.

185

The bell above the door rang out, announcing that a customer had entered, hopefully seeking to be outfitted. The smell of new clothing, along with leather and suede, filled Samuel's nostrils. He started picking through suits hanging on a rack near the front door, looking for something that might be worn by a man in his profession.

"May I help you?"

Samuel turned around and looked down into the eyes of a small, bald-headed man in his late sixties peering up at him from behind a large pair of gold-rimmed spectacles. The tag pinned on his suit announced him as Oscar Mellencamp. Samuel guessed his height at a smidgen over five feet tall, and that was with him wearing what appeared to be shoes with elevated heels on them.

"Yes. I'm looking for something, not real expensive, that will fit with my profession as a freelance newspaper man."

Oscar stared at Samuel a few moments with a puzzled look on his face. "And exactly what do you think a freelance newspaper man, as you call them, should look like?" The little man was giving Samuel's wrinkled tweed suit a good looking over as he asked the question.

DEADLY ATTACK

"Oh, I guess I would expect me to look a little nerdy, you know, kind of eccentric without appearing to be one who just escaped from some senior institution."

The Gentleman's Apparel Shoppe's proprietor gave Samuel a long, deep, penetrating stare. "Come with me."

Samuel dutifully followed the little man to the back of the store, stopping in front of a rack with a large 40 percent off clearance sign on it.

"These are excellent for a man in your profession and are all offered at a price that will leave you enough money for lunch."

"Why are they marked as clearance? Is something wrong with them?"

"Not at all. They are all freelance newspaper men's outfits just waiting for someone like you to come in and give them a good home. Paw your way through them and let me know if you find some nerdy enough to suit you."

Samuel was left to go through the clearance rack as the little man went back to the front of the shop to answer the bell above the door announcing another man in need.

*****

ALTON LYNN COOPER

"You sure have changed your look since the last time we met." Gregory Lawrence gave Samuel a good looking over after being seated in the Seafood Lovers Restaurant in downtown Los Angeles.

"I had to buy additional outfits since my stay here is turning out to be longer than expected. Have you gotten any leads in the armored car heist?"

"Jimmy Winters hasn't turned up yet. His boss couldn't explain why he would have a large amount of cash left in his apartment or where he would have gotten the money from. He said Jimmy was one of these guys that always lived from paycheck to paycheck. He liked to play a few cards from time to time and wasn't very good at getting other people's money. According to his boss, the other people seemed to always get Jimmy's money."

"So that would cause a person to think that Jimmy Winters may be someone who could be persuaded to help set up an armored car robbery?"

Gregory considered Samuel's question before responding. "I'm of the same mindset as you. I plan on paying a visit to Macrone Pharmaceuticals tomorrow and see what they can share with me concerning the lost shipment."

"You are saying that the prescription drugs in the robbery were from their company?"

DEADLY ATTACK

"Yes."

The two men ate in silence for a few minutes before Samuel spoke up. "I had made myself a note to ask you what company had their stuff on the truck that got robbed. If we believe that Jimmy Winters set all this up, sending the armor truck driver to Macrone's, which wasn't on his normal route, and then alerting the robbers to stick up the truck, why wouldn't they have just waited and hit a full truck leaving on a regular route?"

"Good question. The DEA agents have been monitoring a large number of the pharmaceutical shipments from the drug companies' warehouses to the pharmacies for some time. Maybe the robbers didn't want to take a chance on hitting a truck that could have been under DEA surveillance."

"That makes sense, Gregory. That would necessitate Winters setting up a truck that wouldn't normally be transporting the pharmaceuticals."

Samuel shared the attack on Manuel Alvera and the link back to the illegal drug organization in Los Angeles. He also shared his trip to the port that didn't turn up any useful information in his investigation.

"Samuel, the DEA guys have been monitoring the port and the airport for months and haven't found any illegal drugs coming into the city through them. I'm persuaded that whoever is running this operation is well aware of their observation points and is bringing in the drugs by land. All that being said, my focus is on the armored car robbery itself and not on busting a drug lord."

"I understand that, Gregory. Let me know how your visit to Macrone Laboratories goes tomorrow. I may decide to hit some more of the night spots and see if I can glean any leads on where a person might be able to buy a large quantity of street drugs."

"Watch yourself, Samuel. If you make the wrong contacts, you may end up where the man in the ditch and his buddy in the ravine ended up."

*****

Samuel was sitting in his hotel room before turning in for the night, staring at the photo of the blood markings that Rollie Jenkins had left on the stone. The *M* appeared to be drawn in a way to indicate it was a capital letter and not a lowercase letter. The *1* next to it could either be a number *1* or the lowercase letter *l*. His mind twisted the markings over and over, trying to make sense of the message the dying man had left behind. It dawned on Samuel that perhaps Jenkins died before finishing the second

DEADLY ATTACK

marking. What if the second mark was the beginning of the second letter in Jenkins's message? That could make the second letter either a capital *L* or possibly a capital *P*.

Something struck deep inside Samuel's brain at that moment that sent the familiar tingles up his spine. He was getting close to something important in the case, but he couldn't see it clearly. His thoughts were interrupted by the vibration of his cell phone in his pants pocket, causing him to jump up out of the chair. He silently promised himself to change his call signal away from the vibration to a ring tone, avoiding the feeling of being bitten by a snake.

Samuel was pleased to hear Joe Halstead's voice on the other end of the line. He had stopped his daily calls after a few days back from the island in Los Angeles and needed to catch up on the latest from back home.

"How are things going in Amarillo, Joe?"

"Quiet for the most part. How are things in LA?"

"About the same, I'm afraid. I feel like I'm spinning my wheels getting nowhere. If something doesn't break soon in this case, I may just head back home and wait for the goons to come to me."

ALTON LYNN COOPER

"I think they are already here searching for you. That's why I'm calling."

"My deputy was having lunch in his favorite restaurant across the street from your office when he noticed two men in the restaurant that appeared to be strangers in Amarillo as far as he could tell. They were sitting at a table near the front of the restaurant having lunch, talking quietly between them. He noticed they would occasionally look out the window toward your office. That in itself wasn't enough to know for sure if they were casing the place, so he kept an eye on them and watched as they left the restaurant. They walked down the street to the feed store and sat down on the sidewalk bench, still looking in the direction of your office. He approached them and struck up a conversation, asking if they were new in town. He got the impression that his talking with them caused them a certain level of uneasiness. They indicated that they were passing through town on their way to a business meeting in Albuquerque, New Mexico. They quickly stood up, bidding him good day, and got into a dark late-model BMW sedan and drove away."

"What did they look like?"

"He said they looked like 'Mutt and Jeff' to him. One was very short and small-built, and the other was a medium-built, taller individual. He snapped their picture on his phone as they were walking to their car. I'll have him shoot a copy to your cell phone."

Samuel stared at the picture on his phone, trying to remember whether or not he had met the men in the past. The small man was indeed short and delicately built next to his taller counterpart. The deputy had snapped the picture from a distance, with the sun coming at him, partially obscuring their facial features. Samuel stared at the tall man's blurry face for some time, trying to remember if he had ever seen him before. He seemed familiar, but it was the same feeling that had come to him when he saw the side view of Rollie Jenkins's face in the Denver airport video. He was sure that they had crossed paths in the past but couldn't put his finger on when or why. He doctored his sore skin with a mild facial crème that he picked up from the pharmacy down the street and turned in for the night. He found the Gideon's Bible in the desk drawer and read Psalm 121 before turning out the bedside lamp. He determined to do something to draw those up to no good his way, hoping it would lead him to some top-level drug dealers in Los Angeles. If he was successful, he would need

God's protection in the coming days if he was ever again going to return home to Amarillo.

*****

Samuel woke up with a throbbing headache after a rough night's sleep, dreaming of men chasing him and shooting in his direction. He had tried to turn toward them to see who they were, but his neck was stiff, keeping his face forward as they kept shooting and yelling, "Die, Garcia, die." He had pulled the covers loose from the mattress on his bed and woke up in a cold sweat with his head pounding a rhythm that reminded him of the gunfire coming his way in the dream. He stopped by the front desk, getting a small packet of Bayer aspirin on his way into the restaurant for breakfast. Gregory Lawrence had called him just as he was boarding the elevator, letting him know he was on his way to the hotel. Samuel had just gotten his second cup of hot black coffee when the FBI agent sat down at his table, letting out a low wheeze.

"You sound like I feel. Did you have a rough night too?"

"No, just having a little bit of lower back trouble. I lift weights and tried to increase my bench presses up to the next level. Problem is my back was not ready to go with me. Now let's talk about Macrone Pharmaceuticals."

"Have you eaten yet, Gregory?"

"No, I came here thinking you might want to buy my breakfast while I give you some free insight into what may be pertinent to your snooping around."

Samuel gave his friend a faint smile. "Let's get our morning grub, then you can spill your guts while I add your upkeep to the tab on my hotel room."

The two men ate in silence for a few moments before Lawrence opened up, sharing his latest activities.

"I tried to meet with Macrone's top man but was put in a conference room with one of their lower-level managers. A man named Felix Lowery. He seemed reluctant to discuss the details of the armored car robbery and the pharmaceuticals that were taken. It struck me as strange that his company losing two million dollars in their drug shipment didn't cause them to be more cooperative in trying to help catch the thieves involved. According to him, all their shipments are insured and the losses due to the robbery were covered by their insurance company. As far as Macrone is concerned, it's a closed subject."

Samuel finished swallowing his bite of sausage and egg before speaking. His mother had always chastised her boys growing up if they spoke with their mouths full. Some things a boy, or a man for that matter, never forgets.

"Why would that seem strange? If they are insured for any losses, whether by theft or any other reason, that relieves their company and results in the loss being placed on the insurance company, right?"

"True. One other thing, when I was preparing to leave, I noticed three individuals that seemed out of place making their way toward the head man's office. They just had that look about them that spoke *mafia* to me. I may be completely off base, but they didn't appear to be the corporate type."

"What would *mafia* men be doing meeting with the head man at Macrone Pharmaceuticals?"

"I don't know if they are mafia-related. It was just a hunch at the time, and in my business, I've learned to pay attention to my hunches in certain situations."

"I understand that, Gregory. I react to tingles running up and down my spine. When those come upon me, it normally means there's a rat's nest close by." Samuel thought for a moment and then threw two proposals Lawrence's way.

DEADLY ATTACK

"What if I spend my time finding out where our Mr. Jimmy Winters has disappeared to, along with using my journalistic credentials to write a glowing story of the Macrone Pharmaceutical Company? I'm sure they wouldn't mind a world-traveled journalist like me bragging on their positive impact on society, developing all their leading-edge pharmaceuticals and saving untold numbers of lives. During my digging for info for my article, maybe I can find out why your man Felix seemed reluctant to share information on the robbery."

"Samuel, I don't want to sidetrack your investigation into finding out who tried to kill you. I don't know if anything strange is going on at Macrone's, and I wouldn't want you to get distracted from your own reason for being here in LA. I'm going to connect with the DEA agents in Sacramento who have been working the illegal drug investigation for a number of years to see if the gang war here in LA may have been drug-related. If there was a connection, that might be why they hit the armored car, taking the street-legal drugs to recoup losses from a blown illegal drug deal gone bad. These guys can't lose some drug lord's money and keep on living. They may have been desperate to generate a lot of cash quickly to pay off someone. If you indeed try to

ALTON LYNN COOPER

find out more information on our man Winters, see if he had any drug connections in his background. Our agents who investigated him previously didn't turn up anything. I'll get you some information on his known associates."

*****

Gregory Lawrence mentioning the DEA agents in Sacramento nudged something in Samuel's brain. He had gone back upstairs to his hotel room to put on one of his newly purchased reporter outfits and pay a visit to Macrone's corporate offices. His face was somewhat better after smearing the crème on it the night before, but the spirit gum still sent a burning sensation through his skin, causing him to whimper while sticking the beard and mustache on. He promised himself that once his would-be assassins were put out of commission, he would never wear false facial hair again. If he needed hair on his face, he would grow his own and stop keeping the spirit gum people in business. Before leaving his room, he stared at the pictures on his cell phone that Joe Halstead had sent him.

"Nah. It couldn't be. Why would a DEA agent be in Amarillo looking for me?"

"What did you say your name is?"

DEADLY ATTACK

"Francis Bennett."

"And what is your business with Mr. Macrone?"

"I'm a freelance journalist, and I am interested in doing an exposé on your company. I'm impressed with all of the company's achievements in helping people with your pharmaceuticals and would like to make it a great American success story."

The nameplate on the desk identified the receptionist as Ms. Sally Greensboro. She gave Samuel a thorough looking over and then asked to see his identification. Samuel produced his doctored driver's license provided to him by Raymond Stevens and then showed her his press identification.

"Mr. Macrone is an extremely busy man, and his appointments must be scheduled in advance."

"I'm sorry to hear that. I'm also in great demand as a world-renowned writer and have a limited amount of time to conduct this interview promoting your company in prestigious publications around the world." Samuel flashed Ms. Greensboro one of his most brilliant smiles and waited for her response.

"Please have a seat in the lobby, and I'll see what time may be available for you with one of our vice presidents."

"Thank you for that offer, but I prefer to speak to Mr. Macrone himself."

The receptionist gave Samuel a less-than-welcoming stare, flipping open her desk calendar and searching through it before speaking. "How does two months from today on the twenty-third fit your schedule, Mr. Bennett?"

Samuel gave a quick, tight-lipped smile before responding, "I can start with your vice president and go from there as needed."

"The lobby awaits you, Mr. Bennett. I'm sure you will find the seating comfortable." Ms. Greensboro gave Samuel a satisfied smirk as if she had just put the world-class reporter before her in his place.

Samuel sat watching the hustle and bustle going on around him, realizing that Macrone Pharmaceuticals was indeed a busy place. Numerous men and women came scurrying in and out of the expansive lobby attired in the latest business apparel, all carrying leather briefcases, including some with an additional leather bag with a strap slung over their shoulder. Samuel kept glancing at his watch and was beginning to get a little impatient after he had enjoyed the nice seating for almost an hour.

Two men making their way through the marble-floored lobby caught his attention when he heard the larger man say to his counterpart, "You stay quiet.

DEADLY ATTACK

I'll handle this the way the boss wants." They disappeared down a wood-paneled hallway, bypassing Ms. Greensboro's receptionist station, with her staring in their direction. Samuel decided he had waited long enough for a vice president to make time for him and headed back to the receptionist to let her know his thoughts. He was approaching her station just as she rose, taking her handbag with her. The small metal plaque placed on the edge of her desk announced, "Please be seated in the lobby. Returning at 2:00 p.m."

Samuel gave out a sigh of exasperation and headed back to his place in the lobby. Before he could ease himself into his comfortable seat, a man came toward him, asking if he was Mr. Bennett. Samuel almost slipped up, starting to respond, "My name is Garcia." He caught himself and gave the man a faint smile, sticking out his hand.

"I'm David Welker. Sorry for your wait. Busy day. Please follow me." Samuel followed dutifully behind his guide down the long wood-paneled hallway with the plush carpeting squeezing up around the soles of his reporter's shoes. After traveling around a number of turns in the hallway, Welker opened a set of thick mahogany doors, ushering Samuel into an exquisite conference room that was also covered

ALTON LYNN COOPER

in the rich dark wood. The smell of leather mingled with wood polish filled the room, giving Samuel the feeling he had just been let into the inner sanctum of a millionaire's palace. He quickly realized that these pharmaceutical people spared no expense providing themselves with the best surroundings while charging the regular class a fortune for their prescription concoctions.

David Welker was attired in a suit that no doubt cost ten times the amount of the one Samuel was cloaked in. He was in his mid-thirties with wavy blonde hair and a perfectly trimmed mustache with gold-rimmed glasses resting on his long slender nose. Samuel thought that Mr. Welker fit the role of a corporate vice president to a tee.

"Would you like coffee, Mr. Bennett? Or is tea more to your liking?"

"Coffee is fine. Black and strong." Samuel flashed the young man a toothy smile as he exited the room, leaving Samuel seated at the long mahogany conference table. A few minutes later, Welker returned carrying a silver tray with a pot of coffee on it next to a plate of sugarcoated wafers accompanied by a small container of honey. Samuel thought it strange that a vice president would be waiting on him, just when his host announced, "Mr. Willmar will be with you shortly."

"Is he another vice president?"

David Welker gave Samuel a puzzled look. "He is one of our vice presidents. We have a number of them. I am Mr. Willmar's secretary."

Samuel had polished off half of the stack of delicious sweet wafers and drained the last of the coffee into his cup from the silver pot when the door swung silently open on its well-oiled hinges.

"No, tell him I'll see him shortly after I finish with this newspaper man." The comments were cast behind the man's back to someone in the hallway. Samuel stood to his feet as the Macrone Vice President entered the room. The man turned, staring at Samuel from dark, brooding eyes held in place by a chiseled square-jawed face that looked like it should be in a prizefighting ring.

"Bennett, Willmar." He extended his arm, sticking out his index finger toward Samuel, pointing for him to be seated. "I'm told you're some kind of a reporter, is that right?"

The gold name tag on the man's dark pinstripe suit announced him as Jeremiah Willmar— Executive Vice President, Macrone Pharmaceuticals. He appeared to be in his late forties with slight graying at the temples in his raven-black hair. He was a muscular, broad-shouldered man and carried himself with an air of importance that could easily turn to impatience toward the person in his presence.

"Now what do you want?"

Samuel gave his best speech, plying the vice president with his desire to hold their company up before the world as an example of success that all could follow. He tried not to lay the compliments on too thick, hoping to keep from sounding overly anxious to get an interview. He finished his speech and sat uncomfortably in the silence that followed. Jeremiah Willmar stared deeply into Samuel's face as if he were inspecting a bug that had crawled into his presence.

"And just what makes a world-traveled man like you think that Macrone Pharmaceuticals could give a *sow's ear* about what others think about us?"

Samuel stared back silently and at a loss for words. He hadn't expected that kind of response from Willmar and searched his brain quickly for what he hoped would be a good reason for the gruff man before him to give him the time of day.

"Many in our world are searching for success. It's indeed a help to society when a company like yours, that has found success, shares your knowledge

DEADLY ATTACK

with those coming along behind you." Samuel went silent, feeling the sweat popping out under his false mustache and beard. He wanted desperately to start scratching at the hair on his face but knew he might end up ripping it off, exposing the red splotched skin underneath.

It seemed forever before Willmar gave Samuel a slight grin, breaking the silence between them. "Well spoken, Bennett. Now what do you want to know about our amazing success here at Macrone?"

Over the next hour, Samuel found out that Macrone hadn't always been the picture of a corporate giant. Willmar shared with him how just a few years ago the company had almost gone bankrupt. The founder of the company, Stephen Macrone, had been a very astute businessman and knew when to cut his losses on prescription drug development. Samuel learned that it cost millions of dollars to develop and bring a new drug to market. The current owner, William Macrone II, was the strong-headed nephew of the founder, Stephen Macrone, and was prone to ignoring his company's experts, many times pursuing drugs that never gained FDA approval, costing the company millions in the process.

When Stephen Macrone passed on, he left the company in the hands of his younger brother,

William Macrone. Under William, the company continued to expand and enjoyed a number of new drug successes that put the firm on solid footing. William met an untimely death in a skiing accident at Lake Tahoe, leaving the company in the hands of his ill-prepared son.

"What brought the company back from the brink? Looking around, it's obvious that you are once again a very prosperous company and enjoy being one of the top drug-producing companies in the world."

"Young William graduated from one of the nation's most prestigious business schools and made a number of high-level friends. When he was desperate to keep the company afloat, he called upon some of them to bail him out. They swooped in and invested heavily based on what we were told."

Samuel considered Willmar's last comment before responding, "What do you mean 'based on what you were told'? Were there other sources of money involved in saving the company?"

Jeremiah rose from his seat, looking quickly at the gold Rolex watch on his wrist. "Sorry, Mr. Bennett, but I have other meetings to attend to. I've given you what time I had available and the amount of information that can be used for public consumption. My secretary will see you out."

Samuel was escorted back down the winding hallway toward the lobby. On his way out, he noticed the gold nameplate on a different set of thick double doors announcing "William Macrone II, President." He lingered just a moment, hearing muffled voices coming out of the president's office. They sounded angry to Samuel, and he desperately wanted to get close to the door and try to make out what was being said.

"Mr. Bennett. This way, please."

He reluctantly continued down the hall, following David Welker to the exit. He felt a tingling inside that let him know all was not well at Macrone Pharmaceuticals. He needed to get back to his whiteboard, updating it and then spending some quality time with Gregory Lawrence.

*****

"I'm telling you, hanging around here in Amarillo isn't worth our time. He's obviously not in town and hasn't been for a number of days now."

"If he's not in Amarillo, where is he? He didn't just disappear without leaving a trace. Don't be idi-

ALTON LYNN COOPER

ots. Check the airport and see if some of the local workers there may give you information concerning his destination if he flew out of town."

"Okay. And just what reason can I give for wanting to track down their local private investigator who almost got killed a few weeks back without bringing unwanted attention our way from the local law enforcement?"

"I'm sure if you use that brain of yours, you can come up with something. How about this? Tell them you were hoping to meet up with him at his office on some urgent business. It's imperative that you reach him soon. Our mutual boss doesn't like unfinished business. Samuel Garcia is unfinished business, and the boss's patience is growing thin waiting on you to finish the job. Don't disappoint him. That never turns out well. We all know he will go to any length to protect the big man."

*****

Samuel finished making a few notes on his Post-it pad, sticking them on the whiteboard. They weren't very definitive, simply mentioning that he had observed some non-business appearing individuals entering Macrone's inner sanctum, overhearing

DEADLY ATTACK

the big man's comment about handling something the way the boss wanted. He had a strong feeling that something strange was going on at the pharmaceutical company, especially when Jeremiah Willmar ended their meeting abruptly when he asked about the source of money that bailed the company out, saving it from bankruptcy. Samuel finished preparing for the day ahead and headed down to the lobby to meet Gregory Lawrence for breakfast. The two men had found meeting often early in the day was a good way to share notes, hoping that their joint efforts might break open the cases they were working on. Lawrence had just entered the hotel lobby when Samuel exited the elevator, heading toward the restaurant. Neither of them noticed the man seated near a small statuette in the corner of the lobby as he snapped pictures of them on his cell phone. He slipped the phone back into his pocket, folded his newspaper, and exited the hotel.

"You recognize these men?" Samuel held up his cell phone in front of Gregory with the two men's pictures on it that Joe Halstead had sent him. The agent took the phone from Samuel's hands, staring at the blurry picture before responding.

"The tall one looks like Lemuel Rollins from the Sacramento DEA office. I don't know who the short guy is. Why?"

ALTON LYNN COOPER

"Joe Halstead's deputy snapped their picture in Amarillo after he observed them keeping an eye on my office. When he questioned them, they gave him a story about passing through town on their way to a meeting in New Mexico."

"And you don't think that was true?"

"Gregory, why would a DEA agent be in Amarillo checking out my office when he was one of those who investigated Davey and me on Kalmajo Island? Something doesn't feel right."

Lawrence took the phone from Samuel and stared at the short man's picture for a few moments. "Samuel, there's something here. I can't put my finger on it, but I agree there seems to be some connection to the attack on you and the armored car robbery here in LA. We know the two men who shot up your bunkhouse are both dead. We know that the man who sent Rollie Jenkins to the bottom of the ravine had little feet because of the footprints left behind. We know that whoever is behind this is eliminating individuals who had some connection to the drug trade. I have a hunch about the armored car robbery, but I need to do some more digging before I come to any conclusions. I'm thinking there's a link to the gang war and how they knew to hit that truck on that particular day. Have you done any snooping involving Jimmy Winters yet?"

210

DEADLY ATTACK

"Not yet. I'm working myself in that direction."

Lawrence handed Samuel a small piece of paper with various notes written on it. "Here are some of his known associates along with info on his family members. His parents were out of the country during the time of his disappearance and couldn't give the investigators any worthwhile information when they got back to the States. Maybe you could take another run at them and try to stir up some leads concerning his whereabouts."

*****

"Bobby, Samuel Garcia here. How is Manuel Alvera doing?"

"He's hanging on. The doctors don't know how he's lasted this long, as shot up as he was. I've kept an around-the-clock guard on him at the hospital. I'm sure those that tried to take him out are aware that he's still alive. I haven't been able to interview him yet because they're keeping him heavily sedated. When he is out of the woods, if he ever is, I want to question him to learn whether or not he recognized his attackers."

"I'll keep checking back with you, Bobby. Were you able to find out whether or not someone had

ALTON LYNN COOPER

come onto the island through the airport from LA prior to the attack?"

"Not from LA. There was a flight that came in from the Sacramento International Airport."

Samuel's radar sent strong signals up and down his spine. "Were you able to get the names of those on the passenger manifest?"

"We did. There were three families along with four single men on the flight. Two of the men hooked up with your people, sending supplies out to the missionaries on the islands. The other two men were here looking at some vacant buildings downtown that had been advertised stateside."

"Can you send me a list of the names that came in on that flight?"

"I'll send it to your cell. My deputy and I checked all of them out, and everything appeared to be on the up and up."

Samuel hung up the phone, knowing that a definite pattern was forming. His problem was that he had no indication of where it was leading. There were a number of different players moving around, but he needed to be able to connect them to a central source to hopefully open up the case.

*****

DEADLY ATTACK

Samuel parked the rental car in front of a small, well-maintained home on the outskirts of Los Angeles. He rang the doorbell and waited, hearing movement inside. An older lady slowly swung the door open, looking up into Samuel's face.

"Are you Mrs. Winters?"

"Yes."

"My name is Francis Bennett. I'm a newspaper reporter and would like to ask you some questions concerning your son, Jimmy, who I understand has come up missing."

"The police have already been here on multiple occasions. We couldn't help them. What makes you think we can share anything of value with you?"

"I may be able to write a story that would help locate him and bring him back home." Mrs. Winters turned, going back into her home, leaving the door open for Samuel to follow her in.

"Oliver, there's another man here asking about Jimmy."

"Have a seat, young man, and I will get us something to drink." Samuel sat down on the sofa, with the cushions sinking down toward the floor, causing his knees to almost come up even with his chest.

"You might want to crawl out of that thing and sit at the table. Been trying to convince Rose to throw

213

it out for years. She's attached to it, so it's still here."
Oliver Winters was a man in his late seventies and
walked bent over with a slight limp. His wife, Rose,
was also in her late years but stood erect and moved
around the kitchen with ease.

Oliver sat down at the table, staring at Samuel
with a sad look on his face. "What can we tell you
about our boy that might help bring him home?"

"Do you have any ideas why he may have left
his apartment without taking some of his possessions
with him?"

"None. He's never come up missing before and
certainly wouldn't leave the amount of cash behind
that they said was in his safe."

"They being the police?"

"Yes."

"Do you know how he may have come up with
ten thousand dollars in cash?"

"He was a gambler. I tried to warn him about
it, but he followed that road most of the time, losing
his own money. I don't know if he won it gambling
or what else he would have done to get that much
money. He lived mostly paycheck to paycheck as far
as I know. I would have to occasionally help him if
his car broke down or he got behind on his rent."

"Did anything unusual happen before his disappearance?"

"Not that I know of. His two buddies from work came by to see if he wanted to go fishing with them. Said he wasn't at his apartment and they were going out on a charter boat that afternoon leaving out of Newport Beach. Thought he might have been here visiting us. We were packing for a trip to Italy and left shortly after those guys stopped by the house."

Rose Winters sat three steaming cups of hot chocolate on the table beside a small bowl of miniature marshmallows. "Scoop yourself some in there, Mr. Bennett. Makes it sweeter when they melt and you suck them in."

"Oliver, I told you before that Jimmy didn't hang with those people at work. I don't know why they would show up trying to track him down to go fishing with them. Jimmy never liked eating fish, let alone catching them. He didn't like going out on the water either."

Samuel knew that he was close to another piece of information that hopefully would shed some light on his case. "What did these friends of his from work look like?"

Oliver swallowed his mouthful of melted marshmallows before speaking. "One of them was

ALTON LYNN COOPER

big enough to sink any fishing boat I've ever been in. Heavy-set fellow. The other was the exact opposite."

"What do you mean the exact opposite?"

"Little fellow. Next to the big guy, he almost looked like a kid. Small built. Had a nasty look about him, though. Scowled all the time he was here. When the big fellow mentioned going fishing from Newport Beach, the little man gave him a hateful look. I wouldn't want to be out in a boat with him for sure."

"Do you know if your son had any close friends at work that he might have confided in?"

Oliver's face appeared to start searching somewhere in the past, trying to bring up a lost memory. Rose went over to the stove to bring the pot of hot chocolate back to the table for a refill.

"Oliver, you remember that funny-looking guy that came by one time with Jimmy. Oh, for the life of me, I can't remember that fellow's name." Samuel could almost hear the wheels changing gears in Oliver's brain shortly before he blurted out, "Mickey Gosling. That's it, Mickey Gosling. Funny little old guy. That must be why he became Jimmy's friend. Our Jimmy had a way of attracting those kinds of people."

DEADLY ATTACK

"Oh, Oliver, don't say that. He had kids at school who came over to play, remember?"

"Yes, Rose, and I also remember that most of them were strange in the head. Remember the one that you caught trying to eat a nightcrawler out in the flower bed? Your Jimmy had told the boy it would solve his bad breath problems and clear up the acne covering his face. That kid didn't know any better, neither did that boy of ours."

Samuel excused himself from his visit with Jimmy's parents and headed for the armored car office. He wanted to track down this Mickey Gosling and see if he had any information concerning Jimmy's disappearance. He also made a note concerning the two men who came looking for Jimmy shortly before he came up missing. He wondered to himself if the big man could have been none other than the late Rollie Jenkins. If that was true, then the little man could be the one who left his footprints near the edge of the ravine when he sent Jenkins out of this life into the world beyond. He also made a note of the little man's reaction when Jenkins mentioned going fishing on a charter boat leaving from Newport Beach.

*****

"Leroy, is your little rat still here?"

The man behind the counter at the armored car office waited on the line, evidently for the person on the other end to check for the little rat's presence. "He's here. Why do you wanna know?"

The counter man turned back to Samuel, asking why he wanted to know if the little rat was still present at work.

"I'm doing a story on Jimmy Winters's disappearance, and I need to ask him some questions."

The counter man stared deep into Samuel's eyes as if he were trying to pick information out of his brain. "And just who would want to waste their time reading a story about that loser's disappearance?"

"Why do you call him a loser?"

"Because that's what he always did. Lost his paychecks to the gambling bunch, lost his would-be girlfriend to one of the route drivers, and then lost the respect of his uncle."

"How do you know he lost the respect of his uncle?"

"You doing a story on me or him?"

"Just trying to get inside Jimmy's head to hopefully understand where he's at."

"I pity anyone with the desire to understand Winters's mind. His uncle stopped in here one day,

DEADLY ATTACK

saying he wanted to reconnect with his nephew and let bygones be bygones."

"Did his uncle say what those bygones were?"

"No, and I don't care. I'm not behind this counter to counsel all the misfits that work here. Just to remind the nerds to remember to put gas in the trucks they service so the deliveries remain on schedule."

"What did his uncle look like?"

"How many questions you got in that brain of yours? He was a big guy. Didn't exactly look like the loving type. What else you wanna know?"

"Do you know who the big and little men were here at work that Jimmy hung out with?"

"He didn't hang out with anyone here except the little rat out back, and he's the only little one on our payroll that resembles a rat. You'll find him out back, hopefully doing what he gets paid to do."

Samuel made his way down a short hall leading into the large back room of the armored car depot. He heard the blast of a country song coming out of a radio somewhere, with the singer wailing forth a sorrowful set of lyrics because someone had stolen his best coon dog. "I'll never hunt another coon now my coon dog's long gone. Someone took my coon dog and now I'm left here all alone. I'll just sit in my

219

old porch chair and grieve away my time. Someone stole my coon dog and I'm so heartbroken I forgot to report the crime."

Samuel could hear a shrill voice singing along with the radio somewhere in the midst of a number of armored trucks waiting their turn to be washed. He went around the last truck and saw the little rat bent over, scrubbing the rear wheel on one of the trucks as he continued to wail the mournful words grieving the stolen dog.

"Are you Mickey Gosling?"

The small, heavyset man kept scrubbing away, not hearing the person that had entered his workspace.

"Are you Mickey Gosling?" Samuel raised his voice to hopefully drown out the radio man still missing his coon dog, but the little man kept on washing and wailing on his own. Samuel reached down and tapped the bent-over truck washer on the back, causing him to scream before spinning around and sitting down on the wet, sudsy floor near the truck.

"Are you Mickey Gosling?"

"What?" The little man's eyes were wide as saucers behind the thick glasses resting on his nose. Samuel left him in the suds and went to shut off the radio, allowing the singer to grieve his missing coon dog in private. He returned just as Mickey was pushing himself up, with the seat of his work pants sodden from his trip to the floor.

"Are you Mickey Gosling?"

The small man was a little over five feet tall, heavyset for his short frame, and completely bald-headed. He had a pinched look on his face with the thick glasses resting on his short pudgy nose, causing his eyes to appear extremely large, resulting in a rat-like appearance.

"Who are you? Does Joey know you're back here?"

"Who's Joey?"

"My boss out front."

"You mean the counter man?"

"Yeah, the counter man, Joey."

Mickey Gosling shared with Samuel Jimmy Winters's struggle with his gambling addiction. It had gotten so bad that not only was he losing his paycheck on a regular basis, but he was also getting deeper and deeper in debt to his gambling buddies. Mickey indicated that Jimmy had told him that the main man had let him run up a tab at the gambling house, trying to give him more opportunities to win his money back. Samuel asked Mickey if Jimmy ever mentioned the main man's name and was told that he hadn't said who the man was or why he would let Jimmy go deeper and deeper into debt.

He shared how a few weeks before the armored car robbery, two tough-looking men showed up at the depot looking for Jimmy. Jimmy was off that day, so they went searching for him. The next time he came to work, he had been beaten up pretty bad and refused to talk about what happened to him. After that, he stopped sharing any information with people at work, staying completely to himself. According to Mickey, he became more and more nervous and paranoid shortly before he came up missing.

Samuel returned to his hotel and added a few notes to the whiteboard concerning Jimmy's gambling addiction, his apparent beatdown for not paying his gambling debts, and his receiving ten thousand dollars in cash before he came up missing. He still couldn't figure out why the man would leave his apartment and not take the money with him if he was intending to disappear. It seemed the obvious conclusion was that he didn't leave on his own accord and was carried off against his will. Samuel inspected the red splotches on his skin and then lathered up his face with the medicated ointment before turning in for the night. He was hoping to keep his face stable enough to continue adorning it with spirit gum and

DEADLY ATTACK

phony hair each morning. He was becoming more homesick as the days went by and sent several prayers up to the Lord asking for His guidance in solving the case that had been thrust upon him.

*****

Samuel woke with a start at the sound of a weather warning coming from the clock radio next to his bed. "Yes siree, folks, it's coming in off the Pacific and could work itself up into quite a blow. Be careful out there today and keep your umbrella ready for deployment."

Samuel crawled out of bed to begin preparing for his day, just as his cell phone started buzzing on the bedside nightstand. He had changed the vibration to the buzzing sound and was still trying to figure out which one he hated the most.

"Is this Mr. Bennett?"

"Yes."

"This is Sally Greensboro from Macrone Pharmaceuticals." Samuel worked his early morning brain trying to remember who Sally Greensboro was.

"I'm sorry, I don't remember meeting you."

"I'm the receptionist. We met when you wanted to set up a meeting with Mr. Macrone, remember?"

ALTON LYNN COOPER

"Ah, yes. What can I do for you, Ms. Greensboro?"

"It's not what you can do for me but, on the contrary, what I can do for you, Mr. Bennett."

"And just what might that be, Ms. Greensboro?"

"As it turns out, Mr. Macrone's schedule has opened up somewhat, and he would like to meet with you concerning your interest in our company."

"You mean all those appointments for the next two months have all vanished away, Ms. Greensboro?" The momentary silence on the other end of the line let Samuel know he had scored a direct hit on the Macrone receptionist.

"Are you interested in meeting with Mr. Macrone or not?"

"Why, of course, Ms. Greensboro. When is his next available opening?"

"Today at 9:00 a.m. sharp."

"Sharp as in I should interrupt my busy schedule at the last minute to make time for Mr. Macrone at such an early hour in my busy day?"

The dial tone on the other end of the line let Samuel know that his conversation with the Macrone Pharmaceutical receptionist had ended. He thought once again that he really should make time to attend some personal relationship group sessions back in

224

Amarillo. After all, a man in his position as a high-level private investigator should learn how to get the most out of those coming across his path. Having a good bedside manner wasn't only necessary for an elite doctor but also for an elite private eye.

Samuel was preparing to go to the hotel restaurant for a quick breakfast when his phone buzzed again, popping up Gregory Lawrence's number on the screen.

"Sorry, Samuel. I can't meet with you this morning, although I dearly love eating breakfast on your dime. I've got some interesting new leads on the gang war and its possible connection to the armored car robbery. I want to run down as many as possible, then we can hook up. Were you able to get any information on Jimmy Winters's whereabouts?"

"I met with his parents. It seems that a big man accompanied by a small man showed up at their house trying to find Jimmy just before he came up missing. They claimed to be buddies of his at work, but no one there remembers him hanging with anyone like that. The little man working for the armored car company that befriended Jimmy is a truck washer and doesn't fit the description given to me by Jimmy's father as one of the men that stopped at their home, looking for Jimmy. I have a strong feeling about who

ALTON LYNN COOPER

those two men were, but I'll wait for our get-together to discuss that with you. Do you know anything about fishing charters going out of Newport Beach?"

"Why do you ask?"

"Just curious for now."

Lawrence was quiet for a moment. "It's interesting you ask that. Let's plan dinner tonight and I'll fill you in."

"Sounds good. Oh, by the way, I have a meeting this morning at 9:00 a.m. with William Macrone II. I'm hoping that may give some insight into the state of affairs inside the company. One of their vice presidents clammed up when I asked him to clarify where the money came from a few years ago that helped Macrone avoid bankruptcy."

"Okay. Stay safe. I'll call you this evening."

*****

Samuel's reception at Macrone Pharmaceutical was one to remember. When Ms. Greensboro saw him entering the lobby, she immediately left her receptionist desk and came toward him. "This way, Mr. Bennett." She led him down the hallway and stopped, giving a soft knock on the door of William Macrone II's office door. "You wait here." The recep-

DEADLY ATTACK

tionist opened the door and disappeared inside, shutting it behind her, leaving Samuel in the hallway.

Samuel looked up and down the long hallway, not seeing any other action going on, and was just about to knock on the president's door when it opened with Sally Greensboro motioning for him to enter. "Mr. Macrone will see you now."

Samuel entered the room and was struck once again with the grandeur of the furnishings surrounding him. The air exuded the rich smell of leather and wood polish, letting him know that the janitorial staff was alive and well. William Macrone II sat behind an ornate carved wooden desk that could just as easily fit in at the White House in the Oval Office. He was a solid-built man in his late forties with a head full of wavy black hair, matched by a large mustache that was perfectly trimmed. He had dark, brooding eyes that locked onto Samuel's face as he entered the room.

"Have a seat, Mr. Bennett, and we'll get started. I'm sure both our schedules don't permit small talk, so let's get to the point quickly. Why are you interested in my company?"

Before Samuel could answer Macrone's question, the door opened behind his seat in front of the president's desk, ushering in someone else. Samuel didn't turn to see who it was initially, instead keeping his eyes fixed on Macrone's face. He saw a visible change spread across it that indicated whoever had entered his presence had not been welcomed in by him. Samuel turned, looking into the face that Jimmy's father had described to him during their visit. The man was short and delicately built, but his face showed forth a permanent scowl that no doubt had resided there for years.

"Mr. Bennett, it appears that Mr. Caston will join us in our meeting."

Caston made his way over to the large conference table and pulled out a chair, turning it toward Samuel. He made no effort to either introduce himself or speak to Samuel, as courtesy required, so Samuel decided to jump right in and see just how sinister the little man was.

"Mr. Macrone, why would I want to allow another individual such as Mr. Caston to intrude on our personal meeting?" Samuel saw the ashen look immediately spread across Macrone's face.

Caston spoke up with the sound of hatred filling his voice. "I am not required to be invited in. I decide when and where to interject myself at will."

Samuel didn't give the small man the pleasure of looking in his direction but kept his eyes on Macrone's face.

DEADLY ATTACK

"Tell me, Mr. Macrone, what position does this man hold in your firm? I thought you were the main person running this company. If I'm going to do an exposé on your company, and I did say if, I want the information coming straight from the top and not from one of the hired staff." Samuel knew that he had just put a target on himself from the scowling little man at the table. He felt the old familiar tingles running up and down his spine, assuring him that at last he was getting the opening in the investigation that he needed.

Macrone quickly spoke, trying to relieve the tension in the room and draw Samuel's attention back to the subject at hand. "I ask you again, Mr. Bennett, why do you want to do a story on Macrone Pharmaceuticals?"

"I am always interested in a company such as yours that almost collapsed into bankruptcy but then was miraculously able to right the ship and become successful again. That must have taken a small fortune to stave off the creditors and then once again regain the trust of future investors. I understand that you were fortunate enough to have gone to business school, making some high-level friends that were able to advance you the necessary funds to keep your company afloat. Is that correct?"

ALTON LYNN COOPER

Macrone's facial expression was one that Samuel had not seen often from a man in his position. It appeared that he was deathly afraid of the little man sitting at the table and completely unable to come up with an answer to Samuel's question. The tension in the room was palpable.

"Of course, if the money came from another source, that would add much interest to the story as well. I would like to include your financier's information in the exposé and interview them as well."

William Macrone finally regained his ability to speak, letting Samuel know that he wasn't interested in his vision of writing the success story for Macrone Pharmaceuticals.

"I prefer to keep our company strictly focused on the development of world-leading pharmaceuticals and avoid the limelight concerning our rate of success. The quality of our products is all the exposure we need to remain one of the top companies in our field."

Samuel was measured in his response. "I respect your viewpoint, Mr. Macrone, but I'm sure that I could still gather information concerning your company's background, allowing me to write a positive piece concerning your success story. Thank you for your time. I have other appointments as I'm sure you do as well." Samuel rose to leave and then stopped, asking the little man at the table a question. "I noticed your shoes. I admire a person with small enough feet to wear those very attractive business loafers. I'm afraid my feet send me into other types of footwear. I'm guessing you're a size six and a half to seven, is that correct?"

The question went unanswered as Caston fired his own question back at Samuel. "Do you know a man named Gregory Lawrence?"

"Why do you ask?"

"Yes or no, Mr. Bennett?"

"Again, I repeat myself, why is that any of your business?"

"Mr. Macrone's business and mine is the same. We want to know who we are getting involved with, and you apparently want to press forward with your ill-advised story with or without our approval."

"I wasn't aware you were part of the decision-making process for Mr. Macrone. However, if you must know, yes, I know Mr. Lawrence. He is with the FBI. I find getting to know people in his line of work gives me more exciting writing opportunities as time goes on. Good day, gentlemen." Samuel turned and showed himself out, closing the door behind him. He knew without a doubt that he had just found a major link in his investigation tracking down those responsible for the attack on the bunkhouse. He just needed to figure out what triggered the attack, what Caston and Macrone's involvement was, and who the other players were. The thought of one of America's leading pharmaceutical companies possibly being involved in the illegal drug business was hard to fathom.

*****

Samuel decided to throw caution to the wind and meet with Gregory Lawrence at one of Los Angeles's best Mexican restaurants. He needed his dose of three tacos dripping in mild sauce to help focus his mind on the various pieces of information he had gleaned so far. He knew without a doubt that Macrone Pharmaceuticals was somehow involved not only in producing legitimate drugs but could very well be linked to the illegal side of the business as well. It didn't seem possible that a company of their stature could possibly be tied up in illegal activities, but his gut told him something at the company wasn't what it appeared to be.

Samuel seated himself at a table in the back of the Los Señorita restaurant and waited for Gregory

DEADLY ATTACK

to show up. He noticed a heavyset man across the room talking on a cell phone, staring in his direction. He wasn't paranoid, but he knew he had stepped on Caston's toes hard and would need to be cautious going forward during his time in Los Angeles. He glanced at the man off and on and caught him looking his way a number of times. Gregory Lawrence entered the restaurant and made his way to Samuel's table.

"Hey, buddy, how was your day?"

"Interesting. How was yours?"

"Same. Let's get our orders in and then we can catch up. What's good in these places?"

Samuel stared at his friend before answering, "Are you a daring individual or do you prefer to stay on the safe side, keeping your stomach intact?"

"I'm up for something that will challenge my palate without destroying it."

"I understand."

Their waitress finished with the people at another table and headed in their direction. "Hello and welcome to Los Señorita. Are you ready to order?"

Gregory ordered first, asking what was safe but still something that would challenge his taste buds. "Just how daring are your taste buds, señor?"

ALTON LYNN COOPER

"I've had them for a long time and want to give them something to think about without causing them to leave home."

"I recommend the special. Our very own Crazy Gringo's Delight enchiladas. They will satisfy the daring side of you and leave the rest intact for your return visit."

"Let's go for it along with your very best unsweetened iced tea."

"And for you, señor?"

Samuel noticed a curious look come over the waitress's face as he felt his mustache start to slide off his lip on the right side. He quickly shoved it back in place, pressing it into his sore lip, trying to avoid letting out a low-pitched scream. "Make mine the same."

Gregory sent a smile in Samuel's direction. "You using enough of that spirit gum or is that thing starting to take on a life of its own?"

The men shared their day's activities with Samuel describing his meeting at Macrone's.

"I'm sure that the little man in Macrone's office could have been involved in Rollie Jenkins's death. His shoe size is small, possibly matching those at the edge of the ravine, and his features were sinister, matching the description Jimmy Winters's father gave me concerning the man who came looking for their son. He certainly had some sway over Macrone to the point I think he feared the little man."

"Was his last name Caston?"

"Yes. How did you know?"

"The DEA has an informant inside one of the drug cartels here in town. I found out that the supposed gang war that occurred shortly before the armored car robbery was actually a conflict between two of the leading dealers controlling the drug business here and in other parts of the country. It seems that one group got wind of a major shipment involving the other group and ripped it off, starting the war. The strange thing that I don't understand is that the armored car robbery was a payback from the group that got ripped off. If that is true, then why would they steal a load of legal pharmaceuticals belonging to Macrone as payback for a shipment of illegal drugs being taken? The informant heard of a man named Benjamin Caston who supposedly was instrumental in directing the attack on the armored car. He had no proof of that, only that the name popped up in one of his conversations with another drug runner here in LA. He said the man is known on the street as Benny Caston and has the reputation of being a vicious individual controlling a large part of the illegal drugs coming into the state. Their problem is Caston has managed to stay above the fray, so there's no evidence linking him to any illegal activities."

"Gregory, was the informant sure that it was Caston who directed the attack on the armored car?"

"No. It could have been one of the members from one of the other cartels operating here in LA. These drug wars are a mess. It's hard to figure out which gang started the war and the reason behind it."

Samuel thought for a few moments about Gregory's comments before continuing. "What would a man like that be doing in Macrone's office, concerned about me doing a story on the company?"

"Samuel, I believe there is a connection between the illegal drugs being distributed here in LA and throughout the states and the Macrone Pharmaceutical Company. We need a strategy between the two of us to tie these pieces together going forward."

Samuel pulled the notepad from his pocket just as the waitress came back to refill their drinks. "How was the special? Do we have room for dessert?"

"What kind of desserts are we talking about?" Samuel asked, thinking of a giant bowl of strawberry ice cream.

DEADLY ATTACK

"Our chef has prepared a delicious sweet jalapeño pepper pie guaranteed to send you home satisfied."

Samuel stared at the waitress in disbelief. "You're telling me there's such a thing as sweet jalapeño peppers that found their way into this pie of yours?" Before Samuel could make up his mind whether or not to risk his stomach any further that evening, Gregory spoke up, telling the young lady to bring them two pieces of this amazing dessert.

"Look, I survived that special with only a little burn left over. I don't know about this pepper pie idea."

"You've got to live a little, my friend. The sweet juices from the peppers may just help soothe that burning skin under the hair on your face."

Samuel noticed the man across the room who had been staring in his direction preparing to leave. "Gregory, do you know that guy over there?" Lawrence turned, watching the man making his way out of the restaurant.

"That's interesting. I don't know his name, but I saw him talking to Lemuel Rollins at a gas station in Sacramento when I stopped to gas up my car. They were in a very animated conversation before that guy

ALTON LYNN COOPER

turned, getting into his car, and exiting the station in a huff."

"So Rollins was in Amarillo with a little man scoping out my office, and now a big man is here in LA, keeping an eye on me, and who also happened to have been seen by you arguing with Rollins at a gas station in Sacramento. Interesting. Interesting indeed. Is that guy also with the DEA?"

"When I saw Rollins at his office later on, I asked him about the incident at the gas station, and he said it was a personal matter and didn't say any more about it."

"Okay, Gregory. Let's put our heads together and make us a to-do list. If we coordinate our efforts, hopefully, we can uncover the key elements of both our cases and catch a nice bunch of rats along the way."

*****

Samuel sat in his hotel room at the small desk, reviewing the items that he and Lawrence had come up with for the days ahead. Samuel's items on the list involved finding and questioning William Macrone's friends from his college days about the money they loaned him to keep his company afloat. He also

DEADLY ATTACK

needed to visit some of the more elite men's clothing stores in Los Angeles and ask some leading questions concerning shoes. Gregory's items included hooking up with the DEA agents observing the pharmaceutical deliveries to the many pharmacies in town to verify their legitimacy.

Next, he wanted to investigate the fishing charters working out of Newport Beach. When Samuel had asked him about Newport earlier, it surprised him because there were a number of DEA agents assigned in that area watching out for illegal drugs possibly coming in either overland from Tijuana, Mexico, or on the fishing boats. There were also sightseeing sailboats operating in the Gulf of Catalina that may be involved as well. Gregory indicated that he would be out of town checking on those leads for the next three days and then meet with Samuel to compare notes after returning to Los Angeles.

CHAPTER 11

Shocking Revelations

Samuel watched as the secretary searched through files on her computer, pausing occasionally to answer the phone and route calls to various departments. He had gone to the UCLA Lakewood School of Business to inquire about William Macrone II's years as a student there.

"Does Mr. Macrone know that you are doing an exposé on his business?" she asked.

"Yes. I was in a meeting with him yesterday. I want to make sure that only the facts make their way into the final writing of his company's amazing track record." Samuel gave the young woman one of his most gracious smiles as she continued her work on the computer.

"Here we have it. He graduated slightly above the middle of his class. What was the other information you wanted?"

"The names of some of his classmates. Preferably those that he may have been close to, if you have that information. I'd like to track them down and include their recollections on the young Mr. Macrone."

"Take a seat in the lobby. This is going to take some time."

Samuel found a comfortable leather chair in the corner of the lobby and pulled out his cell phone, placing a call to Bobby Lambers on Kalmajo Island. The police chief's secretary answered, putting Samuel on hold. A pleasant rendition of island music played softly in his ear as he waited for the chief to come on the line. The music and the soft leather cushion holding him in its grip caused his eyelids to begin slowly shutting and sliding open again.

"Chief Lambers here. How may I help you?" Samuel jerked himself alert, asking the chief how Manuel Alvera was doing.

"He has improved somewhat. He's still in and out of it. I tried to question him two days ago, but his mind is still foggy concerning the shooting. He mumbled something that sounded like 'badge' to me, but it could have been another word. His voice was pretty slurred from all the pain medication they've got him on."

"So you're not sure if it was 'badge' or not?"

ALTON LYNN COOPER

"No, I can't say for sure. I plan on giving him a few more days and then try again."

"Okay, Chief, I'll stay in touch."

"Samuel, how is your investigation going there in LA? Got any good leads yet?"

Samuel filled the chief in on the latest and had just hung up when the secretary motioned him back to her desk across the lobby.

"Hope this helps. It was the graduates' parting shots at their buddies here during their graduation party. Some of the comments are quite funny, others not so much." Samuel took the yearbook from her hand, seeing three young men's notes under their pictures making verbal jabs at "Willy Macaroni, our aspiring business nerd." One of their comments stated, "To our ole' college pal who is destined to go far. That's away, of course." It showed them in a group with their arms draped around one another with Macrone in the middle. All were smiling, leading Samuel to believe these could be his college buddies that sprang into action, bailing out his fledgling pharmaceutical company.

"Can I get the names and addresses of these three men?"

The secretary took the yearbook out of Samuel's hand and directed him back to his chair in the lobby. After enjoying three cups of the college's day-old

242

DEADLY ATTACK

lukewarm coffee, the secretary motioned him to her desk once again and handed him the requested information. Samuel reviewed the list, seeing that two of Macrone's friends resided in the city while the third one was located in the country a few miles south of Los Angeles. He decided to head for the country first and then work his way back into town.

*****

"What did you say your business is with Mr. Whitley?"

"I am a freelance writer, and I'm doing an exposé on the Macrone Pharmaceutical Company. Mr. Whitley was a friend of the young Mr. Macrone in college. I'm interested in his insight into the company's success."

The housekeeper told Samuel to wait there on the small stoop and shut the door behind her as she went to relay his message to the head of the house.

Samuel had surveyed the place as he drove down the stone driveway leading to the rather modest house. He thought that this was evidently one of William Macrone's buddies who hadn't made it to the big time yet. The house was small and well-kept but not one reflecting a person of wealth. The door swung open with the housekeeper motioning Samuel to enter.

243

ALTON LYNN COOPER

"Please have a seat in the living room, and Mr. Whitley will be with you soon." Samuel could hear a man's voice coming from the room across the hall as he was finishing a phone call discussing stock options, deciding whether to hold or sell.

A short, muscular man entered the living room, coming over to Samuel with his right hand extended. "George Whitley here. What was your name again?"

"Francis Bennett."

"Ah, yes. My housekeeper tells me you're doing a story on Willie, is that right?"

"Willie?"

"That's what we called William in school. I understand you want information on his company?"

"I'm interested in the difficult years when he almost went bankrupt. I understand that you and two of his other friends were able to provide some critical financial assistance to help him save the company, is that right?"

George Whitley gave Samuel a concerned look. "Why do you ask?"

"I think it reveals an interesting part of the company's history, showing the grit and determination of Mr. Macrone to keep the company afloat through hard times."

DEADLY ATTACK

"Mr. Bennett, can I trust you to be discreet with the information I give you? I don't want Willie to be hurt in any way with what I may tell you."

"Yes. I am interested in writing a constructive story on the company, realizing it is one of the leading pharmaceutical companies in America."

"Willie was a risk-taker. He got into trouble for always going it on his own. When he took over the business after his father died suddenly, he didn't listen to the knowledgeable experts inside the company concerning the long process of drug development and the cost involved. By the time he called me and his other buddies from our college days, he was in way over his head. We didn't want to see him go under, but there was no way any of us had the necessary funds to pull him out. We are still working today developing our own businesses."

"So, Mr. Whitley, you're telling me that William got financial help from another source to save the company?"

"He must have. He's still in business."

"Do you know who may have been able to provide him the funding?"

"No. Sorry, I can't help you there."

*****

ALTON LYNN COOPER

Samuel drove back to Los Angeles in search of William Macrone's other two friends, realizing that they probably would confirm what George Whitley had already told him. The question now was, where did the vast amount of money come from that saved Macrone from bankruptcy? He knew at that moment the answer to that question was a significant part of his investigation. Macrone's two other friends from college did indeed confirm Whitley's information. Samuel found one of them at his office, where he was operating a financial investment firm catering to private investors, and the other friend at his home, preparing to leave on a business trip to London. They all lent William Macrone their deep concern for his troubles but did not have the financial capacity at the time to help him out. Samuel decided to stop at Macrone's office before heading back to his hotel. He still needed to find out what a specific individual did for their company.

"Is Mr. Macrone in?" Sally Greensboro looked up at Samuel from behind her receptionist desk, where she was busy filling in dates on a desk calendar.

"Do you have an appointment with him, Mr.—aaaaah, what was your name?"

"Francis Bennett, Ms. Greensboro. And remember, when I write the story of Mr. Macrone's company, it will include excerpts concerning his staff and their professionalism."

The receptionist gave Samuel an icy stare and told him to be seated in the lobby. A few minutes later, Samuel was escorted down the hall to an empty conference room and told to wait there. After enjoying the silence of the room for almost forty-five minutes, the door swung open, and the short, sinister little man who had been in William Macrone's office during Samuel's first visit entered the room. Benjamin Caston gave Samuel a hateful look that could very easily kill if it was a loaded gun ready to go off.

"What is it now, Mr. Bennett? I believe that is your name or do you prefer to go by another name?"

"Am I to assume that you are involved enough in the company's business to answer questions concerning past employees?"

"I'm involved enough to tell you what I may and also what I may not if it isn't any of your business."

"What did Rollie Jenkins do for Macrone Pharmaceuticals? I know that he worked here for a short period and then either quit or was let go."

Caston gave Samuel a look that let him know he had scored a direct hit. "How do you know about someone who worked here before? What has that got to do with this so-called story of yours?"

"I became curious when I saw his sad demise in the ravine on the news. You can understand my surprise when I later learned that he worked for Mr. Macrone's company."

"And just how did you learn that he worked for this company?"

"As an investigative reporter, I am always interested in someone's suspicious death. Mr. Jenkins was obviously murdered, being shot in the back. I'm sure that you can understand how that might interest law enforcement and a person in my profession."

"And just what profession are you in, Mr. Bennett? Are you a journalist or are you part of law enforcement? I have no information on this individual. What did you say his name was?"

"Rollie Jenkins, Mr. Caston. Rollie Jenkins!"

Caston turned, leaving the room, letting Samuel know that he could show himself out. Samuel stopped by the receptionist's desk and picked up one of the company's business cards. Something about the name of the company kept trying to send a message to his brain. He wanted to put the card on his whiteboard, hoping that if he looked at it long enough, the message would break through.

*****

DEADLY ATTACK

Samuel was having a small supper in the hotel restaurant and was just finishing up when his cell phone buzzed.

"How are things back in LA?"

"Not much different than when you were here in town, Gregory. How's your trip to the seaports?"

"That's the reason I'm calling you. There are some DEA agents who have been watching the charter boats and sailboats for some time. They got onto some other information that indicated there were potentially some overland routes that may be bringing drugs in from Tijuana, Mexico. It seems that when they get a tip to watch the boats, the drugs get in through the overland routes. When they watch the overland routes, because of a specific tip, the drugs evidently come in on the boats. That's the assumption anyway. The thing that is concerning the higher-ups in the DEA's office is that it seems the drug traffickers are being tipped off as to what places are being watched."

Samuel considered Gregory's comments before responding, "What office do the agents work out of that have been monitoring those activities there?"

"The Sacramento office. Why?"

Samuel felt a chill spread up his spine. He knew at that moment that some very important pieces of their investigation were coming together.

ALTON LYNN COOPER

"When will you be back in LA?"

"I plan on heading back the day after tomorrow. I'm going on a little driving trip to scope out a place in the Cleveland National Forest. I want to get some information on their campgrounds."

"Are you planning some downtime? I didn't know you were a camper."

"I'll fill you in later. I'm interested in what you've found out concerning Macrone Labs. I'll run some things by you when I get back into town."

*****

Samuel sat in his hotel room staring at the whiteboard and the information on it. He read his previous notes over and over, trying to establish some connections between them. He kept going back and forth between the picture of the letters in blood on the stone in the ravine and the business card that he had picked up from the receptionist's desk.

"Ah, yes. Good job, Rollie. Good job indeed." There was a definite pattern forming now in Samuel's mind that should lead him to those responsible for the attack on his bunkhouse. He just needed to understand certain connections and figure out how and why those connections came together. He headed for

DEADLY ATTACK

the bathroom to doctor the skin on his face that by now was becoming one of his major concerns. He was contemplating whether or not to abandon his disguise and expose himself to those in Los Angeles, letting them know that he was in town and very much on their trail. He decided that it might be a little premature to put himself out there since he still didn't know all the key players involved in the drug ring or rings in Los Angeles.

*****

Samuel woke up early, hearing the thunder crashing over the hotel, sending its bolts of lightning splitting the sky overhead. He began his daily activity of painfully smearing on enough spirit gum to hopefully keep the hair in place on his burning skin. He knew that he was quickly coming to a time when his face wouldn't survive many more applications of the stuff he had come to hate. He hoped that the weather would calm down enough outside to allow him to visit some of the men's stores downtown. He pulled open the nightstand drawer next to his bed, taking out the Gideon's Bible to spend some time in God's Word before beginning his day. A sense of foreboding spread through him as he felt sure he was nearing the head of the snake that had sent out its deadly venom against him back at the ranch. He had no doubt that the drug business on the island and now here in Los Angeles was definitely connected, and his involvement on the island had created a deep hatred in someone close by.

Samuel opened the book and began reading one of his favorite portions of scripture. *"And the work of righteousness shall be peace; and the effect of righteousness quietness and assurance forever. And my people shall dwell in a peaceable habitation, and in sure dwellings, and in quiet resting places" (Isaiah 32:17–18).* He closed the Bible and bowed his head in prayer, asking God to protect him in the days ahead. He truly believed he was doing a work of righteousness tracking down and bringing to justice those spreading death and destruction against others. They had tried to kill him, but he knew the drugs they were selling were destroying many lives, tearing apart homes and families across the land. He longed for the peace that God promised in His Word, but those times wouldn't come into his life until he finished the task at hand.

*****

DEADLY ATTACK

The attendant in the men's store smiled as he came in Samuel's direction.

"How may I assist you today?"

"I'm interested in a particular type of shoe." Samuel did his best to describe the shoes that he had seen on Benjamin Caston's feet. They had appeared to be a set of Florsheim shoes that Samuel had observed on the feet of Larson Maxwell during his investigation on the cattle rustling case. He had admired Maxwell's footwear at the time and remembered them when he saw the ones on Caston's feet in Macrone's office.

"Ah yes, an excellent choice in a gentleman's footwear, yes."

"I believe those are the same ones that Benjamin Caston wears, is that correct?"

"Benjamin Caston, sir?"

"Yes, Benjamin Caston. Isn't this the store where he purchases his attire?"

"I'm not familiar with a Mr. Caston. What does he have to do with you buying yourself a new pair of shoes?"

"I have admired his in the past and was hoping to buy the same brand and style as he wears."

"Have you asked him where he shops?"

"No. I don't want him to know how much I admire his choice in shoes." Samuel bade the confused salesman good day and headed to the next elite men's store in downtown Los Angeles. He was visiting his fourth store when the salesman there beamed and said, "Yes, Mr. Caston. A very discerning customer. He does have excellent taste in menswear."

Samuel did his best to sound discreet, asking his next question. "I've not been blessed with feet his size, I'm afraid. I think that style of shoe looks better on someone with size seven than on my ten and a half."

The salesman gave Samuel an odd look before responding, "I've never heard that comment in all my years of selling shoes. But I do understand your point. Mr. Caston's size six and a half are small for a man's foot, I'm sure."

"Well, let me think about what I might do before rushing into any hasty decisions today." Samuel turned, leaving the salesman staring in his direction as he made his way out of the store.

Samuel noticed the heavyset man that had been in the Los Señorita restaurant sitting in a black sedan across the street when he exited the men's store. He waited for the traffic to clear and started to cross the street toward the car when it started up and pulled out into the stream of traffic. A vehicle stopped in front of the big man's car, waiting for another car to pull away from the curb, allowing Samuel to get the tag plate number of the dark sedan. He pulled out his notepad, jotting down the number, and made two quick notes before heading to his rental car parked down the block. Gregory Lawrence would be back in town in the morning, and the two of them had a lot of catching up to do.

*****

"I have my suspicions about Francis Bennett. I'm not convinced that he's this world-traveled reporter that he pretends to be. I've checked with all my sources, and no one has ever heard of him in the literary world."

"Who do you think he is?"

"I'm not sure, but he's working closely with Gregory Lawrence. Do you want me to take him out?"

"Not yet. I need to know what he is after and why. See if you can find out where he came to LA from. With your contacts, you should be able to get access to the passenger lists from the airport. If we know where he came from, that might shed some light on why he's here asking all these questions."

"I'll check with my favorite tailor and see what he was doing at the men's shop where I do my business. If he needs to be quickly disposed of, be ready."

"You may need to make a room service call on him at his hotel. There's no need for the boss to be aware of this for now. With his paranoia, he may decide that you and I are becoming liabilities, and that wouldn't bode well for either of us."

*****

Samuel stopped at a local delicatessen and picked up six boiled eggs, a bag of potato chips, a ring of bologna, and a two-liter of diet Pepsi. He planned on dining in his hotel room while writing down what he believed were the major pieces of the case thus far. He wanted to be prepared for his breakfast meeting with Lawrence, running his thoughts by him. He could sense the picture coming together but still didn't know exactly who the head man or men were. He felt that William Macrone II was being used more than being a major player in the drug business going on around him. He was fairly certain that Macrone Pharmaceuticals was being used in the movement of illegal drugs as well as their prescription medications. He fully believed that Benjamin Caston was a key

DEADLY ATTACK

player in not only the illegal drug business but in the murder of Rollie Jenkins. He had reviewed the picture of the two men that Joe Halstead sent him, who were seen in Amarillo checking out his office, and was persuaded that the little man in the picture was Caston. That would mean that the DEA agent working out of the Sacramento office, Lemuel Rollins, was somehow involved with Caston. Samuel wasn't sure if Rollins was acting undercover gathering incriminating information on Caston or if he was, in fact, a dirty agent dealing in the drug business himself.

Samuel sat at the small desk in his hotel room with a paper plate piled high with sliced ring bologna, potato chips, and two boiled eggs. He was washing all of that down with his diet Pepsi. He could kick himself for not picking up a bag of chocolate chip cookies. If his dear mother could see him now, she would wring his ears for eating what was before him. He tried to avoid the fast-food restaurants except for an occasional cheeseburger, but he dearly loved his boiled eggs and ring bologna. He completed his list of items to cover with Gregory Lawrence just as his cell phone buzzed.

Samuel answered, hearing Bobby Lambers's voice on the other end. "How are things going on the island?"

ALTON LYNN COOPER

"Quiet for the most part. I was able to get the names of a few passengers new to the island who came in on the last flight before Manuel Alvera was gunned down. I've checked them out and found them to be legit except for a couple of them. The ones that checked out had business here on the island and were on the up and up. The two that appeared to be mysterious were a man named Jack Quinlyn and Horace Donaldson. They were the two that supposedly came here to check out vacant property downtown. They sat next to each other on the plane, and I couldn't find any connection here on the island of them making contact with anyone involving property up for sale. They flew off the island two days after Alvera was shot. They probably would have left the very next day, but that flight got delayed due to a mechanical issue with the plane. They stayed at a small motel near the airport and paid cash."

"How is Manuel doing?"

"By the grace of God, he is slowly improving. He is still sedated for the most part, but his doctor said he expects a full recovery, barring any unforeseen circumstances."

"Bobby, are you keeping a guard at the hospital?"

"Yes. I've had to pull him off a couple of times because of some of my guys being out sick, but other than that, I've kept an eye out for him."

DEADLY ATTACK

"There's a lot going on here in LA involving the illegal drug business. I can't go into everything right now, but Gregory Lawrence and I are meeting in the morning, and I think between the two of us, we are getting close to the head of the snake. Please keep an eye on Alvera. I believe they will try again to kill him if they find out he's improving."

Samuel hung up the phone and wrote the two names that Bobby Lambers had given him in his notepad. He didn't recognize either one of them but would see what Gregory could come up with on them along with the tag plate number he got off the big man's car that had been tailing him. He felt strongly that Lemuel Rollins's association with Benjamin Caston and his previous argument with the big man at the gas station in Sacramento were key pieces of the puzzle coming together. He pulled out his notepad and jotted down another question for his meeting with Lawrence.

*****

Samuel took his shower, letting the hot water run over his sore face with his eyes closed. He was getting close to throwing off his disguise and becoming Samuel Garcia, Private Eye, once again. He would bounce it

259

ALTON LYNN COOPER

off Lawrence, but he thought that might just be the next step to pull his attackers to him. If they knew that he was there in Los Angeles, that should spook them enough to come after him. He propped himself up in bed and pulled out his cell phone, calling home.

"It's about time you came back from the dead and called your mother. You and this so-called snooping of yours are going to send me to meet your dear papa in heaven sooner than the good Lord plans if you keep this up."

"Why would you leave us and go to be with Papa before your time? I'm doing fine here, getting close to the bottom of who blew up Papa's bunkhouse, and then by God's good grace, I'll be back home with you and Ms. Valentina's cooking."

"Don't you answer this question wrong or when you show your face at this ranch again, I will wring those ears off that head of yours! Which do you miss the most, your dear mother or Ms. Valentina's cooking?"

"Is it possible to answer both without losing my ears? I mean, after all, they have been attached to me since my precious mother gave birth to me, no?"

"You're a scoundrel, Samuel Garcia. But I love you anyway. Hurry home and stop putting gray hairs in this old head of mine."

DEADLY ATTACK

"I love you too, Mama. Tell my brothers hello for me and give Ms. Valentina a good hug for me."

"Do you want me to hug your brothers for you also or just say hello to them? If they know you sent the hug to Valentina and not to them, they may be hurt, don't you think?"

"I'll leave that to you, Mother. Normally, we give each other a good pop on the shoulder, then enter into a foot race when I'm there. That is, of course, when you're not watching." Samuel heard his mother's familiar snort on the other end of the line before she bade him good night, ending their conversation.

*****

The clock radio went off, blasting out an old tune from the past, almost blowing Samuel out of bed. He had apparently turned the volume up louder than he planned the night before. Ever since he overslept that one time and had to rush to meet Gregory for breakfast, he wanted to be sure to always be up and ready to go on time. The song was squealing out the sad story of some hobo taking the wrong train north when he intended to go south back home to his wife and dog that he had left behind. He flicked off the radio and sat up on the edge of the bed, scratching his scalp through his thick mane of rich black hair. He hated the wig that was beginning to flatten out his natural locks, causing it to have that permanent smashed down appearance. He padded over to the TV, turning it on to the morning news and headed to the bathroom to prepare for his day.

When he came back into the room, the newsman was giving praise to one of California's most prominent senators, Gerald McPherson, who had brought forty-five million dollars back to the state to expand the pharmaceutical industry for the purpose of lowering drug costs for the consumers. The senator took to the microphone and began to bloviate on all that he was doing for the great state of California. The newsman asked him if there was any truth to the rumor he might be considering a run for the White House in the next presidential campaign. The senator guffawed and tried to look humbled by the question and stated his heart was to keep on doing what he was doing for the great people of the state of California. Samuel was amused when the story was over and the senator angrily snatched the lapel microphone from his suit jacket, thinking the cameras were turned off. He was overheard on the hot microphone telling the newsman to stop talking about his support for the pharmaceutical companies

DEADLY ATTACK

in the state. His facial expression completely changed from his on-air smile to a vicious snarl as he disappeared off the screen.

McPherson was a square-jawed, burly man who came across as someone used to always getting his way. Samuel wondered to himself if all politicians had hidden aspirations and two different personalities or if it was only a select few that hid that from their admiring voters. It was somewhat puzzling as to why the senator thought the pharmaceutical industry needed his help bringing in additional finances from the federal government. They seemed to be doing well enough on their own, at least as far as Macrone Pharmaceuticals was concerned.

*****

"Looks like you enjoyed some sun while you were checking out the boats." Samuel noticed that Gregory Lawrence had returned from his time at Newport Beach sporting a deep tan on his face.

"I actually took a sightseeing trip on one of the sailboats. That gave me an opportunity to talk with a couple of the workers on the boat and give it a good looking over. The small bathroom was in the lower level, giving me an opportunity to check out things down below. There were some medium-sized rectangular boxes tucked away under the stairs. I was preparing to see if I could lift one of their lids when a worker started down the stairs. I scooted away from the boxes and stepped aside, letting him pass by me on his way to the small galley kitchen.

"I was able to make contact with Jeremy Simmons from the Sacramento DEA's office at Imperial Beach. He indicated that they were going to assign more agents to the area, hoping to cover the waterfront areas as well as the overland routes coming in from Tijuana. He's frustrated, feeling like they're being set up, watching certain hot spots only to have the drug mules bring in their loads from another direction. How have things been back here in LA?"

"I need to bounce a number of things off you and also ask for your help on a couple of items. I am convinced that Benjamin Caston at Macrone Pharmaceuticals is a key player in the illegal drug business here and probably also involved in the murder of Rollie Jenkins and maybe others as well."

"What makes you think he's caught up in this mess?"

"His attitude is extremely hostile, and it appears to me that he doesn't actually work for Macrone from a pharmaceutical standpoint but is there, keeping

DEADLY ATTACK

check on William Macrone II. I need you to find out what the shoe size was of the small footprints at the edge of the ravine where Jenkins met his end and whether or not the lab could make out the brand of the shoe. I would also appreciate it if you could have the DMV check out this license plate number."

"You sure are giving me a lot of job assignments. When are you going to get rid of that phony wig and hair on your face and go back to being the fellow I know who is a private investigator?"

"I'm very close to doing that. This spirit gum has almost seen its end. A few more days using that stuff, and you won't recognize me as that fellow you knew from before."

"Take a look at this." Samuel brought up the picture on his cell phone of the letter *M* painted in blood on the rock with the *l* next to it near Jenkins's body and then laid the Macrone Pharmaceutical business card down next to the phone. "Gregory, what do you see there?" The business card had large capital letters of *MPL* in the center of the card with Macrone Pharmaceutical Laboratories printed underneath the logo.

"Are you thinking Jenkins was trying to write those initials on the rock and died before he could finish the P and the L?"

"I believe that's possible. He worked for Macrone Pharmaceutical for a short period of time. When I tried to find out what he was doing there, Caston became belligerent and began questioning me, wanting to know why I would be asking about someone who worked there. I noticed that Caston has small feet and was wearing a set of fancy shoes when I first met him in Macrone's office. I tracked down the men's store here in LA where he shops and found out his shoe size and what brand he wears. If I'm correct, when you get the information from the crime lab, we will know who owned the small footprints at the ravine that killed Rollie Jenkins. I'm persuaded that Macrone Pharmaceuticals is mixed up in this illegal drug business. The problem I'm having is trying to figure out why a successful company producing legal medications would end up in that kind of business."

"Samuel, I need to check in with my people in DC and ask them to look into a certain DEA agent. Let's plan dinner tonight and I'll try to have the info you requested."

Samuel latched on to Gregory's comment concerning one of the DEA agents. "What agent are you looking into?"

"Can't say right now. I'll fill you in later."

DEADLY ATTACK

Samuel went back to his room and decided that it was time to scrap the disguise and go back to being Samuel Garcia, master detective. He felt that he knew who enough of the rats were to take it to them face-to-face. He believed that Benjamin Caston was the head man who had orchestrated the murders and the attack on his bunkhouse. If he was indeed the one who killed Rollie Jenkins, then he believed that the DEA agent Gregory Lawrence was talking about must be Lemuel Rollins. He was the one seen with Caston in the picture snapped by Joe Halstead's deputy in Amarillo. If Rollins was involved with Caston, it would either be as an undercover DEA agent or as an accomplice in the illegal drug business. He didn't want to jump to any premature decisions, but something about Rollins had always rubbed him the wrong way. His demeanor during the investigation involving Davey Gibson and himself on Kalmajo Island had left a sour taste in Samuel's mouth concerning the agent. A thought surged through Samuel's mind at that moment, causing him to take out his cell phone and place a call to Bobby Lambers.

"Well, have you trapped all the rats there in LA yet?"

"Getting close, Bobby. When you tried to interview Manuel Alvera at the hospital, what was the word you thought he was trying to say?"

ALTON LYNN COOPER

"I can do you one better than that. He was alert enough for me to talk with him again yesterday afternoon, and he said the person that came into the mission the night of the shooting had a badge on his belt. It had been covered when he first entered the room, but after he shot Alvera, he reached behind him to holster his gun, and that's when Manuel saw the badge."

"What kind of badge was it?"

"He remembered it as a gold eagle above a blue circle with the capital letters *US* in the middle of the circle."

Coldness spread through Samuel, filling his being. "Was he sure of what he saw?"

"Said he would never forget it. Made him think some law enforcement person tried to kill him."

"Thanks, Bobby. I'll keep you informed of what we find out here. I believe we are getting very close to wrapping up this whole sordid affair."

Samuel hung up the phone wondering if Lemuel Rollins was actually capable of going back to Kalmajo Island as a killer instead of as a drug enforcement officer.

Samuel took his blue jeans and brightly colored silk shirt to the hotel laundry room and tumble dried them for a few minutes, getting the wrinkles out.

DEADLY ATTACK

He was glad at last to put away the tweed suit along with the wig and false beard and mustache. His face was still sore with some areas of red splotches on it from the "evil spirit gum." He had started referring to it as "evil spirit gum" as day after day, it worked under the beard to permanently destroy the skin on his handsome Spanish face. He took the tube from the bathroom medicine cabinet and threw it into the small trash can under the sink. "Goodbye, spirit gum. May you rest in peace." He couldn't imagine what Ms. Valentina would think if she saw his face in its present condition.

Something kept troubling his mind when he thought of Caston as the mastermind behind all that was going on. He was indeed a dangerous individual, but if he was trying to wipe out all those who would be able to identify him, why would he be operating out in the open?

*****

Samuel stood in front of the mirror in his room, admiring the new person before him. He hadn't realized until that moment how much he had missed his blue jeans and favorite silk shirt. He remembered a promise that he had made to himself at the beginning of this case and would be sure to collect what was coming to him. The dress loafers on his feet did not do his blue jeans justice. He set out to find the right shop in LA to correct that condition.

Samuel waited patiently for the salesman at the Western Leather Shop to finish up with a mother and her young son so that he could be fitted with a new pair of cowboy boots that he had admired in the shop window. The mother was trying to decide how to outfit her little man with his own boots, allowing him to play the lead part in his school's western adventure school play. The salesman placed boot after boot on the little guy's feet, letting him clop his way around the shop before complaining that they were trying to choke his toes. Samuel was thinking that he'd like to choke more than the little fellow's toes after he stepped on Samuel's sock feet a number of times as he sat waiting to try on his own boot selection. The salesman led the mother across the store to another boot rack just as the little boot-clad villain stopped in front of Samuel, looking up into his face.

"Does it hurt?"

"Does what hurt?"

"Your face."

Samuel curled up his upper lip and leaned close to the little cowboy's face and snarled out his

DEADLY ATTACK

own question, "Do you wanna know what really hurts me?"

The little man's eyes grew big as he stepped back quickly, shaking his head from side to side.

"Your face in my space."

Samuel let his red splotched face twist itself to one side just as the little man ran yelling to his mother's side. After trying on more boots from the rack across the store, she finally took her squealing wannabe cowboy toward the exit, announcing that he could lead the western show wearing his tennis shoes. Samuel finally left the store walking gently as his feet settled into a new set of richly carved cowboy boots that would surely need some break-in time in the days ahead. Before heading for lunch, he stopped in at another western apparel shop and bought four new pairs of boot-cut blue jeans along with four brightly decorated silk western shirts. He tucked the receipt into his wallet, smiling to himself. *You go, Garcia. You go.*

Samuel stopped in at the Shrimp Lovers restaurant for a quick lunch, taking a table in the back, allowing him a full view of the room and the street out front. He was determined to show his true identity for the rest of his stay in Los Angeles and would take every precaution to protect himself in doing so.

271

He wanted to do all he could to draw the rats out into the open, close this case down, and get back to Amarillo, hopefully in one piece. He took out his notepad and wrote down his summation of the case and would share his plans to expose the villains with Gregory Lawrence when they met for dinner that evening. He decided to stop by Macrone Pharmaceutical's headquarters on his way back to his hotel and put his plans into action. He intended to let anyone interested know that Samuel Garcia was in town seeking out those involved in the blowing up of his office in Amarillo. This would put Benny Caston on his trail and hopefully expose the head man along the way.

"What did you say your name is?" Sally Greensboro, Macrone's receptionist, stared deeply into Samuel's red splotched face.

"Garcia. Samuel Garcia."

"And what is your business with Mr. Macrone?"

"I'm a private investigator from Amarillo, Texas. My office was shot up a few weeks ago, and I believe someone here at Macrone Pharmaceuticals may have information as to who the culprit or culprits were that attacked me."

The receptionist's face took on a look of disbelief. "You think our company was involved in an attack on your office in Texas?"

DEADLY ATTACK

"I think that someone here involved in this company may be a suspect in the attack. Absolutely."

"Please take a seat in the lobby." Samuel took his place in the lobby as he watched the receptionist set the small sign on her desk announcing her return and then disappeared down the hall toward the corporate offices. She returned shortly, letting Samuel know that none of the company's managers were available currently but that Mr. Macrone could be available to meet with him the next day before noon.

"What time before noon?"

"Please leave me your contact information and I will call you when his schedule is firmed up."

"I'm staying at the Hyatt Regency near the LA International Airport. Leave a message at the desk for me. I'll pick it up in the morning."

Samuel left Macrone's corporate headquarters knowing that he had just moved his investigation into full gear. He felt sure that he would have the opportunity to meet one or more of Benny Caston's associates in the near future.

*****

Gregory Lawrence met Samuel at one of LA's premier steakhouses for supper. It was time for a

273

good old full-blown steak and potato dinner with a nice salad piled high and smothered in ranch dressing. The two men ate in silence for a few minutes before entering into their conversation concerning the cases they were working on. Samuel patted his face with his napkin and prepared to share his version of what he believed was going on at Macrone Pharmaceuticals.

"Those red splotches still bothering you?" Gregory gave Samuel a sideways grin.

"Only when I touch them. Shall I start or do you want to go first?"

"You go first."

Samuel pulled out his notepad along with the paper that he had written out in his hotel room the night before. "I'll try to take things in order for clarity's sake.

"First, Jimmy Winters was a heavy gambler. He got in deep with some very unsavory characters. I believe they forced him into setting up the delivery truck schedule the day of the armored car robbery. I believe the robbery was focused on taking the Macrone Pharmaceutical shipment and not the money on board. I don't know the reason why, however. Second, William Macrone II's buddies couldn't come up with enough money to bail out the com-

DEADLY ATTACK

pany when it almost went belly up. Benjamin Caston showed up on the scene and has some kind of a hold over William Macrone. I suspect that he and his associates provided the funding to save the company and are now using it to cover up their illegal drug operations while washing huge amounts of illegal drug money through the legitimate pharmaceutical business. I believe it was Benny Caston who shot and killed Rollie Jenkins at the ravine.

"When I tried to find out what Jenkins did in his short stay at the company, Caston got very agitated by my asking. I still don't know what Jenkins did there, but I'm sure it was tied to the illegal drug business knowing his past history from Kalmajo Island. I believe that Caston, and possibly someone over him, took out Jenkins after they used him to kill the ditch man in Denver to cover their tracks concerning the attack on my office in the beginning of this sordid mess. I also have a suspicion that Lemuel Rollins may be a compromised DEA agent being used by Caston and whoever is above him. I stopped by Macrone's office today, introducing myself, making them aware of my investigation of their company as to their possible involvement in the attack on me. I figure that should stir up the rat's nest, hopefully leading me to the head man himself. I still have some

ALTON LYNN COOPER

loose ends, but I think this centers around Macrone Pharmaceuticals."

Gregory Lawrence was quiet as he considered Samuel's information. "Interesting. Now let me share what I know along with what I suspect.

"I just got a report this afternoon that our man Jimmy Winters is alive and well. It seems that you are right about them getting their hooks into him because of his gambling addiction. He was apprehended bringing illegal drugs in overland from Tijuana, Mexico, passing through the national forest nearby. His handlers snatched him from his home and turned him into one of their mules bringing the drugs into the country. Lemuel Rollins has been identified, through his cell phone records, as the agent who was feeding the drug gangs the DEA information, helping them to avoid detection while using the boats and the overland routes out of Mexico. He was getting paid off in cash, left at agreed-upon locations, and never actually met who it was that was sending the money his way. His problem was he always cared a lot more for money and high living than he did for law and order. Now here is where things really get interesting. The man's name that belongs to that tag plate that you gave me is Jack Quinlyn. He's another minor league DEA agent who got hooked up with Lemuel Rollins taking payoffs from the drug guys."

Samuel interrupted Gregory, letting him know that Quinlyn was one of the men who was on Kalmajo Island at the time Manuel Alvera was shot.

"I know. It was three days after Alvera was shot that I saw Rollins arguing with Quinlyn at the gas station in Sacramento. I suspect that he botched the job on Alvera or that he was not supposed to have tried to kill him in the first place. I'm not sure which. He may have gone off on his own trying to impress whoever is the head man in all this. He has always been known as a loose cannon since he's been with the DEA in Sacramento. They would have probably cut him loose a long time ago, but Rollins took him under his wing, supposedly to straighten him out. We can see how that turned out. Our agents here in LA believe that the armored car robbery was, as you suggested, payback for someone operating out of Macrone Pharmaceuticals, taking possession of another organization's major illegal drug shipment coming into the city, trying to cut in on their territory.

"Our problem is we have Lemuel Rollins and Jimmy Winters in custody, but they have no idea who the actual head of the organization is. Jack Quinlyn has disappeared from sight for the time being, and

Benny Caston has covered his tracks to the point that no evidence has surfaced that can definitely tie him to the illegal drug activity. We know he is involved, but we need more hard evidence to bring him in."

"Gregory, what about a man named Horace Donaldson? According to Bobby Lambers, he was on the flight to Kalmajo Island along with Jack Quinlyn. The flight information revealed that they sat together on the plane and flew out together after Alvera was attacked."

"That name hasn't come up in my investigation, Samuel. He's not an agent with the DEA that I am aware of."

Samuel looked at his notes again before asking his next question. "Did you get information on the shoe prints left near the ravine?"

Lawrence pulled his own notepad from his pocket before responding. "They appeared to be six and a half in size. They seemed to have a pad in the middle of the front portion of the sole and what could have been a brand name stamped in the heel of the sole."

"You say they appeared to be six and a half. Does that mean the lab can't be sure?"

"The dirt near the edge of the ravine was a little moist when the footprints were left. The person leav-

DEADLY ATTACK

ing the prints twisted their feet slightly when they turned to leave the scene, causing the left print to have a smudged appearance. The right print showed the shoe detail a little more clearly."

"So you're saying we couldn't definitely tie Caston's shoes to the prints?"

"We would need to get his shoes and have the lab see if they could match them up. If they're not a perfect match, they could still serve as circumstantial evidence. I'm sure that by now he would have cleaned them enough to not have left traces of the dirt from the ravine on them."

"So what are our next steps, Gregory? We have a lot of suspicions but still can't get to the top man or men running this nasty business."

"It seems to me, Samuel, that you've stepped forward and made yourself a target. I recommend that we put a couple of our undercover guys on you and hopefully nab anyone sent your way. Our agents and the DEA guys here in LA are monitoring all of Macrone Pharmaceuticals' drug shipments. They are making sure they are going to legitimate drug stores. They have become aware that Macrone is using a warehouse in East LA to store large amounts of their products before sending them out of state to pharmacies around the country. We have eyes on Benny

Caston 24–7, hoping that he will lead us to whomever is above him if he is, in fact, a key player in the illegal drug business here in LA. The top players always use burner phones, making it more difficult for the authorities to track them down. They stay on the move, not pinging the same towers multiple times in the areas where their business is going down.

"When they do communicate, it's normally using code language discussing family members' vacation plans with the person on the other end knowing which words to spin the spelling around and which locations actually mean other places. They have their own secret network of code language that makes it tough for anyone outside their organization to make sense of their conversations. For now, we have shut off their shipments coming in by land or sea, so we should start to see some action here in town when the major dealers try to find other supply methods to keep their customers happy. Well, do you have any other thoughts going forward?"

Samuel considered Gregory's question before responding. "Two things. First, why would a prominent politician, Senator Gerald McPherson, lobby to get millions of dollars for these pharmaceutical companies when they are already getting wealthy selling

DEADLY ATTACK

their products? Second, can you set me up with a firearm while I'm here in town? I left my arsenal back in Amarillo when I traveled as a reporter instead of an elite detective. Not only that, I would have been arrested myself if I tried to bring my weapons of choice aboard the flight here."

Gregory eyed Samuel for a moment before responding. "Can you be trusted to not ruin my career if I grant your request?"

"I promise to only use it to save my own skin in case of dire circumstances."

Gregory looked around the restaurant before bending down and pulling a small revolver out of an ankle holster on his left leg. "My personal backup. I have others in my office. That, by the way, is not traceable. I know you won't do anything crazy with it. If you have to use it, wipe it clean and ditch it. And Samuel, we never had this conversation."

*****

Samuel and Gregory parted ways, planning to meet up at the hotel for breakfast the next morning. Lawrence indicated that he had some leads to check out based on his and Samuel's discussion. Samuel had a name of interest himself and headed for the

ALTON LYNN COOPER

library downtown to do some snooping on one of their public computers.

"May I help you?"

"Are there any other terminals available somewhere else in the library?"

"No. Why do you ask?"

"There are kids occupying the ones off the lobby. They appear to be rooted to the seats, not planning to move anytime soon."

The librarian gave Samuel a broad, toothy smile. "It's teachers' meetings at the local schools all this week. We get the little geniuses here at our place while their parents are at work. They seem to think that since they pay taxes to support the public library, we should babysit their kids when school is out."

"Do you think one of the future presidents would be willing to let an older citizen use one of the units for a few minutes?"

"They're pretty possessive once they commandeer one of the machines. Some of them promise others the contents of their lunch boxes when school gets back into session just to weasel their way onto their favorite terminal."

Samuel determined that it would be risky to try and dislodge one of Los Angeles's future leaders off their favorite machine and decided to head back to

DEADLY ATTACK

the hotel. There were guest machines available there, and hopefully, the younger generation out of school for the week hadn't discovered those awaiting him back at his home base.

Samuel first noticed the large SUV behind him when it darted in and out of traffic, working its way closer to his rental vehicle. He had sped up going through an intersection when the yellow light changed to red, only to have the vehicle behind him continue on through the red light, staying within distance of Samuel's vehicle. He fingered the small pistol tucked in the belt of his jeans, pulling it out and laying it in his lap. He could see that there were two men in the vehicle tailing him but couldn't clearly make out their facial features. He felt sure that his fishing expedition at Macrone Pharmaceuticals had brought those behind him his way.

"Let the fun begin, my little pigeons, let the fun begin."

Samuel swung in front of the car in the left lane and quickly turned left into the path of an oncoming delivery truck. There were multiple horns blaring at him as he narrowly escaped being smashed by the oncoming truck. The SUV passed on through the intersection, stuck in the right lane with its left blinker on. Samuel swung the rental into the first

ALTON LYNN COOPER

available driveway and immediately backed out onto the street, heading back to the intersection where he had almost become part of the delivery truck's front grill. He turned right at the red light, heading toward the library, taking the long way back to his hotel.

As he approached the hotel parking lot, he saw the SUV sitting in the back of the lot, facing the main hotel entrance. Samuel continued on down the side street and parked his car, getting out and working his way back along the houses toward the back of the parking lot. He palmed the small pistol as he worked his way up to the back of the vehicle, hearing the men inside in an ongoing discussion.

"Excuse me. Were you the two seeking to make my acquaintance?"

The small man behind the wheel jumped at the sound of Samuel's voice and stared wide-eyed at the pistol pointed in his direction. The man in the passenger seat called out, "Whoa, hold on, Garcia. We're not your enemies. Harold here is young on the force and not accustomed to following at a safe distance. I'm going to show you my badge. Don't shoot."

Samuel watched closely as the man pulled out his wallet, opening it and revealing his FBI badge.

"How do I know that badge is for real? I normally shoot people who try to chase me down."

DEADLY ATTACK

Samuel made his voice sound as threatening as possible.

"Call Gregory Lawrence. He assigned us to watch over you. Maybe he should have given me a better driver."

Samuel bade his would-be protectors a good day and went to retrieve his rental car, moving it into the hotel parking lot. "Watch my ride. Make sure no one puts a bomb in it."

*****

"Are all of the terminals available for use?"

The desk clerk eyed Samuel from behind large black-rimmed glasses.

"Why wouldn't they be?"

"I don't know. I thought perhaps a person needed to reserve one before all the schoolkids come charging in."

The clerk gave Samuel a quizzical look before responding, "Aren't you the same man that had different color hair and a beard two days ago?"

"Yes. I was undercover. Now I've come out in the open."

"Why the change?"

ALTON LYNN COOPER

"There are people wanting to kill me, but they were having a hard time finding me. I wanted to try and help them as much as possible."

The desk clerk stared at Samuel wide-eyed as he removed a note from the key slot behind the counter, handing it to the strange man before him. Samuel took the note and headed for one of the empty computer terminals off the lobby.

The screen flashed a few times before bringing up the picture of Horace Donaldson. He wasn't someone that Samuel remembered meeting at any time in the past. He was a heavyset man with deep jowls on his face with dark, brooding eyes. He had a full head of grey curly hair and a heavy handlebar mustache along with mutton chop sideburns. Samuel thought that he could easily pass as one of the villains on the daytime soap operas. Samuel moved down through the information on the screen, letting out a low whistle when he saw the name of Donaldson's employer.

"Interesting. Very interesting indeed."

He was sure that Horace Donaldson fit into the tangled web involving Macrone Pharmaceuticals but couldn't immediately figure out how. The other question in Samuel's mind was why someone in Donaldson's position would accompany Jack Quinlyn to Kalmajo Island and carry out the attack

DEADLY ATTACK

on Manuel Alvera. As Samuel reached the bottom of the screen, one last picture showed Donaldson at a black-tie dinner party sitting at one of the head tables next to the man who had become a hero to the pharmaceutical industry in California.

"And so the plot thickens."

Samuel shut down the computer and pulled the note that the desk clerk had given him from his pocket. He unfolded the paper and read the printed words, "Don't use your hotel room tonight." He flipped the paper over, seeing it blank on the back, and then headed to the front desk.

"Who left this for me?"

"I don't know. It came in while Charlie was covering the desk."

"Where is Charlie now?"

"Don't know. He's done for the day. Be back tomorrow morning."

"I need to book another room for tonight."

"Do you want to cancel the room you're in and move to a new room? Why?"

"No. I want to keep my same room but book another room three doors down from my present room."

The desk clerk continued to stare at Samuel as if he thought the man before him might be passing

ALTON LYNN COOPER

through some kind of identity crisis. "Is this room for a friend of yours coming in for the night?"

"No. Just book me the room."

The desk clerk looked at the registration book on the counter before announcing, "I don't have a vacancy three doors down from your present room. Would five doors down be acceptable?"

"Yes."

"What name shall I show the room under?"

"Harry Postman."

"Who is Harry Postman?"

"He was a young, wild-haired, hippy mailman that delivered our mail when I was still back home at Mama's place. Never put it in the box. Always threw it on the front porch."

The desk clerk stared in amazement at Samuel as he handed him the room key to his new room.

Samuel grabbed a quick supper in the hotel restaurant before heading up to his old room to move some of his supplies into his new room down the hall. He wanted to settle in and give Gregory Lawrence a heads-up call. Someone knew that an attack would be made on his room that night. He didn't know where the note had come from, but he truly wanted to catch the culprit in action and hope that they would be one of the links leading back to the head rat here in Los Angeles.

*****

"Sorry about Larry."

"Larry?"

"Yes. Larry Edmonds, he's one of our new agents in training. He and his exasperated partner, Jerome Levinson, were the only two the bureau could loan me for a few days to keep an eye on you. Levinson is already yelling about taking an early retirement if he keeps getting stuck with these wannabe agents who can't follow someone without almost getting them both shot."

"I didn't know if they were friend or foe at first. I can understand Levinson's frustration with Edmonds. He's lucky he didn't get the both of them killed running red lights, trying to stay on my tail."

"What do I owe the pleasure of this call to?"

Samuel had called Gregory Lawrence to make him aware of the possible attack on his room that evening and share the information on Horace Donaldson.

"That's interesting, Samuel. His potential connection to Senator McPherson adds a new twist to what I found out concerning our esteemed public servant. I'm waiting on some more information in the morning and may be able to piece the story together then. In the meantime, I will alert my two assignees to your potential attack and have them monitor the hallways on your floor tonight. I sure hope it doesn't come in the form of a bomb."

Samuel left the light and the TV on in his old room and closed and locked the door. He positioned himself down the hall in his new room by pulling the recliner chair over by the door, hoping that it would help him to hear footsteps in the hall should his attacker or attackers pass by his door in the night. He wheeled the desk chair over, facing it toward the recliner, settling into his makeshift bed for the night. He dozed off and on with the small pistol resting in his lap, occasionally jerking awake, hearing other patrons going in and out of their rooms. The clock radio showed 3:00 a.m. the last time he looked across the room before he fell into a fitful sleep, seeing Valentina riding off in a bright red Ferrari with Hector Marie Gonzales Lopez's arm drawing her close to him. He was chasing the car down his mother's driveway on foot, yelling, "You do know he's your cousin, right?"

He was pulled from his dream and his foot-race with the red machine by loud yelling out in the

DEADLY ATTACK

hallway. He scrambled up, pulling open his door slightly, peering down the hall in the direction of his old room. Larry Edmonds was on top of a swarthy little man, rolling back and forth in the hallway. Jerome Levinson pulled his agent in training off the man before kneeling down, placing the man on his stomach, and handcuffing him. Samuel scrambled up from his chair, making his way down the hall to get a good look at his would-be attacker. A canister lay against the wall in the hallway that looked like a sprayer that a person would use to spray weeds in their lawn.

"Caught him as he was preparing to empty the contents underneath your doorway."

Levinson was winded from their struggle to bring the twisting little man under control as he kept screaming, "Lemego!" while pumping his legs in every direction. Samuel reached down and rolled the hollering culprit over, looking into a small twisted-up face that he had never seen before.

"Who sent you here tonight?"

"Lemego, lemego!"

"You're not going anywhere except to jail. Who sent you here?"

Levinson put his hand on Samuel's chest to let him know it was time to back off. "He's not going to

ALTON LYNN COOPER

spill his guts. We'll take him downtown and do what we can to squeeze him. We have our ways of getting little fellows like him to dump what they know."

The swarthy little man's eyes grew so large Samuel thought that they might pop out of his head. "Oh, yeah. That's right. I've heard about what you guys do to those that you take downtown." Samuel twisted up his face in a grimace, shaking his head back and forth as he looked into the terrified eyes of the little man being led away in handcuffs. Samuel returned to his new room, stretching out on the bed after setting the clock radio for 6:00 a.m. He and Gregory Lawrence should be able to begin consolidating their information at breakfast, hopefully leading them to some significant conclusions in their two cases.

*****

"You idiot! The man waltzes in there, making his presence known right under your nose, and you send an imbecile to carry out an attack on him! What were you thinking?"

"Don't you get so high and mighty? It was your first two idiots that blew this whole thing up in Texas when the only thing they could do was to shoot up an old bunkhouse. You've been using me as cleanup

DEADLY ATTACK

ever since. Now the person you hate most has come looking for you. You should have left well enough alone. Your greed and insane desire to get even will be the end of you yet. I'm not going down with you."

"Shut your mouth. You're already in over your head. Do you think I don't keep compelling information on all those that go against the law? You need to settle your head down and think of how to eliminate Garcia. There's nothing tying you or me to any wrongdoing. Let's keep it that way. You and I both have become very wealthy men through the years, and there's still a lot of money to be had as long as we stick together. There are plenty of other stoolies that can go down for the robbery and the unfortunate deaths along the way. Just don't use inexperienced idiots to do what a skilled assassin could have pulled off last night without a hitch."

*****

"So I hear from my associates that you had quite a bit of action here last night." Gregory Lawrence looked at Samuel across the breakfast table in the hotel restaurant.

"My little trip to Macrone's office yesterday had the desired effect. They're not all bad over there.

ALTON LYNN COOPER

Someone sent a note here to the hotel, alerting me to last night's attack. If not for that note, whatever the little man had in that spray canister may have found its way into my lungs."

"Samuel, if that would have happened, I wouldn't be here having breakfast with you this morning. His canister was filled with hydrogen cyanide gas. Breathe that stuff in and say goodbye to the world."

Samuel stared silently at Lawrence before responding, "Is there any way to track where the stuff came from?"

"The lab here in town has it now. My guess is that the canister is not traceable. The little fellow that was hired to give you the special delivery is some stooge that apparently was picked up off the street and promised a good payday to deliver you the gas. He claims that he didn't know what was in the canister. The person that set him up told him the room was infested with bedbugs and that the spray was ordered by the hotel to cleanse the room in the middle of the night. The little sucker was told that the hotel wanted it done in the early hours of the morning so as not to alarm other guests about the bedbugs."

"Was he able to describe who it was that hired him?"

DEADLY ATTACK

"He said he never saw the person before. The only description that he gave my guys was that the man was stocky built, wearing blue jeans, a black leather jacket, and an LA Dodgers baseball cap. He said the guy had hair sticking out from under the cap and a lot of hair on his face."

"I'm not sure, Gregory, but that description could very well fit Horace Donaldson."

"That's an interesting possibility. The guy told Gus—that's our little man's name, Gus Wilson—that he worked for an exterminating company and they needed extra help for the evening."

"Let's finish our breakfast and then compare notes. I reserved a meeting room off the lobby where we can have some privacy and hopefully avoid any more gas canisters coming my way."

*****

Samuel ordered a pot of coffee to be sent to their meeting room and then went upstairs, bringing his whiteboard down to share with Lawrence. "Before you get into your board, let me share some news from yesterday. You mentioned our state senator, Gerald McPherson, that you saw being interviewed on TV. That sparked something in my mind,

ALTON LYNN COOPER

so I did a little digging on him last night. He has gotten reelected through the years with his campaign receiving millions of dollars from the pharmaceutical industry along with others. That in itself wouldn't be newsworthy, but when I dug a little deeper, Macrone Pharmaceuticals has by far been his greatest contributor. Along with that, the bulk of these millions that he's brought back into the state in support of the industry have gone to Macrone far and above any of the other pharmaceutical companies. The way he has directed those funds has been under investigation by the Food and Drug Administration after they received multiple complaints from the other drug companies in the state. That must have provoked his anger toward the newsman for bringing that up in the recent interview. Lately, he's been accused of trying to favor Macrone over other companies that he represents as a state senator, with these actions threatening his 'do-gooder' reputation."

Samuel set up his whiteboard on an easel in the room and began walking Lawrence through what he believed were the facts in the case. "I believe it is obvious that Macrone has been compromised. I'm convinced that Benny Caston was instrumental in bailing out William Macrone II using illegal drug money. I think that the company is being used to

DEADLY ATTACK

launder millions of dollars of cartel money through the guise of developing new prescription medications. I may be wrong, but I think that Senator McPherson is somehow caught up in this whole affair. I did some checking, and this guy named Horace Donaldson is a member of the Gaming Board for the state of California. There's a picture of him at a black-tie dinner party sitting alongside Senator McPherson.

"This may be a wild thought, but what if Donaldson becomes aware of certain individuals that get in over their heads in gambling debt and then recruits them to do the illegal drug guys' dirty work. I think that's what happened to Jimmy Winters. They knew he worked for the armored truck company and sucked him into their web as needed. It's possible they kept getting him in deeper by letting him run up a tab that he could never pay off. Then they come in and make him an offer he can't refuse. Either do their bidding or end up in a ditch somewhere. My problem is trying to figure out who the actual head of all this mess is. If Donaldson's guys actually recruited Jimmy Winters to assist them in setting up the armored truck robbery after rerouting it to pick up Macrone's pharmaceutical shipment, how would that benefit Senator McPherson if he is indeed in tight with Benny Caston and the drug cartels? That's what I have, Gregory. What are your thoughts?"

"I'm going to share some things with you that are not for public consumption yet. That means that you have to keep all this confidential for now. Senator McPherson is under investigation not only by the Food and Drug Administration for his handling of taxpayer money but also by the US Senate Ethics Board. They're looking into millions of dollars of dark money that has flowed into his campaign coffers through the years and what he has done to be in receipt of those funds. It is believed that he has used his office to set up winners and losers in the public sector for some time based on monies received. In other words, they are looking into whether he's been bought off by some powerful individuals.

"Next, there are a number of Mexican DTOs or drug-trafficking organizations operating in southern California. There are constant turf wars here in LA and across the state to gain or keep control of their individual markets. I believe that Benny Caston hijacked one or more major drug shipments entering the state from Mexico, and that is why the cartels that he stole from robbed the Macrone Pharmaceutical shipment. They weren't actually interested in the cash on the truck or the prescription drugs on board.

DEADLY ATTACK

They somehow got wind of the truck's load that day and hit it to send a message to Caston. That shows that whoever they are, they know that Caston is using Macrone's company to cover his illegal drug operations."

"They may also know of Senator McPherson's involvement with Benny Caston. Two years ago, there was an attempt on his life from a supposed disgruntled political actor that actually turned out to be a low-level dealer in one of the Mexican cartels. The senator brushed it off as an individual that wanted to get even with him for his support in the war on drugs. The problem with that statement is there's no evidence that McPherson ever supported the government's feeble attempt to crack down on illegal drugs. Now as far as Horace Donaldson is concerned, I am aware of him. I think he got sucked into all this either by Benny Caston or Senator McPherson. He has an invalid wife and three sons in prep school, two at Harvard and one at Dartmouth. He has spent large amounts of money both for his wife's ongoing medical difficulties and his sons' education. We are planning on bringing him in and squeezing him concerning his involvement with Senator McPherson. I think he may be the weak link that could open all this up for us.

ALTON LYNN COOPER

"We recently looked into his financials, and he has deposited a lot more into his banking accounts and spent a considerable amount more than what his salary from the Gaming Commission has paid him over the last four years. His lifestyle and his income don't add up. We are also preparing a subpoena for Macrone's financial records. We need to take a close look at the timing of the federal monies funneled to them through McPherson's senatorial efforts, the cost of their doing business, and their income over the last few years.

"On the outside, they look very successful. However, a cursory look at their new drug development processes over the last few years has shown many promising new drugs being sidelined because of the lack of approval by the FDA. A company their size can lose billions of dollars in a short period of time in these types of situations. If we can identify discrepancies in their income between legitimate drug sales and monies coming in from other undisclosed sources, that will give us a way to squeeze their financial people. It's come to our attention that their books have not had an outside independent audit in the last five years. The auditing company that they have been using is actually owned by one of William Macrone II's distant third cousins. That connection wasn't discovered until a short time ago."

DEADLY ATTACK

Samuel poured himself and Gregory a fresh cup of coffee before summing up what Lawrence had told him. "So our plan is to shake up Horace Donaldson and see if he will spill his guts while at the same time throwing a subpoena Macrone's way, hoping to find some interesting discrepancies in their financial records. Are there any leads on Jack Quinlyn's whereabouts?"

"Not at this time, Samuel. When we bring Donaldson in, he may know where he's disappeared to. When we slap Donaldson with our knowledge of him accompanying Quinlyn to Kalmajo Island and Manuel Alvera's attempted murder, that may cause him to rat out Quinlyn. We're going to take another run at Lemuel Rollins, our disgraced DEA agent. When he finds out what all we have on Quinlyn and Donaldson being tied to Alvera's shooting, that may loosen his tongue as well. When you begin to threaten people with the charge of conspiracy to commit murder, that normally causes them to squeal pretty loud. We've got to hope that one of our culprits kept some kind of records on how they got sucked into all this and who pulled them in."

CHAPTER 12

Justice at Last

William Macrone II's face turned pasty white when the DEA agents swooped into Macrone's Pharmaceutical Headquarters, armed with a subpoena allowing them to begin taking possession of their financial records. The records were packed into boxes along with computer terminals that had been removed from the desks of the accountants in the financial department.

Meanwhile, across town at the offices of the State Gaming Commission, Horace Donaldson was led out of his office in handcuffs while his staff looked on in shock. The FBI agent was reading him his rights, letting him know if he couldn't afford an attorney, he could petition the court to appoint one for him. His face was drained of color as his world began to collapse around him.

DEADLY ATTACK

Benny Caston slammed his phone down in a rage and prepared to leave his home office just as there was a loud knock on his front door.

"Don't open that!"

Caston's startled manservant had already pulled the door open and turned to look back at his boss as two DEA agents brushed past him on their way into his boss's office. Three other agents came into the house heading for Caston's bedroom, carrying plastic bags to begin collecting items for their investigation.

"You can't do this. I'll have every one of your jobs and sue this whole *stinking* state for this intrusion!"

"Turn around, Mr. Caston. We have some new jewelry custom-fitted just for you." The lead agent handcuffed Benny Caston and began reading him his rights while his associate tucked a subpoena into Caston's suit coat pocket. Caston's face was red and twisted in rage as the agents led him out of his mansion toward a waiting government vehicle. The neighbors in the upscale neighborhood watched as the secretive little man was led away. His vile language echoed across the expansive lawns, with one of the agents reminding him that he had the right to remain silent.

*****

ALTON LYNN COOPER

"I'm sorry, Mr. Lawrence, but Senator McPherson is in a closed-door meeting not to be disturbed." The startled receptionist stared at the FBI badge being held up before her.

"I'll let myself in. No problem." Gregory Lawrence knocked loudly on the thick wooden door and then opened it, walking into the senator's office.

"What's the meaning of this? You leave this office immediately!"

Lawrence ignored the senator as he held up his badge while telling the three well-dressed men at the conference table their meeting was over. After the office emptied out, Lawrence turned to the senator with a smile on his face while handing him a subpoena.

"What is this? You don't have the authority to come in here and serve me. I'm a United States senator. Who sent you here?"

"I have all the authority I need to do exactly what I have done and more. Make this easy on both of us, Senator. That is a Rule 17-C Subpoena ordering you to produce books, papers, documents, data, or other objects as stated in the subpoena. I have authority from the Senate Ethics Committee to secure these records in support of our ongoing investigation into your use of federal funds along with

DEADLY ATTACK

your involvement in questionable campaign finance irregularities." While Lawrence spoke, three FBI agents entered the senator's office and began opening up the file cabinets along the back wall, removing their contents.

"Those are governmental records. You have no authority to remove them." Senator McPherson's face was red with rage as small droplets of spittle covered his chin.

"I'd advise you to calm down, Senator, and let us do our job. You're not being placed under arrest yet, but that could change if it becomes necessary."

McPherson stormed out of his office, shouting for his secretary to call his personal attorney and then get the Ethics Committee chairman on the phone.

*****

Horace Donaldson sat at the table in the small FBI interrogation room, staring at the agents across from him. His face still maintained the sickly shallow look along with his mouth being dry, causing his words to come out low and quavering.

"Mr. Donaldson, we believe you got caught up in something way over your head. We understand that you were desperate for money to care for your invalid wife and keep your sons in expensive schools. These are noble things to do, but not at the expense of breaking the law. Should you go to prison, possibly for the rest of your life, what will happen to your wife and sons then?"

"Prison? What would I go to prison for?"

"Do you know a man named Jack Quinlyn?"

Donaldson's face turned an even paler shade of white. "Why do you ask?"

"We know you accompanied him to Kalmajo Island, and we believe you may have been the one that shot a man named Manuel Alvera on the island. That is at least an attempted murder charge, and if Mr. Alvera doesn't survive, that will be a capital murder charge calling for the death penalty."

Donaldson appeared to become faint as he slumped forward, putting his head down on the table. He began to shake and weep as the words poured forth from his mouth in one long mournful sound.

"Mr. Donaldson, we need you to sit up, calm down, and tell us what you know. If you weren't the one that pulled the trigger, then maybe it can go a lot easier on you if you cooperate with us. Now tell us, do you know where we may find Jack Quinlyn?"

Donaldson's voice came out in a whisper.

"Speak up, man, we can't hear you."

DEADLY ATTACK

"He's dead."

"How do you know he's dead? Did you kill him?"

"I have a tape recording. Can you help me if I give you the tape recording?"

*****

Samuel sat across the desk from William Macrone II in his office. The man before him seemed in a daze and in a complete state of despair.

"Tell me, William—I may call you William, right?"

Macrone didn't answer. He just stared blankly in Samuel's direction.

"William, I think you got used by Benny Caston and possibly a state senator when they came along offering to save your family's company a few years back. I think you have been under their control ever since. There have been a number of arrests today and probably more to come. You could be on that list as well. My advice to you is to come clean and tell us what you know. If you were an innocent bystander being taken advantage of by these other lawbreakers, perhaps you can avoid prison time."

ALTON LYNN COOPER

Macrone stared at Samuel out of bloodshot eyes. "Caston."

"What?"

"Caston. He came to me, offering to be an investor in my company. I thought he was on the up and up. Said his investment firm wanted to expand into the pharmaceutical industry. I didn't know until a few months later that his investment money was coming through the Mexican cartels. By then, it was too late. He threatened my family. Said if I didn't go along and keep my mouth shut, my family would end up like a lot of the others that kept popping up on the news."

"Do you have any evidence of what you're telling me that will implicate Caston in the illegal drug business?"

"No. He was always very careful not to incriminate himself. A few weeks back, he came into my office and turned on the TV set. The news was on with a reporter pointing to the place in a ravine outside of town where that man's body was found. They showed the red blood marks on the stone. He smiled at me and said we might need to change the company's logo in the future. That man who was found there was in my office with Caston three days before he ended up in the ravine."

DEADLY ATTACK

Samuel spoke up, "That man was Rollie Jenkins. I knew him. Do you know what his connection to Benny Caston was?"

"No. Caston met him somewhere and brought him into my company, telling him that he would serve as a security guard here. I think Jenkins was trying to go straight, and Caston found out about his past and wanted to pull him into the drug business. Jenkins was resistant at first, but the money offered to him caused him to succumb to Caston's demands. Caston sent him to Denver, Colorado, for some reason, and when Jenkins returned, they had a major blowout. That argument took place the last time he was in here, a few days before he was killed. That's all I know."

"Knock, knock."

Samuel turned around from Macrone's desk to see Jeremiah Willmar entering the office.

"Mr. Francis Bennett? Or is it Samuel Garcia?"

Samuel remembered meeting Macrone's executive vice president on one of his earlier visits to the company.

"Mr. Willmar, is that correct?"

Jeremiah Willmar reached out, shaking hands with Samuel. "That's correct. Pardon me for intruding, but I couldn't help overhearing your and William's conversation concerning Benny Caston. That's because I heard that you were here in the office with William and I've been eavesdropping out in the hall. I always believed that Caston was trouble. William here put the day-to-day running of the company under my control while William himself remained under Caston's control. I sat back and watched, not knowing exactly what the relationship was, but one thing I noticed: even when we were slow in getting FDA approval on new drug development programs, the company remained flush with money. There always seemed to be large infusions of cash passing through our financial department. I was preparing to leave for the evening a few nights back and got out to my car and remembered that I left my briefcase in my office. I was going back down the hallway when I heard Caston's voice telling someone to pay a visit to a special guest over at the Hyatt Regency Hotel. I remembered that when you and I met, discussing you working as Francis Bennett doing a story on our company, you shared with me you were staying at the Hyatt. Something in Caston's voice that night sounded sinister to me. I sent a note to your hotel suggesting that you avoid your room that night. I trust you got it."

DEADLY ATTACK

"I got it. You saved my life with that note. Do you have any other irregularities that you have noticed that I could follow up on?"

"Review the contents of a warehouse on the south side of town. I believe the shipments of our medicines being sent there for distribution around the nation may be enhanced by other products not produced here in our labs. I've reviewed the pharmaceuticals that we ship out with some recent inventory records our people filled out on what was shipped into the warehouse, and something is awry."

Samuel rose to leave, shaking hands with Willmar. He turned and reached his hand across the desk to William Macrone II, who remained seated without extending his hand in Samuel's direction. He appeared to be a man who had just been drained of his reason for living.

"Mr. Macrone, if you were pulled into this unknowingly, the law will take that into account. I suggest that you let Mr. Willmar do what he can, going forward, to place your company on a more honest and sound footing. You still have a reputation for producing quality products. That's worth preserving."

*****

ALTON LYNN COOPER

Three pairs of shoes had been removed from Benny Caston's home, with their soles being compared to the prints found by the ravine. The lab was able to identify the shoe brand as Florsheim. The cast of the prints revealed that there was indeed a rubber pad attached to the leather on the front of the sole and the brand name stamped into the rubber on the heel of the shoe. The shoes had all been cleaned and polished recently, but the lab technician noticed that one of the pairs had a small section of the front rubber pad pulling loose from the bottom of the leather sole. It was a very small area but did reveal a few grains of dirt stuck underneath the rubber pad. Further testing revealed that the small amounts of soil could have indeed come from the edge of the ravine. The problem was that different areas around Los Angeles had the same soil composition as that near the ravine. At best, the soil could add to the circumstantial evidence combined with the matching shoe size and brand name stamped in the heel.

"They hit pay dirt at the warehouse."

Gregory Lawrence sat with Samuel at a corner table at the Shrimp Lovers restaurant in downtown Los Angeles.

"What do you mean pay dirt?"

DEADLY ATTACK

"The tip that Jeremiah Willmar gave you concerning the amount of product the company was sending out and the incoming inventory records at the warehouse didn't match up. That was one of Benny Caston's major oversights, and it's going to cost him big. Caston hired some of his cartel guys on at Macrone's to drive the delivery trucks to the various pharmacies. He always used one of his men to send the shipments to the warehouse. Somewhere along the way, the truck was sidelined and the shipment had illegal drugs loaded on board along with the legal pharmaceuticals sent by Macrone. Caston's oversight was in not realizing that Macrone employees at the warehouse took their own incoming inventory, sending it back to Jeremiah Willmar at the main office. This was to hopefully avoid any drugs shipped to the warehouse being interfered with during the delivery process. Willmar began to notice the discrepancies but kept it to himself, hoping to dig into the specifics before sharing the information with William Macrone II. That was a few days before we raided the Macrone offices. The DEA guys took a team over there this morning, and guess what they found?"

Samuel waited for Lawrence to go on but quickly realized that his FBI friend was relishing the moment, wanting him to respond.

ALTON LYNN COOPER

"Okay, Gregory, what did they find?"

"I thought you would never ask. They opened up the shipments in the warehouse and started sampling some of the bottles inside the shipping containers. They found that certain containers had illegal drugs being shipped inside what appeared to be Macrone prescription-marked medication bottles. They observed that there was a yellow dot on the outside of all the containers that had the illegal drugs in the company's bottles. They arrested two of Caston's men who worked at the warehouse that arranged to ship the yellow dot containers out on special trucks, distributing the illegal drugs around the states. If law enforcement didn't know of Caston's illegal drug connections inside Macrone's, they would never suspect that there were shipments leaving the warehouse containing illegal drugs labeled as legitimate prescription medications. It was a perfect setup that worked for the past five years."

Samuel considered Lawrence's information before responding, "So you're saying the two warehouse workers gave Caston up?"

"Not so much. They didn't know exactly who it was that commandeered the shipments coming from Macrone's to the warehouse. They only knew to separate the yellow dotted containers and have them shipped out on certain trucks. They got paid by the warehouse and then also took loads of cash under the table to keep the shipments moving."

"So they can't give us Benny Caston?"

"Afraid not. Are you ready for some good news?"

Samuel waited for Lawrence to go on as he dug his fork deep into the baked salmon plank on his plate, resting above a thick bed of wild rice.

"Horace Donaldson was concerned enough for his own skin that he secretly taped his private meetings with our dear friend Senator Gerald McPherson. It seems that Donaldson was in deep enough with him that McPherson let his guard down during those private conversations and gave us some very incriminating evidence. Our man McPherson is indeed the head snake in all this illegal drug business. It seems that he and Benny Caston got to know one another years ago when Caston volunteered to work on McPherson's reelection campaign. McPherson was a power-hungry young man who would do anything to remain in office. Caston evidently persuaded him that he could guarantee him millions of dollars for his campaigns going forward if he didn't mind getting his hands a little dirty.

"Caston told him that if he wasn't interested, he was sure another junior senator would be more than willing to receive the millions of dollars to maintain

ALTON LYNN COOPER

his own career in the Senate. They were very clever in setting up a number of LLCs to funnel the illegal drug monies into McPherson's campaign coffers, but the FEC is hard at work following the money trail. McPherson secured federal taxpayer dollars to supposedly assist the pharmaceutical companies in becoming more efficient in their operations, lowering drug costs for the consumers. The bulk of that money found its way back to Macrone, replacing the illegal drug dollars that had been made available to McPherson during his reelection campaigns."

"So what was the incriminating information on McPherson in Donaldson's tape recordings?"

"On two separate occasions, he told Donaldson to contact Caston if he needed more cash for either his wife's condition or his son's college endeavors. On the tape, McPherson can be heard telling Donaldson, 'I told you not to worry. Stick with me and all your needs will be met. Just give me names when I request them. Remember, I need certain losers in certain companies when I need them. You suck them in and set them up. I'll tell you who and when. You pass their information on to Benny when that time comes. He'll know what to do next.'"

*****

DEADLY ATTACK

The next four days resulted in the local news flashing Senator Gerald McPherson's face across the screen at every newscast. Benny Caston's picture was likewise repeatedly on the screen, with the news reporters announcing the dismantling of a major drug operation taking place in Los Angeles and throughout the nation. All the defendants were being held in the county jail without bail. The news also announced that William Macrone II had stepped down as the head of the pharmaceutical company bearing his family's name at the request of the board and that a Mr. Jeremiah Willmar had been appointed as the new CEO of the company, replacing William Macrone II. The company's name was also being changed to American Pharmaceutical Laboratories in an attempt to give the company a fresh start and renew its image toward its stockholders and its customers. William Macrone II's fate was still unknown and would be determined when the investigation into his involvement with Benny Caston was wrapped up.

Samuel had one last task to perform before he left Los Angeles, heading back to the serenity of his hometown in Amarillo and back to Ms. Valentina's wonderful cooking.

"I don't know about this. We're busy closing down the senator's office. I don't know if that would be appropriate."

Samuel flashed his most brilliant smile in the direction of Gerald McPherson's executive assistant. "It will be fine. Mr. McPherson will receive an official receipt from my office in Amarillo along with the receipt that I'm giving you here."

The young woman took the receipt from Samuel's hand, reading it before staring at him in wonder. "And this is an expense against the senator's account that he would approve?"

"Absolutely. No questions asked. I know he's embroiled in his own problems now, but with him wanting to be known as an honest representative of the public, I'm confident that he would want this bill paid."

Samuel tucked the senator's check into his wallet and headed to the nearest bank to cash it before Gerald McPherson's office accounts were officially closed down. He planned one last lunch with Gregory Lawrence before heading for the airport and home.

"You may see my check listed in the senator's checkbook register when his office turns over all their remaining documents."

"What receipt?"

DEADLY ATTACK

"Four hundred seventy-six dollars and thirty-nine cents."

"And exactly what is that money for?"

"Four pairs of new boot-cut western blue jeans and four exquisitely designed silk shirts adorned in bright colors with cowboy scenes."

"I know that I shouldn't ask, but why would the senator want to pay for your new clothes?"

"His *ruffians* shot holes in my other ones back at my bunkhouse. I made myself a promise early on to have the culprit buy me new ones once I identified who the responsible party was. Case closed."

"You may say case closed, but all these court cases will be pending for a long time. McPherson has some very powerful friends in high places that might not turn their backs on him so quickly. Benny Caston's case is mostly circumstantial. I think we have enough to convict him, but nothing surprises me anymore. Watch your back, my friend. You may go back to Amarillo and forget about these lowlifes here in LA, but you will stay in their memory for a long time to come."

Samuel bade his good friend farewell and thanked him for all his help. They both agreed that their two cases were overlapping and each was solved because of their combined efforts.

ALTON LYNN COOPER

Samuel's face was almost back to normal and the mustache on his upper lip was starting to slowly fill in. It would take some time to get back to its full handlebar beauty, but he was thankful for being able to leave the tube of "evil spirit gum" in the trash can back in his hotel room in Los Angeles. His flight back to Amarillo was, for the most part, uneventful. He swallowed his two Dramamine tablets while he was sitting at the airport café with a large cinnamon roll and hot cup of black coffee. He had asked the café worker for two boiled eggs, only to have her look at him with one eyebrow raised high.

*****

During the flight, a small, twisty little girl with double pigtails tied with pink bows kept staring at him and twisting up her face while sticking out her tongue, letting it hang low on her petite chin.

"Can you do this?"

"Do what?" Samuel looked at his little admirer, waiting for an answer.

She stuck her tongue out as far as she could stretch it and then curled it upward with its tip going inside her right nostril for a short distance.

DEADLY ATTACK

"Sally Mae, leave that man alone and get back in your seat. You hear me? Right now or no gum when we land."

Sally Mae winked at Samuel and climbed over her mother, settling back down in the window seat in the row behind him. Samuel crossed his eyes and pulled the corners of his mouth wide with his index fingers while hanging out his own tongue as he turned toward Sally Mae, wiggling both his ears back and forth.

"Hey, how'd you do that?"

"Sally Mae. No gum."

CHAPTER 13

Back Home at the Ranch

Samuel arrived back at Rick Husband International Airport in Amarillo, Texas, at 5:45 p.m., Wednesday evening. As he departed the plane, he drew his lungs full of good old Texas air.

"Ah, yes, it sure is good to be home again."

"What was that, young man?"

Samuel looked down at a man rolling himself toward the terminal in a wheelchair.

"Just expressing how good it is to be back home in Texas."

"I know that feeling. The war put me in this chair a few years back when I was your age. Thought I'd never see home again when I got blown up. Had some good doctors and nurses that put me back together enough to let me touch this place again."

"Would you like me to push you to the terminal?"

DEADLY ATTACK

"Nope! Before I got blown up, I walked everywhere I went just like you. Now I get to ride wherever I go. Got wheels under me, and I intend to wear them out before I take my last ride home to heaven. The Lord has a new set of legs waiting for me up there. I can wait on Him to set me on my feet again. Be blessed, young man."

Samuel watched with a tear in his eye as the old soldier kept turning the wheels on the chair with his hands, making his way to the terminal and home.

Samuel called Joe Halstead to hitch a ride from the terminal back to his office in downtown Amarillo. He had left his jeep tucked away back in his office building when he left for California and didn't really want to take a cab ride if his friend, the sheriff, was available. He decided to stay in town overnight and then meet with the sheriff on Thursday morning to fill him in on his time in Los Angeles.

"Hey. Good to hear your voice again, Samuel. Give me a few minutes, and I'll scoot over and chauffeur you to your office."

"Thanks, Joe. See you soon."

Joe Halstead stared at the remaining red splotches on Samuel's face with a twisted grin covering his own face.

ALTON LYNN COOPER

"That undercover work sure took its toll on that bronze Spanish face of yours. Does it hurt?"

"Only when I think of the leftover tube of spirit gum resting in the trash can back in LA. You should have seen it when it was in full bloom. I looked like a sour cherry tree covered in fruit. You can drop me off at the delicatessen on the corner. I need to stock up my refrigerator for the night. I can walk to my office from there."

"I can wait for you if you need me to."

"Nope. God gave me two strong legs, and the good old Amarillo air will do me good. Been breathing that LA smog far too long."

"Fine by me. I've got a late meeting tonight with the mayor. We can meet up for breakfast tomorrow morning, and you can fill me in on closing out your case. Ms. Carmen is offering a wonderful breakfast burrito. I'll buy."

Samuel enjoyed a long, hot shower and then slipped into his robe before easing himself down into the plush leather chair in his office living area. He had brought the whiteboard with him and had it lying on his desk before filing it away with the others from his previous cases. They served as visual reminders of how his mind had sought out the truth during past investigations. It amazed him that the crooks always

DEADLY ATTACK

thought themselves smarter than the law, but the law seemed to always win in the end.

He stared at Senator Gerald McPherson's name written on the sticky note stuck on the top of the whiteboard. He never would have thought that a multiple-term United States Senator would be the one to send two thugs to Texas to blow up his bunkhouse office in an attempt to take him out. The man's greed for money and power had destroyed him, and now he probably would spend the rest of his life locked up at the government's expense. Samuel pulled the Bible from his desk drawer and copied two verses onto a new sticky note, pinning it to the whiteboard next to the senator's name.

"The righteousness of the perfect shall direct his way, but the wicked shall fall by his own wickedness. The righteousness of the upright shall deliver them: but transgressors shall be taken in their own naughtiness" (Proverbs 11:5–6).

Samuel slept well that night for the first time since the attack on his bunkhouse. It was a great relief to know that those who sought to destroy him were behind bars. He realized, however, that the business he was in would always generate new enemies and that future threats could easily come his way. The clock radio pulled him from sleep, sending him to

ALTON LYNN COOPER

the bathroom to prepare for his first day back in his hometown.

"Well, folks, out thar in radio land, don't fergit that the cattleman's auction is coming to town next month. If ya'll want your beef to be considered in tha auction, ya'll better git them cattle haulers gassed up and ready to go. This is your old pal Colonel Jimmy George from Amarillo station WWTYZ signing off fer now. Ya'll have a good day, ya hear?"

*****

His phone began ringing just as he put on the coffee pot and finished taking two boiled eggs out of the refrigerator for a breakfast snack before meeting Joe Halstead for a more substantial feeding at Ms. Carmen's cantina.

"Well, is it good to be home again?"

"Yes, Gregory. It's also good to know that justice has been served and some major drug dealers will now pay the price for their crimes against humanity."

"I wanted to give you a call and close the loop on a few things from our investigation that might be of interest to you. It always puzzled me as to why Jimmy Winters would set up the armored car with Macrone Pharmaceuticals on it to be robbed by a

DEADLY ATTACK

rival drug gang. You remember that he had ten thousand dollars in his safe, right?"

"Yes, but I thought that came through Horace Donaldson as they were setting him up to use him in Caston's drug business."

"Yes, that's what I thought also. Winters finally told the police that a man from one of the rival drug gangs had approached him to set up the armored truck route that day and was the one who gave him the cash. Winters thought the man was sent by Donaldson, so he did as he was told. As strange as it may seem, Caston never knew that the pigeon they were grooming to become one of their drug mules bringing drugs out of Mexico was used against him by the rival gang to hit the Macrone shipment that day."

"You said a few things. What's the other bit of news?"

"That canister of hydrogen cyanide gas that was delivered to your hotel room came from a nylon factory in north LA that is owned by Horace Donaldson's cousin. They use it in their manufacturing process and reported a break-in at their facility after Gus Wilson tried to empty the canister's contents under your door. They opened shop the next morning and called the police, reporting the break-in from the

ALTON LYNN COOPER

night before. Wilson later identified Donaldson in a lineup as the one who approached him, setting up the delivery to your room. Now here is the most interesting news. Have you considered why Senator McPherson hated you enough that he sent killers trying to take you out?"

"I must admit that thought has crossed my mind."

"Well, it seems that in his thirst for campaign cash, he had sucked a large amount of the drug money out of Macrone's pharmaceutical company to support his reelection that was struggling at the time. Caston was trying to expand the drug business, opening up the South Pacific, hoping to recoup a large portion of the drug money owed to their major suppliers out of Mexico. That's why Manuel Alvera was interested in your proposal to provide him with a large supply of illegal drugs. When you exposed Alvera on Kalmajo Island that shut down that operation, putting McPherson's neck on the line to Caston and the drug lords in Mexico. It almost cost him his life. He was still in the process of replacing the drug money by getting those government grants for the pharmaceutical companies, with almost all of that going to Macrone Pharmaceuticals. His hatred for you was irrational, based on his maniacal desire for

DEADLY ATTACK

money and the power that it provided him. In his warped thinking, you were the one that threatened to expose his connection to the illegal drug operations by causing the Mexican cartels to come hunting for him before he could return the money owed them."

"Thank you, Gregory, for the update. I'm thankful that all this is behind us and that justice has been served."

"Yes, my friend. You have a nice day, and if you're ever in Washington, you can buy me another steak dinner with all the fixings."

"I'm still paying off all those breakfasts you added to my hotel bill."

"It is so good to see you back home again, Señor Samuel. The news has been full of those arrested in California. You have been a very busy boy indeed." Ms. Carmen sent a loving smile Samuel's way.

"I had a lot of help. Yes, it's good to be back where I belong, smelling that wonderful food being prepared in your kitchen."

"Have you heard of my new invention, the Amarillo Grand Breakfast Burrito?"

"Yes. Sheriff Joe was telling me about it last night. It doesn't have a bite to it, does it?" Samuel watched Ms. Carmen's face closely.

ALTON LYNN COOPER

"A master private detective as you shouldn't be afraid of Ms. Carmen's bite, no?"

"We are still talking about the burrito, right?"

Carmen Ortega gave Samuel's cheek a slight pinch along with giving him a wink as she left to turn in his and the sheriff's order.

"Okay. Tell me about your case in LA."

Samuel thoroughly enjoyed Ms. Carmen's breakfast burrito. It had a little burn to it but not enough to prevent the succulent flavor from tantalizing his taste buds. In between mouthfuls, he shared with his good friend Joe Halstead the details of his time in Los Angeles.

"So let me get this right. Manuel Alvera, a past drug dealer, saved your life on Kalmajo Island, and then his previous drug associate left a bloody message on a rock at the bottom of a ravine that finally led you to the individual that sent his goons here to kill you?"

"Yes. This entire experience seems bizarre on its face. How a well-known senator could let himself stoop so low is beyond me. Power and money do indeed take hold of many in this world and send them down the path of destruction. God said it best when He said the love of money is the root of all evil. It's not the money itself. It's the lust in the hearts of corrupt individuals for it that is the true evil."

"What are your plans going forward? Will you continue to use your new office here in town as your main location?"

"I'm not sure, Joe. There's a lot to think about. I'm going out to the ranch to make an appearance this afternoon. Mama wants to see my face at the supper table tonight, and there's a certain young lady at the ranch that has been on my mind throughout this whole ordeal. Do you think it's possible for a man to get married and remain in the business I'm in?"

The sheriff gave Samuel a warm smile.

"Are you telling me you may have wedding plans in your future?"

"I don't know, Joe. I've got to sort out my future first. I dearly love trapping rats, but I've come to realize that there are also other very important things in life to consider."

Samuel donned one of his new silk shirts along with a new pair of boot-cut blue jeans after putting a fresh coat of polish on his trusty cowboy boots that he had left behind when he went to California. The new boots that he bought in LA were nice, but they still needed some more breaking in to quit chewing the skin off the back of his heels. He sprayed a couple of squirts of Gravity cologne on his neck and then went into the garage, firing up the old jeep for his

ALTON LYNN COOPER

ride out to the ranch. Before exiting the garage, he checked the security system cameras just to make sure he had left all the rats back in California.

Thursday afternoon was a beautiful, sunny West Texas day with a warm, soft breeze blowing its way across the open prairie lands. Samuel rode with all the windows down, letting the breeze blow through his thick mane of black, wavy hair. It felt good not to have the false rug on his head or the stick-on beard and mustache on his face. The red splotches were almost gone, with only a faint pink spot here and there. He had the radio on, listening to a bluegrass song about living on the mountainside in an old cabin on the ridge. He wondered to himself why all the bluegrass singers lived in old cabins on a ridge in the mountains. He thought for sure that maybe one or two of them must surely live in a valley somewhere. He did remember a song one time about a red river valley that someone was leaving.

Samuel slowed the jeep to a stop, amazed at what had happened to the entrance of the ranch. There was a ten-foot-tall black wrought iron fence all along the front of the property that ran down the entire length of the road frontage. It was connected at the corners to the ranch fencing, closing in the property. There was a place to turn in off the road

DEADLY ATTACK

into the drive before coming up against two massive gates that were apparently electronically controlled. He sat staring through the gates as a security guard left a small guardhouse that was built inside the gates across the drive from where his bunkhouse sat with a whole new look.

"And you are?" The guard left the large gates closed, calling to Samuel on the other side.

"I'm Samuel. I live here."

"You are Mr. Samuel Garcia?"

"Yes."

"Please exit your vehicle and show me your identification."

Samuel felt put off. He had suffered a number of near-death experiences, and now he was being interrogated by a rented security guard trying to get into his own home.

"Sorry for the inconvenience, sir. Mr. Eduardo has specific requirements for anyone entering the property. There is a keypad located next to the drive. From now on, you only need to establish your passcode and then enter it into the system. When you enter your private code, the gates will automatically open for you. Welcome home."

Samuel stopped inside the gates, staring at the bunkhouse. It was apparent that it had been completely rebuilt and reinforced along the way. It still maintained the outward appearance of what his father Mateo had built, but it looked more stable than the old structure that had graced the entrance to the ranch over the years.

"Okay, Brother Eduardo. I can't wait to hear about what you've done now."

Samuel parked the jeep on the island underneath the large live oak tree, leaving it in the shade, and began his walk up the tree-covered driveway to the hacienda. He noticed a newly constructed chain-link enclosure setting off the driveway underneath a stand of live oak trees near the south pasture. He quickly realized that his younger brother had been very busy during his time away.

Samuel opened the front door and stepped into the entrance hall of his childhood home. The rich odors of Ms. Valentina's supper washed over him, drawing him toward the large, expansive dining room. He stepped into the room and was met by his mother and his brothers, their heads all turned in his direction. The grandfather clock in the hallway began sending out its loud bonging sounds, letting him know that he needed to quickly take his place near the head of the table next to his mother, who sat staring at her watch.

DEADLY ATTACK

"I do trust that those clothes have recently been washed and your hands are clean as well."

All his brothers burst out laughing as each one left their seats, rushing over to hug their eldest brother, welcoming him home. Sofia remained seated and began tapping her fork on her crystal glass as the clock sent out its last bong.

"There will be time for your emotional outburst later. Now it is time for my wayward son to ask grace on our food after he seats himself."

Samuel finished asking God's blessing on the food and opened his eyes as Valentina and her two lady servants began bringing the supper meal to the table. She had prepared Samuel's favorite roast beef with mashed potatoes that had been whipped smooth with onion and garlic mixed in. Valentina's homemade gravy was the best that Samuel had ever experienced, having her family's secret ingredients blended into its creamy richness. He laid his napkin aside, excusing himself from the table, and followed Valentina back into the kitchen, taking her into his arms.

"Señor Samuel, are you sure this is appropriate?"

"Appropriate or not, I have missed you, Valentina."

"Is it me that you have missed, Señor? Or is it the roast beef awaiting you on the table?"

"That roast beef wouldn't be waiting for me on the table if it wasn't for your lovely hands that prepared it."

"I wouldn't want to hurt your feelings in any way, Señor Samuel, but I've taught my assistants how to prepare the beef the way you like it, and it was their hands that sent it to your table."

Samuel pulled Valentina close to him and held her, smelling the sweetness of her long, flowing hair.

"Regardless of what you may think, I missed you and your cooking while I was away. But my dear, most of all, you won out over your cooking when I had dreams of you."

"You need to go eat, Señor. I have dessert to prepare."

Samuel released his hug on Valentina, stepping back, seeing the tears sparkling in her dark ebony eyes. He thought that if there were angels on earth, surely one was standing before him in that very moment.

The supper meal continued with Samuel answering his brothers' questions concerning his time in California. Sofia ate in silence, watching her boys' interactions around the long dining table.

"How can you be sure you left all the bad people in California?" His mother's question cut through the room, causing his brothers' voices to go silent.

DEADLY ATTACK

There were a few moments of uneasy silence before Samuel responded to his mother's question.

"I don't know that it is ever safe to say that we have separated ourselves from the danger abiding on this earth. It is sad indeed, but there are many who don't know the Lord and have their hearts bent on evil. They can come against us at any time in any place. I have learned to go in the protection of our Lord. I trust Him to keep me in all my ways, just as He promised in His Word."

Sofia's face was filled with a warm smile toward her eldest son.

"Well spoken, my son. Your dear papa, rest his soul, used to say those very things to me when he struggled through the difficult years building this ranch up around us. There were threats coming against us from many places in the early days, but your papa kept his eyes on heaven and his hand on the plow. God's Word tells us that very thing. Keep your hand on the plow that God has placed in it and never turn back. Now share with me what happened in my kitchen before you returned to our family's table to enjoy this wonderful supper."

"Walk with me, my brother. I have some things to share with you." Samuel had finished the slice of delicious warm strawberry pie with three large scoops of vanilla bean ice cream piled high on top. When he looked around the table, he noticed that his brothers had two scoops of ice cream on their slice compared to three on his own. He caught a glimpse of Valentina watching him from the kitchen doorway just as she sent a brilliant smile in his direction.

Samuel left the house, walking next to Eduardo down the winding driveway, listening to the sounds of the early night bugs beginning their serenade as dusk began to settle in across the pasture lands. The sweet smells of the air filled his entire being as the peace of being home flooded his soul. He realized in that moment just how precious life was and the blessing that was his, having a family that loved one another and a home that would always welcome him back no matter where he roamed.

Samuel was amazed as he stood in the office area of the bunkhouse, seeing the inside completely rebuilt as if the attack never happened. It looked the same as he remembered it, with the exception that all the materials surrounding him were new.

"I built up a block wall around the outside. The blocks are filled with rebar and concrete. I covered the outside blocks with the same kind of wood that our father used when he first built this place. The interior walls are also reinforced to withstand gunfire

DEADLY ATTACK

blowing them apart. You will find the same high-level security system here as the one I had installed in your office in Amarillo. I rebuilt this place and reinforced it, giving it the protection of a modern-day bomb shelter. If anyone comes visiting again, they won't be able to blow it apart as before. It would take a direct hit from a bomb to do any significant damage. Now tell me, can we expect you to come back and establish your office here at the ranch?"

Samuel was quiet as Eduardo watched him, waiting for his answer.

"I don't know, Eduardo. The attack made me realize just how dangerous my life's occupation can be at times. It's like I told our dear mother, no one can stamp out all the evil around us. That won't happen until Jesus comes back and establishes His kingdom on this earth. I will pray about it and seek the Lord's leading in the matter. Between you and me, I am torn between staying in the detective business versus leaving it behind and marrying a sweet young woman and settling down here on the ranch. By the way, what do you plan on keeping in that new chain-link pen out by the pasture under the live oak trees?"

"The dogs."

"What dogs?"

ALTON LYNN COOPER

"That's part of our new security system. The man at the kennels said we needed to wait for you to return so that the puppies can smell you before growing up to protect the property during the night hours."

"What kind of puppies?"

"Dobermans. They won't try to eat family members that they know, but watch out if you come on the property as a stranger. You better have on steel britches and be able to run fast."

"Eduardo, aren't you taking this security stuff a bit far? It seems like you've turned the ranch into a miniature Fort Knox."

"Not at all, Samuel. While you were gone, Larson Maxwell's place was broken into when they were away on a short trip to his brother's place. The servants were asleep in their quarters when it happened. If they had woken up to investigate, they could have been killed by the intruders. A number of the larger ranches have seen what I've done here, and they have expressed interest in me building similar systems at their places. If you move your office back here, I could lease your new place in town, turning it into my security company. Not only that, you wouldn't have far to go each day to enjoy a certain young woman's company."

DEADLY ATTACK

Eduardo watched Samuel's face expectantly.

"Sounds like to me you have this all figured out. As I said before, I'll pray about it and seek the Lord's leading in the matter. I do enjoy being back at the ranch now that you have restored papa's bunkhouse to its former glory. I appreciate all you've done for me and our family. What would happen to that fancy sign that you hung on my office in town?"

"I already checked with the sign company. It wouldn't take much to convert its message to announce 'Garcia Construction/Security Specialist.'"

"Whoa! Does our mother know about your plans to enter into the construction business? I thought you were waiting to tell her due to Ricardo's heading off to law school."

"After doing this work here at the ranch, Mama understands that a man has got to follow the calling in his heart. I would still live here at the ranch and work with our brothers, helping to run this place in between my construction jobs. Now are you coming home or not?"

*****

Two weeks later, Samuel settled down in his bunkhouse office back at the ranch. He stocked the

ALTON LYNN COOPER

new refrigerator with a dozen boiled eggs, two rings of bologna, three two-liter bottles of diet Pepsi, and a large wedge of cheddar cheese, along with pickles and other condiments. He brought his desk phone from his office in town along with his answering machine that had its red light blinking on and off in rapid signals. He had been busy moving and getting caught up on other pressing matters and hadn't returned any incoming calls made to his office. He felt that a little downtime was in order before he jumped back into the fray. He smiled to himself each time he punched his secret code into the keypad at the gate, letting him into what he now referred to as the Garcia Compound. His dear mother had shared a sweet young lady's date of birth with him, and he decided to turn that into his secret code to facilitate his coming and going on the property. Sofia had hired the necessary number of security guards to keep the small guardhouse across from his bunkhouse occupied at all times. She reasoned that it was a good investment to provide a safe environment for her son, who seemed to make a number of enemies due to his current occupation and to protect the family home in the days ahead.

Samuel left a message for his younger brother Ricardo at his law school dorm, asking him when he

DEADLY ATTACK

would be trained enough to file a civil lawsuit against a certain senator's estate in California. He had written down the cost to outfit his office in Amarillo along with the money that Eduardo had spent rebuilding the bunkhouse and for the replacement of his trusty old jeep's right headlight. He was enjoying his new blue jeans and silk shirts and knew that he would appreciate the rebuilt bunkhouse more knowing that the good senator had paid for it.

Samuel decided to sit out underneath the live oak tree near the old jeep, enjoying the shade that just might lead to a nice nap on a warm West Texas afternoon. He piled his paper plate high with sliced ring bologna, saltine crackers, and chunks of cheddar cheese. He opened the refrigerator and grabbed a bottle of diet Pepsi along with two boiled eggs. He started for the door and then noticed the rapidly blinking light on his answering machine. He had put off checking his messages until guilty feelings started washing over him for possibly neglecting those in trouble needing his help. He set his refreshments down on his desk and began punching buttons on the machine with his pen in hand. There were a number of hang-ups with no messages being left and then an occasional loud breath from some exasperated potential client wanting to know if he was still

ALTON LYNN COOPER

in the detective business. He jotted down their phone numbers and planned to call them after a few days of resting up. The next message sounded promising at first but then took a negative turn at the end.

"She's gone and taken Susan with her, man. I need you to call me right away. I don't know if she's leaving the country or where she might be taking Susan. Call me, Garcia! Call me!" The man's voice had a shrill pitch in it that caused Samuel to jot down the number. He punched the button, waiting for the next message from someone in distress.

"Yes, if this is the detective, I need to hire you to find my Aunt Mildred. She wandered off from 'Molly Bee's Happy Acres' three weeks ago. Wilber Potsworthy lives there also, and he came up missing the same day Aunt Mildred disappeared. I think someone may be stealing the old people to collect their pension checks. Call me as soon as you get this, you hear?"

The last voice caught Samuel's attention immediately.

"Garcia, I always believe in paying back what I owe. I owe you really big, pal. It's not the kind of payback that you're going to enjoy receiving. Trust me. Watch your back, Garcia." The voice was gravelly and nasal at the same time. Samuel didn't recognize it from anyone that he had been involved with

344

before, but that didn't preclude the individual from being another threat on his life.

He picked up the phone and dialed the number that he had written on his pad concerning the missing person.

"Yes, are you the man that left me a message concerning a person that has possibly been kidnapped?"

"What person has been kidnapped?"

"That's what I need you to tell me."

"How can I tell you about a person that's been kidnapped if I don't know a person that's been kidnapped?"

"Can we start over?"

"I think that would be a good idea."

"This is Samuel Garcia. I'm the private detective that you called, leaving a message on my answering machine about a person named Susan that may have been kidnapped, is that right?"

There was an eerie silence coming into Samuel's ear from the man on the other end of the line.

"What makes you think that Susan is a person? And how in the world did you get the idea that she's been kidnapped?"

Samuel tried to keep his voice in an even tone as he sensed that his diet Pepsi, ring bologna, and cheese chunks were becoming warm before his eyes.

ALTON LYNN COOPER

"Sir, you left me the message that Susan was taken, and you didn't know if the person that took her was heading out of the country with her."

"Are you sure you are a detective? Good night, man, Susan is my cat. I've had her for eleven years. Eleanor had no right, man. No right, I tell you."

"Who is Eleanor?"

"My mother, Eleanor, man! She's my mother. Said she was tired of the cat hair plugging up her vacuum cleaner. I woke up from my nap three days ago, and Mama and Susan were gone. I haven't heard from either one of them. I'm afraid that she may be taking Susan somewhere to dump her off so she can never find her way back home. Can you get my cat back or not? Are you a detective or should I call someone else?"

"So do I understand correctly that you still live at home with your mother, and you and your cat, Susan, have lived with Mommy for the past eleven years, is that right? What is your name, sir?"

"My name's Wilber Festerman. That's W-i-l-b-e-r F-e-s-t-e-r-m-a-n. Did you get that? Write it down so you won't forget. How much do you charge, anyway?"

"I'm sorry, Wilber, but I don't accept cases involving cats. Allergies, you know. I'm sure you

DEADLY ATTACK

understand. If I can think of another detective that hunts down missing mothers with kidnapped cats, I'll call you back."

Samuel, remembering something from his time in Los Angeles, jotted a quick note and stuck it on his bulletin board. "Maybe, just maybe! First, we rest awhile."

He picked up his warm bologna and cheese, and headed outside to share the shade with his old jeep resting under the live oak tree.

"I just hope my Pepsi still has its fizz."

ABOUT THE AUTHOR

Alton Lynn Cooper is an ordained minister and has served as pastor to the Deaf at Capitol City Baptist Church in Holt, Michigan, for forty-five years. During this time, Alton served in prison ministry at Carson City Regional Correctional Facility in mid-Michigan for eleven years. His classes at the prison included both deaf and hearing prisoners, with many being saved and discipled in God's Word. Along with serving in ministry, Alton worked as a manufacturing manager in the automobile industry at General Motors Corporation for forty-one years. He is currently serving as pastor emeritus at CCBC, supporting both deaf and hearing ministries throughout the church.

Alton and his wife, Dolly, have begun writing and publishing a number of Christian books to glorify God and encourage His children as they walk with Him. They desire to see many come to Jesus Christ and receive Him as their personal Lord and Saviour and for God's children to be strengthened in their faith.

Together, they have participated in mission trips and educational tours in Israel, Mexico, Honduras, England, Ireland, Scotland, Wales, Egypt, and Jordan, along with trips in the United States, working in vacation Bible schools and building projects at Bible colleges and youth camps.

Alton and Dolly have ten adult children, seven sons and three daughters, along with a host of grandchildren and great-grandchildren. They enjoy travel and spending time with family and friends along the way while being salt and light to those whom they come in contact.

God bless you and keep you in His care. May your pathway be brightened day by day as you walk in our Saviour's love.

BOOKS BY ALTON LYNN COOPER

The Grampa Hal children's series: (color illustrated)
Grampa Hal Comes to Visit
Rooster for Rent
Hats with Headlights
The Fish That Wouldn't Stay Caught
The Frog That Wouldn't Hop
Flies That Don't Burn
Jeepers and Creepers
The Crazy Little Train That Goes in Circles

Tall Tales for Little People (ten illustrated short stories for children)

Full-length novels (Christian fiction)
Wellmington's Cove
The Long Dusty Road
The Bend in the River
On the Wings of Love (Grampa Hal's Davey grown up)
Caleb's Mountain

Christian discipling books
Godly Priorities for Christian Living (released by Alton Cooper—Swordbook.com)
Finding Peace and Joy in a Troubled World (released by Lynn Cooper—Trilogy.TV)
Building Godly Relationships (released by Lynn Cooper—Trilogy.TV)
Salt and Light—America's Greatest Need
The Coming Wars

Samuel Garcia Private Eye Mystery detective series (Christian fiction)
In the Dark of Night
The Case of the Vanishing Masterpieces
Gone Without a Trace
Deadly Attack

GLORY TO GOD PUBLICATIONS LLC
Alton Lynn Cooper—Christian author/speaker
Dolly Jean Cooper—editing/illustrating/technical support
Website: gtgaltonlynncooper.com
Or Gmail: myjesussavesjohn316@gmail.com
(Please title message "Books")

Their books are available through (ChristianFaithPublishing. com/new releases), Amazon, Barnes & Noble, BAM! (Books A Million), E-Book, Ingram, Indigo, iTunes, Kobo, McNally Robinson, Russell Books, Spring Arbor, Sword of the Lord (Swordbook.com), Trilogy Publishing (Trilogy.TV), and in most brick-and-mortar bookstores.

www.ingramcontent.com/pod-product-compliance
Lightning Source LLC
Chambersburg PA
CBHW022305170125
20532CB00033B/213